THE
ARROW
AND THE
IVY

THE COASTAL LANDS OF
ENTEREA

AFTEAN SEA
ENTEREA
STARFALL
VARYN'S PASS
STABLES
WARRIOR'S GUILD
MANA GUILD
TEMPLE OF THE THREE
LORE GUILD
MAIN GUILD HALL
THE IVORY GUILDS
ARCANE GUILD

https://www.authorbreemoore.com/

THE ARROW AND THE IVY

An Innate Ink Publishing Book

Cover art by Just Venture Arts https://www.justventurearts.com/

Map art by Cartography bird https://www.cartographybird.com/

Copy Editing by Claire Ashgrove https://reedsy.com/Claire-Ashgrove

ISBN: 9978-1-956668-29-2 (Hardcover)

ISBN: 978-1-956668-77-3 (Paperback)

ISBN: 978-1-956668-25-4 (Ebook)

CHAPTER ONE

THE DOVER CREAKED BENEATH Jayce, each groan of its weathered timbers a reminder that trees kept secrets—even in death.

Fortunately, the old, dead wood didn't speak as loud as their living counterparts, leaving her unaware of whatever secrets they might hold.

Let the trees keep their secrets. Jayce hadn't begun to unravel the ones that followed her from Loshar.

She sat near the bow, the sun warm on her shoulders, the wooden chair solid beneath her—but even here, the weight of the answers she sought pressed against her spine. The Ivory Guilds of Enterea held answers—about the journal, the plague, maybe the Plague King himself. If she failed to find them in time, she and her companions could face imprisonment for harboring forbidden knowledge.

Or worse—the plague would keep spreading, and there was no telling who it might take from her next.

Jayce tilted her face toward the sky and let herself pretend her troubles didn't exist while the sun's warmth burned off the chill her thoughts left behind.

Footsteps sounded behind her, and Sav approached where she sat sunning herself on deck. He juggled two bowls of watery stew and a gleech for each of them.

Jayce took the bowl and slurped at the tasteless, lukewarm stew, eager to be done with it. By the time she set the bowl aside, Sav handed her a peeled gleech.

She accepted the tangy citrus fruit. "You didn't have to peel it. I can manage."

"It's a small way I can make you more comfortable. I know you don't prefer touching them."

She loved the taste of gleeches, the sweet and tart flavors playing on her tongue. What she didn't like were the whispers that bloomed the moment the juice touched her lips.

He's hiding something.

Such a suspicious fruit. The gleech couldn't mean Sav, could it? After all, dozens of men milled about the ship. It could mean any one of them. But the whispers sounded louder than ever. Was it because Sav had handled the gleech when peeling it for her?

"We will make landfall tomorrow, early afternoon. I've written to a friend to have us picked up at a travel station in town."

"That's convenient," Jayce said around a mouthful of gleech, warm juice running down her chin. Wiping at it with the back of her arm, she reached for another bite of fruit—then paused, catching Sav staring at her.

"Do I still have something on my face?" A second swipe found nothing.

Sav shook his head, ducking away so she couldn't read his face. "No, you got it. You know, the woman I met in Eastmill would have been terribly embarrassed to be seen with gleech juice on her face, by a baron no less. I like to think that means you've grown comfortable with me."

Jayce raised her eyebrows. "And sleeping for several nights within the same tent didn't prove that to you?"

Sav flushed, the pink color deepening the charm in his handsome face. His eyes reflected the blue sky as he leaned against the railing with casual grace.

Jayce wished for more cycles like this—sunlight, quiet conversation, the illusion of safety. And that their journey to the Ivory Guilds might lead to the cure they'd been chasing for so long.

Sav cleared his throat. "It will take several bells to get to the Guilds. I cannot wait to introduce you to my colleagues. We should try to get you into some classes, as well. I think I can pull some strings with the Head Dame."

"It's not a leisure trip, Sav. We need Dagric Wortcunning's book to be translated as quickly as possible."

"Well, yes, but translation takes time. I anticipate being there for cycles, if not several turns. Dire Pell still has teaching responsibilities within his Guild, and I have other business to attend as well. You'd find it boring following me everywhere. It makes sense to find something to engage you. I know how you love learning."

Her obsession with research hadn't done her much good. Even spending her adult life buried in books, searching for a cure or a way to defeat the Plague King, she had never come close.

Despite the lack of answers, she found comfort between the pages. With all the brilliant minds that had come to Enterea to study at the Ivory Guilds since the plague struck the mainland, some of them must have studied it. Perhaps she could consult with them or find notes they left behind. If the queen hadn't already confiscated them in the name of her scholars finding a cure.

She wouldn't waste time with classes or idle talk while Sav sought answers.

"The Guilds have a library, don't they? Just leave me there until you need me," Jayce said.

Sav laughed. "I'd never see you again. Besides, you need to make some friends. You've been lonely far too long, and I'm not the best company."

She bit back the urge to disagree. He was warm and charming and the kind of handsome that made people listen. But liking him didn't fix the fact that she didn't quite know him.

Besides, loneliness wasn't her whole reality. Nels had been in her life since they were children. His merchant parents had stayed in her village every summer through market season in the capital. And after his parents perished from the plague, he stayed in Loshar, visiting her near daily and providing an anchor to the real world while she dug deeper into her books and alchemistry.

She found herself searching the crowd for his familiar, tousled brown hair and lake-blue eyes before she pulled herself back. Sav had a point. Aside from Nels, she didn't have anyone. Not anymore.

The thought coiled tight inside her. Maybe it was loneliness, or something deeper. Something she'd buried in the face of the life debt that she refused to share with anyone else.

Her hands flexed in her lap, fingers curling toward the fading marks left by the dusk ivy on her left palm and trailing up to her elbow. She couldn't be certain whether it was a scar or some other kind of mark. She had never seen anything like it. But she hated that it reminded her of Sir Dray.

Jayce inhaled through her nose, sharp and fast. The traitorous bailiff was gone, stripped of his title and banished to the salt mines, but a threat still existed. The mysterious L.A. that Sir Dray had been working for was still out there.

A familiar voice floated over from behind her, light and teasing.

"Very serious discussion happening over here. I'm offended I wasn't invited," Nels said.

He stood beside her, opposite of Sav.

Jayce smiled at him. Trust Nels to dissolve tension wherever he went.

"Not so serious, trust me. I'm trying to convince Jayce to meet people while we're at the Guilds," Sav explained.

"She's already got me. Who else does she need?" Nels asked, shooting her a grin.

"You just want to keep her for yourself," Sav jibed good-naturedly.

Nels raised his eyebrows. "Admit it. You don't want to share her either."

Sav hesitated. "I might be reluctant to introduce her to... certain individuals. We'll have to be on our guard, Martin, or she'll be married before either of us can have a say."

Jayce burst out laughing. "I'm not getting married while I'm here! You two are ridiculous."

She folded her arms as the banter continued, her eyes lingering on Nels. She searched his face for any flicker of pain, any crack in the easy grin he offered. If her earlier refusal of his marriage offer had left a scar, he hid it well.

She swallowed past the regret looming like dark clouds on the horizon of her heart. Moments like this, she caught herself noticing the way the sunlight caught in his curls, or how relaxed his presence made her feel, or how he never asked anything from her. How much of her rejection

had been fear of Dray and the repercussions of her debt rather than a true lack of attraction?

Something more than friendship lived between them, no matter how she tried to ignore it.

Sav excused himself, leaving her alone with Nels. They sat in comfortable silence, listening to the snap of the sails above and the cursing of sailors carrying about their duties.

After a moment, Nels sighed and crossed to the railing, leaning his forearms against it.

"He's handsome and charming enough, Jayce, but I feel unsettled around him." He put his hand in his pocket and pulled out a stone that glittered golden and translucent in the sun. "Even the rocks are restless."

Jayce snorted. "How can rocks be restless?" She felt a twinge of jealousy. He understood and used his powers without any of the discomfort she experienced when she touched plants.

"They vibrate. During times of danger, or when they want me to pay extra close attention to something. And they want me to pay attention to Savage Alighieri. Where's he from? Who's his family? Where does he get all that money?"

"Do I detect a hint of jealousy?" Jayce teased. "Hard not to. He's good-looking and well-off."

Nels's face grew drawn and serious. He twisted around, turning toward the sea. "You have to admit it's odd, though. That he would seek you out, save you from your debt, and take you with him on this wild journey. What does he want? I'm not sure I believe his only motive is to hear your story with the Plague King."

Jayce sighed and stared upward, noticing the boy crouched in the rigging, silhouetted against the sky. He waved down to the deck, and she glanced down to find a group of sailors gathered, laughing as they looked up at him.

"I don't know, Nels. He means me no harm, if that's what you're getting at," she replied.

"There are more ways to harm a person than just physically. The way he makes people feel like they're the only one in the world... Surely, you've seen it?"

Sav was nice, and people liked him. And yes, she had to admit he made her feel special. After all, he'd paid off her life debt and helped her solve the noxbrosia mystery without asking for much of anything in return.

Jayce shifted in her chair. "Sav is harmless."

"Maybe so, but I'm going to listen to my rocks. You should do the same with your plants. And keep an eye out for each other while we're here. I have a feeling we're about to see a whole other side to Alighieri."

Across the ship, Sav spoke animatedly to the first mate. As if he could sense them talking about him, he glanced back at them over his shoulder. He smiled, waving his hand.

The thought of him as anything more sinister than an over-enthusiastic historian made her want to laugh.

Nels left to play a card game with some of the sailors, leaving Jayce alone with her thoughts.

A tall, heavyset man passed by, his dark coat flaring in the sea breeze. Jayce's eyes passed over him, but a strange twinge in her gut caused her to look a second time, watching as he crossed the ship's deck.

Prickling tension slid down her spine, and the distant hum of the ship's wood and sails increased from a quiet hum to a roar inside her head.

She couldn't make sense of what the dead wood and flaxen fibers of the sails were trying to say. But her hand, the one with the dusk ivy markings, buzzed down to her bones.

Jayce tore her eyes away from the man and eyed her hand, not noticing anything different. Her heart skipped, and she looked back toward the man, but he had already disappeared below deck.

A sea breeze caressed her face, the fresh saltiness of it grounding her back in the present moment. She rubbed at her arm until the buzzing faded, though the echo of it lingered, and turned her mind toward all of the unanswered questions.

It might be nothing. She might have sat too long in the sun, or perhaps the week at sea had her thinking too much. But the unease from the experience refused to settle.

Her gaze drifted toward Sav, drawn by the rise and fall of his voice, his sweeping hand gestures as he joked with the first mate.

What could she expect here in Enterea? Would being here reveal more of his past, and with it his true self? And who else might she meet?

She tried to relax and let go of her suspicious thoughts, but the seeds of doubt had been sown, and something in her already knew they wouldn't stay buried.

CHAPTER TWO

Getting off the ship in Starfall turned out to be a far more lengthy process than getting on the ship in Crotos. Jayce watched in fascination and curiosity as the travelers funneled into a large building and down a long hallway with three checkpoints.

At the first checkpoint, an attendant examined Jayce's papers. They spent an extra-long time scanning the document provided by the physician, approving her for travel.

At the second checkpoint, several assistants managed the crowd, sending individuals one at a time into two rooms. When Jayce's turn came, she slipped through the doorway and was met with a pleasant-faced physician, who prodded her neck and tilted her face toward the light and politely requested that she undress behind a screen, put on a gown, and allow him to check for any gray patches of skin.

Shivering in the cool room, Jayce did as she was told, despite having checked herself that morning, as she always did, for any sign of the plague. This man was doing his job, and this rigorous process was likely part of the reason Enterea was untouched by the plague. In Crotos, they'd only asked if she had any symptoms. They hadn't examined her thoroughly.

The physician lingered upon seeing the whorls decorating her left arm. "What's this?" he asked, curiosity overcoming professionalism.

"It's—" She faltered. How to explain to a stranger? "Magic-caused."

The physician clicked his tongue and eyed it again, jotting a few things down on a piece of paper. "You're clear. You can dress now and exit through there." He gestured at a second door opposite the one she had entered through, then left.

Jayce dressed quickly and rejoined the line, relieved to see Nels and Sav both had made it through ahead of her. They shuffled through the corridor, moving at a snail's pace.

The soft sounds of hushed conversation and shuffling feet filled the concrete space and brought goosebumps to Jayce's arms. Or perhaps that was only due to the chill in the air.

Sav leaned over, his curls brushing Jayce's cheek. "It isn't true that we didn't get the plague here. It came, but sick individuals were swiftly and brutally quarantined."

"What do you mean?" Jayce asked, stunned that the information she'd heard was wrong.

"People would literally disappear from their homes overnight, sometimes never to be seen again, if there was even a rumor they or someone in their household might be ill. Students and graduates from the Mana Guild were trained to detect the sickness. Still don't have a cure, but prevention is half the battle."

On the mainland, and especially in Loshar, too many people had brushed the plague off as mild and harmless for far too long. Moribund appeared quickly, in numbers too large to manage. Hundreds had died that first age.

Could someone have planned that? The more she learned, the more she wondered if the Plague King had been intentionally created. Neldor had been on the brink of civil war between the capital and the southern half of the realm, but the plague seemed to have prevented all-out war and reunited the people.

But who would do such a thing? Risk even more lives for the sake of politics?

Sir Dray's actions had shown her some people would do anything for a bit of fame and status. Is that what his sponsor wanted? If so, why the anonymity?

The line moved forward again, and Jayce realized it was nearly her turn. She watched the three individuals in front of her with interest. Two of them wore magenta vests lined with gold braiding with a white dove stitched onto a pocket on their right breast. The symbol of the Mana Guild. Between them, stood a traveler, a woman Jayce recognized from the boat.

The two healers lifted and lowered a hand in unison while touching their temples with a single finger from their opposite hands, as if scanning the person between them.

Jayce sensed… something. A crackling sort of energy in the air, for the briefest of moments, and then it was gone, and the two healers motioned the woman on.

They gestured for Jayce to step forward.

She closed her eyes, bracing for what she didn't know. But the magic passed over her with only a slight tingling, and her ears popped as a bit of pressure filled the space.

The healers, satisfied with the results, sent her on her way.

A door at the end of the hall glowed with afternoon light. Jayce hurried toward it and flung it open, taking in a huge gulp of fresh air as she passed from the dim concrete building into sunlight.

She could finally take in Starfall. Sunlight glinted off red-tiled rooftops that cascaded toward the glittering harbor, where ships rocked gently against their moorings. Narrow streets wove between tall stone buildings painted in soft pastels, their balconies blooming with trailing plants. Flags fluttered above shop stalls, and somewhere nearby, someone was playing a reed pipe—its airy melody drifting on the breeze.

It wasn't the largest city, or the wealthiest, but it exuded a certain warmth. The kind that seeped into her skin and made her want to linger a little longer.

Jayce inhaled, catching the mix of sea brine and spices in the air. A shoulder shoved her aside, jostling her, and she stumbled back, catching herself on the edge of a stone box filled with flowers.

The man who bumped her muttered an apology, frowning deeply as if it were her fault as he steered the woman on his arm away.

She *had* been standing in the way of those coming from the checkpoint building. Feeling flustered, Jayce straightened and moved off the path, watching the crowd as people greeted loved ones waiting for them, called for wagon drivers to hire for the next leg of their journey, and milled about the market stalls.

To her relief, the large man in the dark coat—the one who had rattled her so deeply on the Dover—was nowhere to be seen.

A whisper brushed at her mind, and a sudden shock of cold went up her left arm.

Speaker.

She startled, jerking her hand back and finding it tangled in a strand of bloomvine that was growing in the planter behind her, the delicate gold-green tendrils reaching under the sleeve of her shirt.

Her heart thudded. The warmth of the city evaporated, and the bright afternoon seemed to dim. She glanced around, but no one had noticed.

The plant recoiled innocently back into the spill of greenery.

Jayce folded her arms tightly across her chest, rubbing her forearm. What had the bloomvine called her? *Speaker?* It was nonsense.

She tried to shake off the fear and shock of the interaction, but the cold lingered longer than usual. She might have gained some control over her abilities with plants, but the effects of interacting with them was getting worse.

Nels joined her underneath a shade tree, passing her luggage to her. "You forgot to grab this in the last room."

"I never saw it," Jayce admitted, relief flooding her at not being alone.

"Are you all right? You look like you've seen a ghost."

"It's nothing," Jayce said. She didn't need to worry him with her obsessive fears.

They stood in silence, taking in the bustle of the market just beyond the docks. A delightful smell wafted toward her, and she breathed it in, her stomach rumbling in response. "I'm starving."

"Me, too. Hope Sav hurries." Nels glanced behind them and waved.

Jayce followed his gaze until her eyes landed on Sav. He carried several bags.

He dropped them with a grunt, wiped his hands on his pants, and grimaced. "Good thing we're not walking to the Guilds. I'd break my back."

Jayce laughed. "That'll teach you to pack light."

"How do you fit all your clothes in just two bags? Dresses take up a lot of space," Sav said, sounding bewildered.

"When you only have two skirts, they don't take up much space," Jayce replied.

"Well then, we'll have to rectify that while we're here. Every lady deserves some nice dresses."

Jayce didn't bother correcting him. She didn't carry a title, but she knew Sav wouldn't have it. He didn't seem to care about the class difference between them. Refusing his offer of new clothes would have been pointless. One thing she had learned was once Sav got an idea in his head, there was little she could do to persuade him otherwise.

"Where do we meet this friend of yours?" Nels asked, swatting at an insect hovering around his face.

Sav craned his head around the tree's trunk to look down the street both ways, then glanced at the sun. "I reckon he'll be here any moment. Bentley is on time for everything. It's uncanny. I suspect the Three blessed him with the ability. They certainly didn't give me any."

Jayce smiled at that. The thought of someone having powers that allowed them to be on time was too ridiculous to entertain, but it was funny.

Nels walked a few paces away to another small, accent garden bed filled with rocks. He knelt and started shuffling through them, muttering to himself.

Oh, Nels. Always with his rocks. Jealousy overshadowed the fondness she felt for her friend. She wished she had such a positive relationship with her own magic. What would it be like to be friends with plants, rather than an uneasy ally?

She tugged on her gloves at the wrist, reassuring herself they were still there. Looking around, she observed all the trees, bushes, and flowers were contained to planter boxes and curated little gardens beside the shops and houses that lined the street near the docks.

Sav stepped up beside her, leaning toward her in a conspiratorial manner. "Does he always talk to rocks like that?"

Jayce laughed quietly. "Always. I can't take him anywhere."

Nels straightened, glancing over his shoulder at them with a grin, a rock in each hand. "Can you blame me? Look at this granite! It has an entirely unique composition compared to what I find in Neldor. I bet the Ivory Guilds have some really fascinating specimens."

"Well, you won't have to wait much longer. There's Bentley," Sav said, wiping his hands on his pants and pointing up the road, to where a mule-drawn wagon clattered up the cobblestones.

The figure driving waved as he saw them, his wide, square face breaking out in a smile.

Jayce liked him instantly.

"Bentley!" Sav called out, approaching the slowing wagon.

Bentley halted the mule and hopped down, still holding the reins in one hand, and embraced Sav with his free arm.

"Savage! You're a sight for sore eyes. Everything has been chaos since you left. It'll be nice to get some proper order back."

Sav opened his mouth to reply, but hesitated.

Jayce suddenly felt like an intruder.

Sav embraced Bentley, then clapped his hands together. "Let's get going, shall we? If we leave now, we can have dinner at the Guilds."

"Not that I disagree, but could we get some lunch first? I'm half-starved," Nels said.

"Me, too," Jayce agreed, picking up two of her bags and hauling them toward the wagon.

Bentley jumped down, pushing his glasses back on his face, and took the bags from her. "Bentley Pell, milady. I don't believe we've been introduced, but I suspect you're the one Sav goes on about in his letters."

Jayce blinked in surprise, in part at Bentley's stature—he was half a head shorter than her—and also at the fact that Sav had talked about her in letters to his friend. What had he said?

"Y-yes, I am," Jayce stammered, so flustered she didn't even correct him about her station. She brushed hair from her eyes and went back to the tree to get the rest of her bags, passing Nels who introduced himself to Bentley as, "Nels Martin, purveyor and speaker for the stones."

Nels and his flamboyant enthusiasm. He never did anything halfway.

Bentley followed Nels back to the dwindling stack of baggage. He picked up an innocuous looking bag and grunted in surprise as he attempted to lift it.

"What's in here? Rocks?" he asked.

"Yes," Nels replied, his expression entirely serious.

"The man tried to single-handedly sink our ship, I think," Sav said, intercepting the bag Jayce lifted over the wagon bed edge.

He gazed down at her, clear blue eyes speaking volumes she wished she understood. It seemed so long since they'd had a moment alone. On the ship, there had always been someone nearby. Nels joining their conversations, inviting them to play games. Sailors, the ship's captain. And Sav seeking solitude, too, leaving Jayce to wonder if she had imagined growing close in their journey together.

She turned away first, her excitement at finally being on land dampening with the thought that with all his friends around, Sav was unlikely to spend much time focusing on her. Not that he owed her anything.

Bags loaded, Jayce accepted Bentley's offer of a hand up to the seat next to him, and Sav and Nels made space for themselves to sit in the wagon bed.

With a jostle of the reins and whoop, the mule reluctantly stopped munching grass and got the wagon moving.

"What's your mule's name?" Jayce asked over the rattle of wheels on cobblestones.

"Berma," Bentley responded. "Been driving her since I was a third level. Came into town on cycles when I didn't have classes and ran errands for people to earn pocket money, and now I do it for a living." he laughed. "Never thought I'd end up here, but life can be surprising."

She murmured her agreement. She'd followed her mother's footsteps, using her knowledge of plants to serve her community. But her path had taken a turn when the plague struck, leading her to chase a cure and the adventures that had happened since then.

Bentley drove them around Starfall, pointing out various places they could stop and eat. Unlike the places Jayce had seen in Neldor, where every tavern was also an inn, several establishments in Starfall only served food and didn't offer room and board. Bentley called them gatherhalls.

"You mean the sole purpose of this place is to eat? Where do people go to sleep?" Nels asked in amazement as they rolled past another gatherhall.

"That'd be what lodges are for," Bentley said, pointing ahead to a multi-story building taller than anything Jayce had seen in her life, other than the castle in Loshar.

They picked up a meal they could travel with, much to Jayce's regret. She would have liked to experience a meal in a gatherhall, but Sav pointed out they were already going to arrive at the Guilds after dark. Reluctantly, she collected her neatly packaged food and climbed back into the wagon.

She could be grateful for a non-ocean view, at least. They left the city behind them and headed for the Eldenreach Forest.

"We'll skirt the edge of the forest for now and be heading through it near dark," Bentley explained around a mouthful of sandwich. He steered the mule and wagon into a narrow, rocky channel.

The sand-colored stone walls of Varyn's Pass—named after the famous adventurer and founder of the Ivory Guilds—rose steeply on either side.

"Let's see what story these walls have, shall we?" Nels said, clapping his hands and rubbing them together.

He stretched his arms out until he touched the closest rough wall. His brow furrowed, and his eyes closed.

How did his magic work? Was it like hers? Could he hear the rocks speak? If so, they didn't seem to bother him the way the plants bothered her.

Moments passed, with the wagon rattling along, and then Nels withdrew his hand and wiped it on the front of his vest.

"Is there any other passage to the Guilds?" Nels asked, his voice higher pitched than normal. He scanned the rock walls, and Jayce looked, too, as if staring hard enough might reveal the warning herself.

"You can enter the forest on the north end of Starfall and go around Varyn's Pass, but it adds nearly an entire cycle to the journey," Bentley offered.

Another cycle would push back the translation of Dagric Wortcunning's journal that much further. But if it kept them safe...

"What's wrong, Nels?" Jayce asked, putting her sandwich down, all appetite suddenly gone.

"I can't be certain. The rocks seem... excited? I just can't get a clear..." Nels closed his eyes again, looking pained.

"We'll be out in a moment," Sav said, gesturing ahead.

The end of the pass was visible, though still some distance off. Looking up to the top of the wall, she couldn't see any loose rocks.

"What could make rocks feel excited? I didn't know they felt anything at all," she said, shifting in her seat.

"It's not that they feel so much as vibrate. Hard to explain. In any case, something isn't right here," Nels replied, pulling his hands off the wall.

"I trust the guy who talks to rocks," Bentley said, and he urged Berma forward at a faster pace.

Jayce gripped the bench, her head knocking like a loose marble as the wagon jostled over the rocky road.

The ground shook, and a loud rumble echoed through the channel.

"Rockslide!" Nels shouted.

She folded in, arms braced and heart hammering. Whatever words she might have offered the Three in supplication for their lives vanished beneath the rumble of the mountainside.

CHAPTER THREE

Rocks pelted Jayce's back like bee stings. Dust poured over her. She gasped in the tight space between her knees and face.

The wagon bucked.

Arms wrapped around her from either side. A warm presence pressed against her, shielding her from the blows.

She glanced to see Sav's dirt-covered face. He met her gaze, managing a quick, pinched smile.

The rumbling of the rockslide stilled, replaced with a deep thrumming sound.

Sav lifted his head, and Jayce followed his gaze, her mouth dropping open at the sight.

Thousands of stones hung mid-cascade above them, trembling in the air.

Sav straightened, his head inches away from a large boulder that might have landed on him if Nels hadn't stopped it.

"Now what?" Sav asked, twisting to look at Nels.

Nel's face beaded with sweat, his chest heaving. "I can hold it until we pass."

"It'll block the channel," Bentley said.

"There's nowhere else to put it," Nels said.

"You can't put it back?" Jayce suggested.

"I can't lift it any higher. Barely... keeping it up..." Nels grunted, arms trembling like he held the weight with his own bones.

"Go," she said to Bentley, sitting back on the bench. "As fast as you can."

The mule, seeming no worse for the wear, took off at a trot, and then increased to a gallop. Nels groaned, and a loud clatter made Jayce glance back. Several of the larger rocks had fallen into the channel. Nels's face was red with exertion, and Jayce exchanged a worried look with Sav.

They were still in range of the rockfall. If Nels let go now, they would get hit with hundreds of stones.

"I... can't... hold it!" Nels bellowed and collapsed.

Jayce's scream was swallowed in the sound of crashing rocks. The wagon jolted and bounced as the mule bolted, barely escaping the avalanche in time.

Bentley reined the mule in once they were free. The chalky smell of dust lingered in the air, and a few rocks clattered down onto the heap now filling the channel.

Jayce shoved past Sav, scrambling to the back of the wagon. She hovered over Nels, her breath catching in her chest.

"Please be all right," she whispered, fingers searching for his pulse.

He came up gasping, and she fell on her bottom in surprise.

Nels rubbed his arms, then stretched them out, watching the tremble set in.

"Can you breathe? Any pain or dark spots in your vision?" she asked, noting his wide eyes and fast, shallow breathing. Shock, she assumed, but she shouldn't let her guard down until she was certain he would recover.

Nels let his arms fall to his sides. "I haven't moved something that large...well, ever. I once moved a boulder that trapped a shepherd's herds, but it wasn't near as big. Good to know I've still got it."

Then he *winked* at her.

Jayce rolled her eyes. He was *fine*. Still, the fear held her. She shifted her hands, suddenly aware of how tightly they'd clenched. If he ever died trying to keep her safe, she would never forgive herself. And she needed to better understand her magic to prevent that from happening, no matter how difficult or uncomfortable it might be.

Up front, Sav talked quietly with Bentley. Whatever they were discussing seemed serious and involved a lot of hand gestures.

"Does it affect you? Using your magic like that?" Jayce asked, turning back to Nels. To her relief, his pupils were less dilated, and his breathing had deepened.

"I'll sleep like a rock tonight. Pun intended," Nels said, shrugging and grinning.

She managed a smile. If he could laugh about it, it probably wasn't that bad.

His face grew more contemplative. "Moving rocks and hearing their tones are two different things. Listening to the tones makes me feel crazy if I do it for too long. I've thought sometimes I might actually go mad."

That sounds like the feeling I get when I listen to plants, Jayce thought, surprised by the similarities. She pursed her lips. "Well, I'll make sure you get plenty of rest as soon as we get to the Guilds. And I have a tea that can help your muscles recover."

"Yes, mum," Nels teased, the seriousness vanishing from his face.

"Yes, *apothecary*," Jayce replied, trying to look stern. But Nels's goofy smile made laughter bubble out of her, erasing some of the stress from her concern.

"I'm glad you're all right, Martin. Thank you for risking your life to save ours," Sav said, his voice somehow deeper, and his presence imposing as he stood beside them in the wagon.

"Of course," Nels said, nodding. "Anyone would do the same."

"No, they wouldn't. But you're a good man for believing it." Sav turned to Jayce. "I've just been informed that someone is waiting to speak with me at the Guilds. Do you mind if we move on?"

There was a gravity in his expression that she wasn't used to, and she wondered what might make him feel so ill at ease.

"As long as Nels is up to traveling, I see no reason to wait," she replied.

"I'll be fine so long as Jayce sits back here with me. To assess me for any injuries we might have missed, of course,"

Nels said. He didn't wink this time but glanced at her with an arched eyebrow that made her want to roll her eyes again. She resisted.

"Very well," Sav said, and he inclined his head before taking Jayce's place up front.

Shadows passed over the wagon as they drove beneath the canopy of the Eldenreach Forest.

Jayce contemplated the trees, then glanced at Nels, who was staring at her.

"What are you thinking about?" he asked.

She struggled to find the words. "I-I'm jealous of the way you love rocks. That you can hear them, understand them. You make it seem so effortless while I muddle through and avoid plants when I can." She held up her gloved hands for emphasis. "I keep thinking it shouldn't be this hard, but I don't know what else to try."

He kept his gaze on her, his blue- gray eyes like deep, still pools. "I've watched you for a long time. Your gift is unusual, but the Three wouldn't have given it to you if they didn't think you could manage it. Perhaps it'll take more time for you than it does others, but I know you're going to master it. And when you do, you'll leave us all in awe of what you can do."

Jayce shifted to find a more comfortable position, then glanced from him down to her gloved hands. "Some days it feels like I'll never understand it."

"Give it time. And hey, who knows? The Three led you here—perhaps there's someone who can help." Nels stretched his legs out and bent his arms back. He yawned. "Yep, there it is. I think I need a nap."

He tilted his head forward, folding his arms over his chest. No one could possibly sleep with the swaying of the wagon on the dirt road, especially after the excitement of nearly getting crushed by a rockslide, but Nels somehow managed, his soft snore carrying to Jayce before too long.

She got out her lunch, now slightly smashed, and picked at it, peeling thinly sliced meat and cheese off the bread so she could eat in peace without being whispered at.

As she chewed, a flicker of motion caught her eye. She froze, a half-eaten piece of cheese still in her hand. Just off the road, beyond a tangle of fern and shadow, something gold-bright moved beyond the trees. A swishing yellow skirt, worn by a dark-skinned woman bending over as she added a bundle of fresh-picked stems to a basket at her feet. She straightened and stared at the passing wagon.

Little pinpoints of light danced around her head. No, not light—bees. Jayce could hear their humming buzz, and she shuddered, rubbing her arms and trying not to remember the blister bees she'd been stung by the turn prior.

Jayce watched until the woman moved out of sight, the bees seeming to follow her as she went deeper into the blue-green shadows of the forest. She had a strange desire to jump down and pursue the woman and caught herself gripping the edge of the wagon as if preparing to jump out.

She shook the thought from her head, settling back and breathing the earthy scents of the forest, listening as the bees' hum faded. There would be time enough to discover the secrets of Enterea. For now, she needed to get to the Ivory Guilds.

Settling back, she tried in vain to nap. Patches of light filtered through her eyelids where the sun broke through the canopy. The hard wood beneath her provided no relief to her back or bottom as she tried to find a comfortable position to sleep in. How *was* Nels sleeping so soundly?

"Are you sure you want them to stay at the Guilds?" Bentley's voice drifted above the wagon's clatter and Berma's hoofbeats.

"Yes, I'm sure," Sav said. "Do you have a better suggestion?"

"The Head Dame has been keeping things much tighter since you last left. She suspects something, I swear she does. Are you certain Fiametta—"

"I trust her," Sav said firmly.

Did he mean the Head Dame or the other woman he had mentioned, Fiametta?

Despite his excitement, Sav hadn't shared any details about his time at the Guilds or who they were going to see. They would be meeting a Dire from the Lore Guild about the translation, but other than that, she knew nothing about what—or who—to expect.

"Given who she is, shouldn't she be at the hive?" Bentley's voice dropped, but not far enough to keep Jayce from hearing, though she couldn't be certain she heard correctly.

The hive? What did he mean by that? She must have misheard, but she couldn't figure out what the word should have been.

"As far as anyone else knows, she's an apothecary interested in studying at the Mana Guild. There's no reason to introduce her as anyone else, and few people will know the part she has played in history," Sav replied.

Jayce stiffened. They were talking about *her*. She scooted further up the wagon bed to get closer to the two men and better hear what they were saying. As she moved, she spotted Nels lifting his head, open eyes meeting hers. He was awake and listening.

"If the Head Dame catches wind of why you're here... what do you plan to tell her, anyway?"

"I'm hoping to avoid her as long as possible," Sav said.

"I don't think that's wise," Bentley replied. "She already has people watching for you. I get asked every few cycles if I've seen you, where you are, whether you'll return, by different people each time. She'll know the moment you enter the grounds. You know, perhaps I should drop you off here. I can give the journal to my uncle—"

"No," Sav said sharply. "It's my responsibility, and I won't have you taking the risk. If the Head Dame asks, you can deny you even saw it, that you don't know anything about it. If her abilities are what I expect they are, I have to keep you and the others in the dark as much as possible."

Silence passed between the two men, and based on the set of Bentley's jaw, Jayce knew he wasn't satisfied with Sav's answer.

"I am sorry," Sav said a moment later. "I've already put all of you at risk as it is."

"We're aware of the risk, and we would all choose it again," Bentley replied.

"I know that," Sav said, putting a hand on his friend's shoulder. "But the fewer people who know, the safer we'll all be." He glanced back then, as if he could sense her watching.

Jayce blinked rapidly and stretched her arms out, as if just waking. "Are we there?"

She looked at Nels, who slumped back against the wagon, pretending to still be asleep.

Sav's mouth quirked up at the corner. “Not yet, I'm afraid. Do you want another turn up front?”

Jayce shook her head. “I'm fine here, thank you.” Her rapid pulse slowed a bit as she relaxed. He didn't know about her eavesdropping.

What could he be hiding from her and Nels? Why did he consider the Head Dame's abilities dangerous? And why did she get the feeling that they were walking into a place where Sav wasn't welcome?

CHAPTER FOUR

NELS LIFTED HIS HEAD, glancing at the two men sitting up front, then gestured for Jayce to come closer.

She obliged, scooting until she sat next to him, their shoulders touching. He leaned his head toward hers.

"Do you know what all that was about?"

"No, he's never mentioned any of it."

Nels's brow furrowed. "Something is going on here. Something Sav doesn't want everyone to know. Bentley is in on it, too."

Jayce agreed, but she didn't know what to do about it. She could demand Sav tell her and Nels, but he wasn't likely to if he wanted to keep the information from spreading.

"You could talk to him," Nels prompted. "He'll listen to you."

"I'm not anyone to him," she replied, flushing. More than ever, she wondered if she was just a means to an end for Sav. The only one he had access to who had seen the Plague King and lived, one who could answer the questions he had.

Nels rolled his eyes. "Come on, I see the way he looks at you. All you would have to do is bat your eyes and he'd tell you."

"It's not like that," Jayce insisted, glancing at the back of Sav's curly blond head. "Besides, he's trying to keep us safe by not telling us. I think we should consider whether we really want to know."

"Of course he's going to say that. But we should know what we're getting into at the Guilds before it becomes a problem."

The intensity of his gaze made Jayce look away. He would do what it took to protect her, from Sav or anyone else. Her stomach erupted with butterflies despite her attempts, and she leaned away from him, breathing deep and collecting her thoughts.

"I will ask him," she said. "But I'm not going to force it if he says no."

Nels looked at the new distance between them as if he regretted it, but he didn't press her or try to close it.

"I don't like the idea of you being alone with him," he said at last. "How well do you really know him?"

"Well enough I know he won't take advantage, if that's what you're asking. Where is this coming from?"

He rubbed the back of his head, flushing. "Never mind. Forget I said anything."

Jayce forced out a thin laugh. "Nels Martin, I'm beginning to think you're jealous."

His head shot up. “Because I’m concerned about you, I’m jealous? I came to Enterea to help you stay safe. The least you could do is take me seriously.”

Jayce crossed her arms, tightening her cloak around herself. Sav had only ever been a gentleman with her. She didn’t want to entertain suspicions about him. He deserved more than that.

“I would take you seriously if you made more sense. Sav isn’t dangerous.”

“He might not be, but he has put you in danger multiple times,” Nels shot back. He held up a hand, ticking off his fingers. “He took you to the restricted section of the monastery library, ate poison, got you chased by a herd of moon stags, left you by yourself in Musport—where you nearly got killed, mind you—then you were imprisoned and faced down Sir Dray with nothing more than a potted plan for protection. He isn’t good for you.”

The last words came out as a hiss as his anger rose.

“You’re forgetting that I caused half of those things to happen with my own determination to find answers about the noxbrosia,” Jayce replied, heat rising to her face. “Sav isn’t reckless, he’s brave. If you weren’t steeped in jealousy, you might see that.”

“Jayce,” Nels said, his tone pleading. He glanced up at Sav, who still had his back turned to them. “You don’t have to listen to me but at least listen to your own good sense. What does your heart say about him?”

She swallowed hard. Her heart? Her heart beat faster whenever Sav got close, or looked at her, or... no, she wasn’t a lovesick fool, and she could prove it.

"Thank you for your concern, but I trust him," she said, the words coming out harsher than she intended.

He searched her eyes and seemed disappointed by what he saw. He slumped back against the side of the wagon, eyes fixed on the forest instead of her. "Fine. Keep lying to yourself. But don't come crying to me the next time you get hurt and he's the cause of it."

"Nels Martin, that isn't fair. You barely know him. I spent weeks traveling with him."

His sharp, blue-eyed gaze turned on her, drilling into her with its intensity. "And how is that weighed more heavily than the words of a friend you've known most of your life, Jayce?"

"Because that friend is being stupid with jealousy," she shot back, so frustrated she thought she might scream. Typical man. To follow her across the ocean to make sure she didn't make a mistake with some man she had just met. Didn't he trust her?

Sav turned around. "Everything all right back there?"

Jayce smiled at him, glancing at Nels to see his expression, but he didn't even look at her. Fine. If he wanted to sulk, she would let him.

"All good," she called up to Sav, who grinned back and faced forward.

She missed his jovial company—anything but Nels's sulking—and hated herself for the comparison.

The wagon ride continued, tension putting a cloud over them. Occasionally, Sav and Bentley shared hushed conversations that Jayce wished she could hear. They seemed so intensely engaged.

Nels hardly said another word to her the entire ride, except the bare essentials as they stopped to relieve themselves, fill water canteens in a burbling river, and answer questions Bentley tossed over his shoulder.

Just when Jayce thought she could bear Nels's silence no longer, Bentley cried out, gesturing above the trees.

"Look there! You can see the northwest tower!"

Sure enough, a pointed, white, stone roof stood over the tops of the trees with a multi-colored flag flapping in the breeze atop it.

Jayce could almost make out the symbols of the four Guilds—Mana, Warrior, Lore, and Arcane. Her heart picked up pace, out of excitement and anxiety both.

Bentley steered the wagon into the courtyard entrance after they all produced papers proving who they were to the guards at the front gate.

Sav hopped down onto the cobblestones and extended his arms up toward Jayce, who hesitated.

"I'm certain you're capable, but it can't be easy climbing over the side in those skirts," he insisted.

Jayce pointedly did not look at Nels and accepted Sav's offer, allowing him to grasp her waist and swing her to the ground.

She laughed as she landed, stumbling into him.

"See, you did need my assistance," he pointed out, still holding on to her and gazing with those crystal blue eyes.

She thought her heart might gallop out of her chest. Is this why some women fainted in the presence of handsome men?

"I would have managed," she finally replied, sliding out of his reach.

"I'll drop your bags off in the ambry," Bentley called, then clicked his tongue and urged Berma forward.

Sav offered Jayce his arm, and after some hesitation, she took it, pointedly not looking at Nels. Let him think what he would of her. She saw no harm in being escorted by a gentleman.

Instead of heading toward the grand, arched entrance to the Guild Hall, Sav led her and Nels along a mossy stone path that veered off from the courtyard ahead. She blinked in confusion as he released her arm and approached a hidden side door. They weren't going through the front?

He knocked in a deliberate rhythm. No response. He knocked again.

A soft buzz of light formed around the handle before the door creaked open, releasing a wave of golden warmth and the smell of roasting meat and spiced greens. Chef Roland greeted Sav with a hug that lifted him off the ground in a crushing hug.

Roland backed away, adjusting his white apron and turning his smile to Jayce and Nels. "You brought new friends!"

"Yes, I did. This is Jayce and Nels. And this," Sav gestured back to the man in the doorway. "Is Chef Rolan, one of the head chefs of the Ivory Guilds, and the most renowned cook in all of Enterea."

She wasn't certain whether to curtsy or offer her hand. How did one greet a renowned cook? But she needn't have wondered, as Chef Roland spread his arms.

"Chef Roland only gives hugs to friends. And friends of Sav's are friends of mine."

She smiled and stepped forward, allowing the hug. To her surprise, it wasn't the same crushing hug he'd given Sav, but a lighter version, complete with a little pat on her back.

He released her and turned to Nels, not sparing him as he had her.

Nels squirmed and laughed and attempted to return the favor and crush the chef in return, but his much skinnier build didn't do much for him, and Chef Roland lifted him off the ground.

Jayce laughed as Nels was set back down, straightening his clothes and sputtering, his face a brilliant apple-red.

Chef Roland clapped his hands. "There, now, we're properly introduced. Shall I set you up in your regular spot, Sav?"

Sav glanced at Jayce, then nodded to Chef Rolan. "Yes, please. Is anyone waiting for us?"

"The usual party," Chef Roland said, winking. "You know the way. I have to get back to the kitchen and cook up something delightful for you."

"Yes, Chef," Sav said, giving another grin. Then he turned to Jayce and Nels and steered them along a brick pathway around the corner of the building to an outdoor sitting area. Students, instructors, and guests alike chatted and ate, filling most of the tables and chairs.

Sav threaded through the tables, ignoring the occupants. *So he doesn't know everyone in the Guilds*, Jayce mused as she followed. The air was scented with rich food and something floral—lilac perhaps? The purple flowers weighed down their branches in several corners of the cozy dining area. Dark green ivy crawled along most of the limestone walls and dangled from the lattice, providing some shade from the bright noon sun.

Her observance cost her, as her foot caught on an uneven section of brick and she tripped.

An arm swooped around her waist from behind, the other catching both of them on a—thankfully—empty table.

For a heartbeat, she wondered what it might be like to close that gap between their faces, to feel his lips on hers.

Nels released her, making sure she was steady on her own two feet before he stepped back, and in a flash, the feeling was gone.

"Thank you," she said, feeling guilty over their earlier argument. He cared for her, had always done so. Accusing him of jealousy wasn't fair, perhaps, but she wouldn't if he didn't keep trying to convince her to distrust Sav.

A look of concentration came over Nels's face, and he held out his arms, pointing them at the ground.

The bricks beneath her feet shifted, the path smoothing.

Nels relaxed, smiling. "There. They were more easily persuaded than I expected."

"Did you... tell the bricks to move?" Jayce asked with wonder, moving her foot over the flawless path.

He flushed and nodded. "Manufactured stone has less will than raw stone, but it also has less power over itself. I can't always manipulate it, but it comes in handy all the same."

Jayce stared at him. If he could do things like this, why didn't he work as a stonemason instead of running his little booth at the market in Loshar?

"What's with that look?" Nels asked, nudging her with his elbow.

"Nothing." She ducked her head. "Thank you, again."

They walked more slowly than Sav, who had already reached their destination. Through a thick, hanging curtain of ivy, Sav greeted three individuals at a longer table. Laughter and hugging and handshakes were passed around.

A twinge of anxiety went through her. Having Sav practically to herself these past few weeks had spoiled her. Now that they were among his friends, where would she fit in?

Nels held up the vines covering the entrance to the private patio, and a chill crossed her face as she walked through the dark ivy. One of the dangling strands escaped from Nels's grip.

"Oh, I'm sorry," he said, reaching to pull it away. It was caught fast.

Common ivy. I cling to the truth, the leaves told her.

Jayce reached up to help and found the vine already tangled in her hair. She struggled, tugging in vain as the vine attempted to wrap around her fingers.

"Making friends, Jayce?" Sav called.

He meant no harm by it, but the sudden attention drawn to her made panic rise in her chest. She swallowed, her throat feeling as if it had a rock stuck in it.

Beware that one, Speaker, the ivy whispered.

Not again. It had called her the same name as the bloomvine.

Jayce yanked it free at last, shaking the clinging tendrils from her skin. What did it know? It was nothing more than a common sort of plant that grew everywhere back home. It couldn't know anything about her. Its warning was so vague as to be laughable, but she couldn't bring herself to ignore it completely. If she listened closely, she might learn something.

"Who are you hiding back there in the vines, Savage? Is this that healer you told us about?" A woman in a lacy lavender-colored gown straightened the gloves on her hands and eyed Jayce in a curious way, her dark brown eyes intelligent and thoughtful as they took her in.

Jayce's body stiffened. She hadn't been a hermit in Loshar, by any means, seeing clients each turn for her work as an apothecary. But she hadn't spent any time in a group of people her own age... ever. Working off her life debt had kept her far too busy for any socializing, something Nels constantly teased her about.

"They won't bite you," Nels said in her ear, so close she felt his breath. "Say the word, and I'll make up any reason I must to get you out of here." He touched her shoulder, breaking the spell her emotions laid on her.

Beware that one, the ivy's words echoed in her mind.

Her gaze lingered on the dark-skinned woman who had spoken, then on Sav. Who could the warning be about? And should she heed the words, or was listening to the ivy making her paranoid?

CHAPTER FIVE

"JAYCE?"

Sav's voice tugged her from her thoughts. He gestured from the occupants of the table to her.

"Everyone, this is Jayce Keenstone, apothecary of Loshar." He offered a reassuring smile, coaxing her from the entrance of the private patio.

The courtyard air pressed down—thick with spice and smoke, too heavy to breathe easily. Her heartbeat thundered in her ears. Eight pairs of eyes stared. Including Sav's clear blue ones.

Take a step. Just one step, she urged. Her feet refused to move.

Nels nudged her gently. The tightness in her chest eased, and her legs responded.

She glanced back to thank him with a smile and froze.

Beyond him, a heavy-set man in formal robes leaned on a cane, watching her with narrowed eyes.

Jayce's stomach twisted.

She knew that face. She'd seen it on the ship—just a glimpse—but the same crawling unease bloomed in her core, as if her body remembered something her mind couldn't place.

A tall, red-haired woman swept in, greeted the man, and gestured to a table beyond view. The two disappeared together.

Jayce turned to Nels. His lake-blue eyes met hers, steady and sure, urging her forward. He nodded and placed a reassuring hand on her back.

The mystery of the man could wait. She was here to meet Sav's friends. And maybe one of them would know who he was.

She stepped closer and gave a small wave. Two women—one in an elegant purple dress, her dark skin dappled with pale patches, the other in cropped white hair and fighting leathers. The third guest, a man with shoulder-length brown hair, kept brushing it from his face as he fidgeted with blue-striped robes, clearly uncomfortable in them.

Sav gestured toward the woman in the dress. "Fiametta Tofana. Recently made a Dame of the Mana Guild."

Jayce turned her full attention to the woman. She wore long sleeves and tights beneath her skirt, a high-necked dress buttoned to her throat. The visible skin on her face was dark—like the southern islanders Jayce had occasionally seen in Loshar—but interrupted by striking patches of pale. Even her dreadlocked hair, adorned with clicking beads, was streaked with white.

Jayce had read about the condition in palace books. It was something one was born with. Seeing it in person took her breath away.

The woman was stunning—her lip and eye paints bold. She made no effort to hide the lighter patches with make-up.

Jayce admired that level of confidence. She must have incredible control over her abilities to serve as a Mana Guild instructor. Were they plant-related, like hers? Or something different?

Perched on the table beside her sat a wiry woman with spiked, silvery-white hair cropped close on the sides. Her green eyes flicked between Jayce and the room, one leg bouncing like a spring-loaded trap.

"Yamalda Reshar, Warrior Guild trainee," Sav said. "Final trial at the end of the cycle, if I recall?"

"Yep! Gotta train hard and earn that shield," Yamalda piped, her grin wide. She never stopped moving.

Jayce waved shyly, then turned to the last guest. He lounged in his chair, arms folded, exuding a casual disdain that made Jayce bristle until she reminded herself that Sav counted him a friend. She set aside her impression and offered a polite smile.

The man raised an eyebrow. "This is what you spent cycles chasing around Neldor for? She doesn't look like much."

Sav coughed, shooting Jayce an apologetic look.

"That brooding beauty in the corner is Corbin. Corbin Thorenvale, Arcane Guildsman."

"Apprentice to Mordain Rithmore," Corbin added, letting the legs of his chair thud to the floor.

Jayce startled. She didn't know this Mordain, but the name sounded important.

Sav rolled his eyes. "He thinks because he passed his Arcane Guild Trials with the highest merits of his age—"

"Highest merits ever," Corbin corrected, narrowing his gaze.

"I stand corrected," Sav said with a grin. "Well, he thinks he's something."

Corbin snorted and sat back. "At least I don't act like my breeches are made of gold." He stood, and Jayce braced for a fight to break out, tension thick in the air.

A wry smile broke out on Corbin's face, and he clasped Sav, bringing him close.

"Who has breeches made of gold?" Bentley's voice carried across the air as he entered the private sitting area behind Nels. "And why are we all standing around?"

"Making introductions, Bentley. Glad you could make it," Sav said, pulling away from Corbin.

"Then who's that guy?" Yamalda asked, pointing at Nels.

"This is Nels Martin," Jayce said, faltering. Everyone else had had some sort of title or achievement attached to their name. What could she say for Nels? She opened her mouth, but didn't get a chance to speak.

"Just call me your rock man," Nels said, flashing his signature grin and flipping a fist-sized stone in his hand. Where had he even gotten it—his pocket?

Rock man hardly covered all he could do. Jayce searched for better words, but silence stretched. Her tongue stalled.

"That's not half of it. I've only known him since this morning, and he's already saved my life," Bentley offered, slicing through the tension.

Sav nodded, clapping Nels on the shoulder. "I wouldn't have asked him to come if I didn't think he'd be useful."

Warmth bloomed in Jayce's chest. She'd thought Nels might feel out of place tagging along with her and Sav on this mission to contact the Cold Tongue translator, but he fit right in. Nels could make a friend out of anyone.

She watched Nels greet Sav's companions, handing out polished stones from his pockets. A smile tugged at her lips.

"He has a natural charm," Sav said, suddenly beside her.

Jayce blinked out of her reverie. "Yes, he does," she said, flustered. "But then again, so do you. I've seen the way you are with people here. Even on the mainland, you had a way of getting everyone to do what you wanted."

"You could say it's a gift I have."

His smile darkened for a flicker of a moment—then returned to a charming, easy expression so quickly she almost doubted she'd seen the change.

She shook her head. No one could truly understand a person after so little time—not even someone as friendly as Sav. She'd spent over a decade with Nels and still uncovered things about him that surprised her. But she had never doubted his trustworthiness. Somehow, she felt the same about Sav. How could such a generous and kind person be hiding something dangerous?

Besides, if she wanted to cure the plague and stop the Plague King, she had to trust someone.

And for now, she was choosing Sav.

When had stopping the Plague King become her goal? When she'd met Sav, all she had wanted was to uncover who was poisoning people with a fake cure for the plague in Loshar. She had found the proof—exposed and convicted Sir Dray, the kingdom's head bailiff.

But Dray hadn't been working alone. They'd discovered another person stood behind it all. The only clue: the initials L.A.

I don't know anyone with those initials, Jayce thought, sifting through memories of past clients and her ages of being tutored at the castle.

And even if I did—what were the odds they'd be the one behind this?

"Despair no longer, your bellies will soon be full!"

Chef Roland's booming voice broke through her thoughts like sunlight. She turned gratefully toward the sound.

He entered with a bronze cart stacked high with covered dishes and flanked by four attendants balancing even more.

Jayce stepped away from the doorway, moving to join the table. Both Sav and Nels stood at the same moment, each pulling out a chair for her on opposite sides.

She flushed at the attention and chose the one Nels offered—he was closer, after all. His hand brushed her shoulder as he helped her scoot forward, then took the chair at her left.

He stared at her for several moments, something flickering in his eyes she couldn't quite name, before Corbin slid into the seat beside him and pulled his focus away into a spirited debate.

Jayce tore her gaze from Sav and cleared her throat. "So, Fiametta, what sort of ability do you have?"

“I can sense and neutralize poisons,” Fiametta replied, her sharp gaze meeting Jayce’s without flinching.

“Oh! Can you hear the plants?” Jayce leaned forward, growing excited. “Is that how your sensing works?”

“No,” Fiametta said flatly. “I feel the poison. It creates a physical sensation—similar to how it would affect a real body. I draw it out and channel it elsewhere without harm to myself.”

An attendant arrived, setting a plate of cooked fowl in front of Jayce. Its aroma was rich and spiced, mouthwatering.

“Is that why you wear gloves?” she asked, dodging the plate as it settled.

“No. I simply like the look of them,” Fiametta said, her tone curt.

Jayce’s shoulders slumped. It was an incredible ability—but she’d hoped, just for a moment, that they might share something in common.

Jayce bit into a dense roll, slightly sweet beneath its herb-crusted top. Bitter notes bloomed on her tongue. She set it down, appetite fading fast.

Poking at her game hen, she debated whether to scrape off the rest of the herbs—then something moved on Fiametta’s arm.

Jayce flinched, dropping her fork and scooting into Nels, bumping his plate so it almost fell off the table.

Nels stopped it with a quick hand. “Jayce? Are you all right?”

“It’s a rat!” she blurted, breath catching as the tiny creature climbed down Fiametta’s arm, amazed that the woman didn’t even flinch.

A burst of laughter and the clatter of dishes erupted across the room. Yamalda had half-fallen off the table in her mirth, righting herself with Corbin's help, her face flushed crimson.

"Your face!" Yamalda cackled. "I've never seen anyone so terrified over something so small!"

"If I'd known Mortimer would cause such a stir, I would've introduced him at the beginning," Sav said, eyes twinkling.

Nels bumped her elbow. "I'd have done the same in your place," he said, smiling with warm understanding.

"This is Mortimer." Fiametta lifted the hand where the rat perched. "He helps me see."

"You're blind?" Jayce asked, still stunned.

"Partially. I can see shapes and motion, but many things are fuzzy. Mortimer can guide my hands. Do you object? I can put him out of sight."

"No, no—it's fine," Jayce said quickly, pushing herself upright. "I was just startled." Her voice came out a bit too loud. She cleared her throat, picked up her fork, and resumed scraping herbs off her meat.

Chef Roland appeared beside her with surprising speed. "Is something wrong with your meal?" he asked, concern creasing his brow.

"I can hear plants," Jayce murmured, keeping her voice low. "Dead ones are quieter, but... it's still uncomfortable."

She didn't want the others to hear. Didn't want them to see someone who couldn't even eat dinner without complaint.

"I'll prepare it without," Chef Roland said. "A cream sauce. No herbs."

"I wouldn't want to troub—"

"She'll take it," Nels cut in, glancing at Jayce. "You can ask for accommodations, you know. You don't have to grin and bear it. Most people want to help."

Jayce hesitated, then nodded, guilt stirring low in her chest. She hadn't done anything wrong—but all this fuss for her felt excessive.

Chef Roland swept up her plate and handed it off to a servant. "I'll send out a yogurt sorbet while you wait," he said, tone brisk and final.

Jayce folded her hands in her lap and sat quietly, listening to the easy flow of conversation between Sav and his companions. They glanced at her often—measuring, perhaps—but no one addressed her directly. And no one mentioned the plague. Or Sav's mission.

"Fiametta, if I ate that, I'd die," Sav said, nodding toward her plate, which was piled high with vegetables, meat, and heavily spiced rice. "What are you, part dragon?"

"Perhaps I am," Fiametta replied, flashing a grin that had been entirely absent during her exchange with Jayce. "I'm certain one bite wouldn't kill you. You should try it." She lifted her fork and pushed it toward him.

"Oh, no you don't. I've been fooled before. Last time, I couldn't taste normal food for two days," Sav said, eyes wide.

Laughter broke out, and even Jayce smiled.

"I'll try it," Bentley offered. He stood, leaned over the table, and speared a piece of meat with his fork. The moment it hit his tongue, he blanched and lunged for his water, gulping like a man dying of thirst.

Jayce sat back, watching the banter pass between friends. Nels joined in easily, earning his share of laughter.

She stayed quiet, arms resting on the table, and tried to enjoy herself. But some part of her couldn't relax.

Her sorbet arrived, and she took the first bite, letting the cold, delicate, and honey-sweet treat melt on her tongue.

"Loreman Alighieri!" The command in the voice snapped through the courtyard like a whip.

Sav shot to his feet, straightening his jacket. Panic flared across his face—then vanished behind a practiced, polite smile.

The chatter died. Laughter dissolved. Warmth drained from the courtyard as the woman stepped through the ivy curtain, her presence slicing through the gathering like a blade.

She was tall and slender, with the brightest red hair Jayce had ever seen. Her angular face curved into something resembling a smile. She tugged at the sleeves of a fitted maroon blouse, her skirt of the same color whispering across the stone floor.

Jayce recognized her instantly—the same woman who had greeted the man with the cane.

That curled smile didn't reach her eyes. Sharp and searching, they swept the room.

Jayce's gaze darted to Sav, who bowed.

"You honor me, Head Dame Tsega."

The Head Dame of the Ivory Guilds. Powerful, clearly. And if the man with the cane had traveled here just to meet her...

Jayce's fingers crushed her cloth napkin. She would ask about him the first chance she got.

"I was told you had arrived," Tsega said. "I thought I'd say hello before your name lands on the daily incident report." She scanned the table, her eyes catching on Fiametta.

Fiametta didn't flinch. Her spoon paused midair, then lowered with practiced grace. She stroked Mortimer and leaned close to whisper into the rat's fur.

"We'll try not to disrupt too much this time," Sav said lightly. "Actually, there's someone I'd like you to meet." He gestured toward Jayce.

Jayce wiped her mouth and rose, every eye suddenly on her. Her stomach churned, and she steadied herself on the table.

"This is Jayce Keenstone, Apothecary of Loshar. Brilliant with plants. She's been invaluable to our work."

Sav's voice had that subtle, coaxing lilt she'd heard him use when he wanted something.

What was he about to ask?

"Invaluable?" the Head Dame echoed, arching one brow. "High praise, Loreman. She's not enrolled, is she?"

"No, but I was hoping she could observe while we're here. Perhaps attend a few sessions in the Mana Guild."

A ripple—soft but undeniable—passed through the air.

Jayce gripped the edge of the table. Her body tingled as if something unseen brushed against her skin. Strong magic, somewhere close.

Sav smiled too easily.

Was it a trick of the light, or did the Head Dame's eyes seem too glassy, vacant even?

Around the table, conversation stilled. Even Nels's alert posture had slackened. Everyone seemed as if they were under some thrall.

"Unorthodox," the Head Dame murmured, folding her hands. "But then again, so are most things associated with you."

Jayce's pulse jumped.

Had Sav just... manipulated the Head Dame?

Her skin prickled with suspicion. Nels's earlier warnings rang loud in her mind. But no, Sav claimed he had no magic. He hadn't used any on their journey together.

The Head Dame spoke again, but Jayce didn't catch the words—not until every gaze around the table turned to her.

"I—I'm sorry," she stammered, cheeks heating. "What did you say?"

Head Dame Tsega studied her like a specimen under glass. Then she smiled—sharp and toothy. "I asked where you studied."

The air thickened again, syrupy and strange. Tension pulled at Jayce's chest and limbs. Her throat tightened. "W-with my mother," she managed. "I learned my business from her. And I spent several turns with the queen's apothecaries."

"Ah. That explains it."

The Head Dame's eyes gleamed. "And your powers? I can sense significant ability."

"Plant magic," Jayce said, shifting beneath that gaze. "I... I can hear them speak."

She felt it again—that subtle tug. As if power coiled around her, trying to pull something more from her lips.

She clamped her mouth shut.

A flicker of something crossed Tsega's face. Approval? Amusement?

"If the Guild can tolerate Sav's presence," she said dryly, "I suppose we can manage one more anomaly. I'll authorize limited access."

"Thank you," Sav said.

"Yes," Tsega replied, brisk now. "You've always had a way of getting what you want, Savage."

The magic could be coming from her, Jayce realized with relief. But she caught Nels's eyes and saw the accusation there. Had he noticed the strange energy, too?

The Head Dame's gaze lingered on Jayce before flicking to Fiametta, who hadn't moved once during the entire exchange.

"Tofana. A word, before I leave."

Fiametta stood smoothly, gloves immaculate, voice calm. "Of course."

Jayce watched them vanish into the courtyard's shadows. Unease curled tight in her gut. Her appetite had long since vanished.

Even the warmth of the evening now felt thin and brittle.

Dishes clinked. Laughter resumed.

Sav leaned in to joke with Corbin and Yamalda—never once glancing her way.

Someone had used magic. She wanted to believe it hadn't been Sav. But she couldn't be sure. Not unless she asked.

Nels met her gaze. His look said it all: *I told you so.*

He glanced at Sav, then back at her, tilting his head with deliberate emphasis.

She didn't want to think the worst—that Sav had lied. Still, she couldn't ignore the evidence.

She would root herself in the truth, even if it took time to bloom.

CHAPTER SIX

"FOR YOUR MIDNIGHT MUSINGS," Chef Roland said with a wink as he handed her a small package. "Food makes the best company. Next to new friends, of course."

Jayce peeked inside the wax paper wrapping. A tart—lemon, judging by the scent. Her belly was full, and her cheeks ached from smiling.

Perhaps she would find friends here.

"Thank you again, Chef Roland. Impeccable service, as always," Sav said, clasping the large man's hands.

"I don't think I'll be able to eat anything I make after this," Nels said, rubbing his stomach with a groan of contentment.

Jayce agreed silently. The replacement dish they'd brought her had no plant matter—no whispers, no chill on her tongue. Just quiet, blessed warmth. Warmer than she'd felt in ages.

After another round of thanks, the group left the courtyard, splitting into smaller knots. Fiametta disappeared into the dark with barely a wave, Mortimer riding on her shoulder. Corbin, Yamalda, and Bentley wandered in the opposite direction, leaving Sav, Nels, and Jayce to walk together.

The evening air was cool and soft against Jayce's skin. Crickets had begun their chorus, and the breeze tugged at her sleeves and hair like a restless child.

"I'll show you to your rooms at the ambry—that's where students and guests stay," Sav said, gesturing ahead to a cluster of single-level buildings. "Bentley already dropped off your luggage."

The building's entry smelled faintly of lavender polish. A lantern flickered beside the front desk, where a woman dipped her quill in ink, the scratch of her pen steady and deliberate. She looked up and smiled.

"Need to get checked in?"

The woman gave them a building number and three keys. Sav took them, thanking her, and led them to the correct building. They stepped through an elegant arched doorway into a softly lit entry hall, where a crystal chandelier glimmered overhead. Behind a polished desk sat another woman, who looked up and asked if they needed help finding their rooms.

Sav offered a slight nod. "That won't be necessary, thank you."

He took them through a second set of doors into a long, carpeted corridor lined with polished doors and lantern sconces. Halfway down, he stopped and unlocked one.

"This is your room, Jayce." He offered her the key.

Her hand hovered—then dropped. "Are we taking the journal to the translator in the morning?"

Nels stepped forward and took the key Sav still held, sparing her the choice. Sav handed him a second one.

"Yours is two doors down," he told Nels, still avoiding Jayce's question. "The tag matches the door's symbol."

"What time should I be awake?" she asked, her voice firmer now.

"I signed you up for a class after breakfast, ninth bell." He fidgeted with the final key. "I can have someone wake you an hour before, if that's enough time for you to get ready?"

"You're not taking me. To see the translator, I mean."

Sav winced and reached a hand toward her but then pulled back and dragged it through his curls instead. "Jayce, he's risking everything. If word gets out—"

"I wouldn't betray him," she said. "I'm the one who found the journal. I deserve to know what it contains." Her own boldness shocked her. She fought the instinct to apologize, to shrink.

Sav's expression tightened. "This man is taking an enormous risk for us. He could be imprisoned, his life's work confiscated or destroyed. I promised him anonymity."

She understood. She did. But disappointment surged anyway, hot and sudden. She crossed her arms, holding it all in. "Will you at least tell me what he says?"

"I'll tell you everything tomorrow," Sav assured, already backing away.

His hand went to his vest, and she caught the gesture, noticed the rectangular outline pressing beneath the fabric. He had the journal with him. Was he going *now*?

Her eyes narrowed, but she said nothing.

Sav turned and unlocked the door across the corridor. “Goodnight, Jayce,” he said, casual as ever. But a sheen of sweat glistened on his brow.

Jayce didn’t respond. Let him think her rude.

Why even bring me here? She could have stayed in Loshar. In her apothecary. Living her peaceful, if dull, life.

Nels glanced between the two of them with a confused frown.

The door clicked shut behind Sav.

With a huff, Jayce held out her hand for the key Nels had taken. When he passed it to her, she unlocked her door and stormed inside.

Nels lingered in the hallway, then peered in. “Do you want company?”

She dropped onto the edge of the bed, still brimming with frustration. After a beat, she motioned for him to enter.

While he closed the door, she took in the room. An off-white woven blanket covered the bed, and the fern-like tendrils of a potted plant on the bedside table bobbed as if in greeting. She inhaled the faint scent of dust and mint, eyes scanning the wardrobe and a screened-off corner for washing.

He leaned against the wall across from her, arms crossed. “What are you going to do?”

“Do?” Jayce echoed. She picked at the fingers of her gloves, peeling them off to let her skin breathe. Some days the leather stifled her—but she couldn't imagine facing the world without them.

He nodded toward the hallway. "About Sav. He's acting suspicious. Don't you want to know why?"

"I—I don't know." The words came out deflated. All her fire, gone. She didn't even have it in her to accuse him of jealousy. Sav *was* acting suspicious, but what could she do about it?

"You could follow him," Nels offered.

She blinked. "I don't know the first thing about following someone." The idea startled her—and intrigued her. *Would I really do that*?

"You listen for his door. Or post a watch. Maybe by enlisting a certain supportive friend?" His brows wagged up and down. "Then you wait a few moments, keep back, duck behind things. Once he's where he's going, decide if you'll confront him or just eavesdrop."

Jayce stared. This was... surprisingly detailed.

"Why do you sound like an expert?" she asked. "Do you have a secret hobby I should know about?"

It felt good to tease him. Her chest lightened, the ache from Sav's dismissal beginning to ease.

"Believe it or not, yes," he said, his face dead serious. "Some types of stone, the most rare ones, if they sense me coming, they'll hide. Not literally, but it's like they turn off the signal they would otherwise let off. So I've learned to sneak up on them. I imagine humans are similar."

"You... sneak up on rocks?" she said, a grin blooming across her face.

Nels rubbed the back of his neck. "It sounds pretty ridiculous when you say it like that." He seemed uncertain about whether she was making fun of him or being genuine.

She let out a small laugh. "No, no! It's... cute," she finished, uncertain what else to call it.

He rolled his eyes. "I'll show myself out."

Jayce reached out and caught his hand.

"I think you're amazing," she said, gazing up at him and getting lost in his lake-blue stare. "Sure, your methods sound quirky, but they work. You're one of the most-requested gem experts in Loshar. That's no small feat."

The flush in his cheeks deepened. He glanced at their clasped hands, then back to her, a full grin on his face. "So, are you turning to espionage?" he asked.

Jayce rubbed at the bald spot at the end of her right eyebrow. She'd thought she'd had her fill of sneaking around after the incident at the Draigh Monastery where she and Sav had nearly been caught in the restricted area of the library. "Do you really think I should?"

Nels studied her. In the silence that passed, the click of a door opening in the corridor outside sounded far too loud.

"If you are, that may be your chance," he said.

"Look for me?" she asked breathlessly.

He walked quickly to the door and cracked it open with painstaking slowness.

"That's him." He pulled his head back and looked at her. "He's leaving out the front. Moving fast."

Jayce hesitated, head spinning. If she followed him and he caught her, he might be angry. But she had seen Sav angry before. She could handle it. If he didn't want her to sneak around, he should have invited her. *She* had found Wortcunning's journal. She deserved to be part of its translation.

She shoved off from the bed, struggling to get her fingers in her gloves. "I'm going," she said. "He has no right to shut me out. But don't take this to mean I don't trust him."

Nels grinned. "We'll see what you think after you get back with more evidence that Mr. Too-good-for-his-britches is hiding something."

Jayce shot him a disapproving look but said nothing as she approached him.

He stepped back and opened the door for her. "Remember to blend in with your surroundings. Act as if you belong there. You're not just tailing him, you have a purpose. Don't hunch or try to hide. If he turns and sees you, you could always claim you're out for a walk."

On a whim, she tip-toed and pressed a kiss to his cheek. "Thank you."

He blinked, looking dazed, and raised a hand to his cheek. "Any time."

She slid past him into the hallway.

"And Jayce?"

She paused, glancing back. His expression had shifted—earnest, almost worried.

"Stay safe."

Her lips parted, but she pressed them shut. This was her choice. Her risk.

She wouldn't ask him to come. Besides, there was a better chance Sav wouldn't see her if she went alone. Straightening her spine, she set off at a brisk pace.

The woman at the front desk barely looked up as Jayce passed. Her blood pounded in her ears.

Surely everyone knew what she was doing.

Surely one of them would call out to her and ruin everything.

But the lady at the desk only smiled and wished her a good evening, and then she was outside, breathing cool night air and walking among a surprising number of people.

Where were they all going? Most were walking the same direction she was, away from sleeping quarters. Could there be some kind of event happening at one of the Guilds?

She stretched her neck side to side, trying to peer past those in front of her until—

There.

Sav's curly blond hair bobbed just ahead in the crowd.

She veered around a chatty group of young women and sped up, walking faster than anyone on a casual stroll.

Most of the people went left.

Sav kept going straight. Hands in his pockets. Relaxed. Unbothered. The picture of a man out for a stroll.

Keeping him in view was easy. Keeping out of his was harder.

Her limbs felt mechanical, her breath shallow. Every step sounded too loud, every glance too exposed. *He'll turn around. He'll see me. He'll know.* Her heart pounded too hard, her mind spun too fast as she tried to predict what he would do next and anticipate the moment when he caught her.

They crossed the grounds, passing under still-lit lanterns, until Sav stopped.

Jayce froze, biting back a yelp, and ducked behind an oak tree, her whole body trembling.

Flattening herself to the trunk, she kept her skin from brushing the bark.

Glancing now would give her away. She didn't dare.

Don't turn around. Don't turn around...

After what felt like a lifetime, she peeked.

Sav was crossing the grass, away from the path, moving toward a tall building of pale stone.

The Lore Guild.

Of course, the translator would be in the Lore Guild; they were experts in languages and cultures.

Jayce's skirt swished across the grass as she stepped quickly, trying to keep her shoes from thudding against the ground. Out here, there were no crowds to hide behind. Only a few stragglers that passed her going the opposite direction, headed back toward the ambry.

The sky deepened from a dusky violet color to an inky blue-black as the last trace of sunlight fading beneath the horizon. Lanterns buzzed with tiny moths, casting pools of honeyed light that flickered and stretched across the path.

Her initial nervousness had dulled, replaced by a shiver as the air cooled. She hugged her arms around herself, wishing for her cloak.

Had she misjudged Sav? Maybe he was just meeting an old friend from his Ivory Guild days.

This had been a mistake. She could still turn around and go back to her room...

Sav mounted steps worn smooth by decades of shuffling boots.

She couldn't follow too closely—he'd spot her for sure. She hung back, heart racing, willing him not to glance behind.

He didn't.

As soon as he reached the doors, she bolted forward, her steps light and quick up the stairs.

If she didn't hurry, she'd lose him.

At the top, she slowed to a walk, trying to breathe normally. Twin owls judged her from the double doors, carved into the wood.

Her hand hesitated on the door.

Why was she doing this? Sav would tell her what the translator said. Wouldn't he?

How well do you really know him? Nels's words entered her mind.

Jayce set her jaw.

She'd spent too long fumbling in the dark. If this translation could help end the plague, she *had* to know what it said.

She tugged open the doors and stepped inside the Lore Guild.

Books filled every wall, bound in silks, leathers, and linen. Some cracked with age, others gleamed like new. The scent of parchment, beeswax, and old ink wrapped around her. Students whispered. Pages turned. Soft footsteps echoed beneath the golden glow of standing lamps.

The collection at the Draigh Monastery had been larger, but this one held all the evidence of decades of wealthy patrons' donations. Plush chairs and gleaming tables stood in tasteful arrangements. Polished statues caught the light, and paintings adorned what little visible wall space wasn't taken up by bookshelves.

A wide staircase rose from the center of the room, a crimson carpet running between polished railings toward the upper level.

Rooms branched off the main entrance, each one filled with more books and chairs and tables. Most of the students looked to be packing up—gathering books and bags, drifting toward the exits.

The smell of parchment and quiet weight of knowledge wrapped around her like a blanket.

She startled back into awareness, catching a glimpse of Sav's curly hair as it winked at her between shelves.

She gathered her nerves and took off after him, not bothering to hide. Would he meet the Dire in plain sight, relying on the crowd for cover? Or slip upstairs to a private office?

She rounded a corner—then halted, heart jumping.

Sav stood in the middle of the aisle, a book in hand. Not the journal. Something he'd pulled from the shelf. He was reading—or pretending to.

Did he know she was following him?

Or maybe he'd arrived early and needed to pass the time. She clung to that thought.

Jayce leaned back against the shelf and forced herself to breathe. She tried to focus on anything else—counting lamps, then statues, then students as they passed.

A young man gawked as he went by, probably wondering why she stood in such an odd spot. She offered a stilted smile, then risked a quick glance toward Sav.

Gone.

Panic surged.

She stepped into the aisle, head swiveling. No Sav by the staircase. None at the tables. Nowhere among the chairs.

Thesleepingfoxy

Darting between more shelves, her heart pounded. He'd find her. He'd send her back to her room. And worst of all—he'd know she didn't trust him.

Still, she didn't dare search too widely. If she made a loop around the room, she might miss him—and he might catch her.

He had to be close. Just a few shelves over...

A book dropped somewhere behind her, the thud oddly sharp in the hush. Then came the sound of a cane, a slow, deliberate tapping as it approached.

"Brave of you to wander the Guilds alone," a gruff male voice said from behind her.

She froze, closing her eyes and taking several breaths. It wasn't Sav.

Spinning, she clasped her hands in front and plastered a pleasant smile on her face. A greeting died on her lips at the sight of the man she faced. Sunken eyes fixed on her. His sallow, sagging cheeks and thin lips stretched into something like a smile. One hand braced on a glossy black cane.

Recognition struck hard enough to make her take a step back.

"You—I saw you on the ship," she stammered. She hadn't meant to speak, only to slip away unnoticed. Sav would vanish if she stayed much longer.

"Yes, I did travel from the mainland with you," the man said. "I've been so curious these past ages how you've fared. You had so much potential."

Jayce opened her mouth to explain she wasn't who he thought she was, but something prickled inside of her, a glimmer of recognition.

“Do I know you?” she whispered.

Her stomach squeezed, heaving at the words. She wouldn’t lose her dinner on the fancy rug beneath her feet. The Three forbid she spatter the books, or his polished shoes, or that cane...

His smile vanished. He muttered something she didn’t catch. Something about memories. Or remembering?

Her stomach clenched again, and pain shot through the center of her chest, right at her sternum. Had she eaten something bad? Chef Roland would be horrified if she got ill from his cooking. Perhaps a sickness she had caught while at sea. She pressed one hand against the pain and held the other hand over her mouth.

“I’m not who you’re looking for. I’m sorry.” She backed into a shelf. Books shifted. She startled—and bolted sideways.

Get to the door, get out, leave before he says anything else.

Those sunken eyes tracked her, even as she fled to the end of the aisle and broke into the open.

Footsteps followed. The cane clicked against the floor. The mumbling. That gruff voice.

“Stop! Girl, stop.” The cane struck the wood with a sharp *crack*.

A cold shimmer prickled across her scalp, and suddenly, her thoughts vanished. Like someone had pulled a thick curtain over her mind. Her feet slowed. Why was she running?

“Always too much,” the man muttered. “Fifty ages, and I haven’t learned to use a lighter hand.”

He stepped in front of her, peering into her eyes.

Her senses stayed intact, but her thoughts slipped from her like smoke. Panic bloomed, wordless and rising.

She knew she should run, but she couldn't remember why.

So she stood frozen in the quiet library, eyes flicking from the man's scarred face to the reflection in the window behind him—

A familiar silhouette. Blond hair. Climbing the stairs.

She focused on him like a lifeline. Something solid. Something real.

"No, no. Come back to me," the man murmured, reaching a trembling hand toward her head. "Stand still… that's good…"

Sav.

The name snapped into place inside her, and thought came flooding back.

Jayce gasped as if she'd stopped breathing. Knocking the man's hand away, she slipped around him, not bothering to apologize or demand an explanation. She could only think of getting as far away from him as possible.

Bursting through the Lore Guild's doors, the cold night air slapped her back to alertness and cooled her burning lungs.

Who *was* that man? And why did every instinct she had beg her to stay far away?

CHAPTER SEVEN

JAYCE DIDN'T STOP RUNNING until her lungs and limbs gave out. Rain had begun while she was in the library, and the light drops spattered her face and arms as she slowed to a walk, trying desperately to catch her breath.

She wanted nothing more than a warm drink and bed, but panic still flooded her system. Sleep would be a long time coming.

Her fingers searched her pockets, finding with relief that the key to her room was still there. She gripped it, frustrated thoughts swirling.

She could have run to Sav. Called out. Demanded he take her to the translator.

Instead, she'd fled from an old man with a cane. Like a coward.

A choked noise escaped her throat. She pressed her palms to her eyes, then let out a sharp, frustrated yell and tore off her gloves. The leather clung, tacky with sweat and rain.

She stared at her hands.

One bare, the other marked with ivy.

Proof she couldn't control what lived inside her. She didn't even understand how it worked, why plants sometimes listened and why other times they overwhelmed her.

The gloves rested limply on the path at her feet. Wind stirred them as the rain grew heavier, swallowing what dry space remained.

Embarrassed by her outburst and grateful no one had seen it, Jayce bent to retrieve them. With slow, dejected steps, she made her way back to the ambry.

The air inside felt still, thick with that cloying scent of lavender. Too clean, too quiet. Her boots squelched softly on the rug. The warmth of the ambry wrapped around her, but it did nothing to ease the ache in her chest.

At the front desk, she barely acknowledged the woman's polite question. Her eyes stayed fixed on the hallway ahead.

She turned the key in the lock.

As if summoned, a door two down opened a crack, then widened.

Jayce paused, forehead resting against the door. She didn't want to see Nels. Didn't want to explain how badly she'd failed.

Maybe talking to Nels will help. A traitorous voice whispered, a little too eager to see him.

She turned.

"How was it?" Nels asked.

Jayce snorted. "Let's just say, I'm not changing careers any time soon."

She opened the door and stepped inside, knowing he would follow. Sitting on the bed, she concentrated on removing her shoes and gloves, avoiding Nels's expectant stare.

The door clicked but didn't close, leaving a sliver of the bright hallway light filtering into the dark room.

Nels took up his spot on the wall, arms over his chest. He cleared his throat, but didn't speak.

Jayce fidgeted. Why didn't he start? He had to be dying to hear how it had gone.

But he waited, and as the moments stretched, she wished he would say something.

"You can't have expected to be good at it the first time."

The first time? She was never doing that again. This time, she meant it.

"I lost him," she admitted, staring at her hands.

Nels sighed and came to sit beside her. "It's all right. You can talk to him tomorrow. We'll corner him. Won't let him leave until you have answers."

Jayce shivered. Goose pimples lifted along her arms. His shoulder radiated steady heat. She hadn't realized how cold she'd gotten until it reached her.

Should I tell him about the man with the cane?

It seemed silly, now. In fact, the more she considered it, the more she was convinced she had overrated him. He must have mistaken her for someone else. She'd panicked, that was all.

That rolling in her stomach had stopped, but she still didn't feel right.

She lay back on the bed. “I don’t feel well.”

If he could tell she was holding back, he didn’t let on.

Part of her wished he would. That he’d challenge her, make her say what she was too afraid to speak aloud.

Instead, he stood and walked around the bed and pulled back the covers.

“Get changed,” he said gently. “I’ll go ask the woman up front if they have any hot packs.”

Jayce stared at the ceiling, unmoving. “What’s it like when you talk to rocks?” she asked.

He didn’t reply right away. Perhaps he was offended that she had never asked until now.

“I listen to their tones,” he said at last. “It’s like music. I can sense when the rhythms shift, when they’re trying to communicate something different. It took a lot of practice to hear them well, and even more to influence them the way I do.”

Jayce propped herself up on her elbows and glanced at him. “Do you think I’ll ever be able to communicate with plants the same way?”

Nels tilted his head, straightening as he finished turning down the bed. “Well, now, that’s another matter. I sometimes wonder if…” He trailed off, shaking his head. “Never mind.”

Now he had her full attention. She sat up, leaning on one hand. “You can’t leave me with that. Tell me what you think.”

He ran a hand through his brown hair, clicking his tongue. “Ah, I should learn to keep my mouth shut one of these days. I don’t want to imply that I know more than you about your own abilities, but I’ve thought about it. A lot.”

She waited, breath shallow.

He shrugged. "It's not straightforward like most other abilities, is it?"

Jayce clenched her jaw to keep from snapping. *Get to the point.* She swallowed, her mouth suddenly dry, and forced herself to wait.

Nels held her gaze, blue eyes sharp with purpose. "I don't think your ability is about plants."

A nervous laugh slipped out before she could stop it.

"What? Of course it's plants. I've heard their voices since I was a child."

But even as she spoke, doubt crawled beneath her skin.

What if he was right?

Her parents used to say she'd claimed that from the moment she could talk—said the plants whispered to her. She remembered it clearly. Voices blooming from roots, leaves, petals, even dried stems. And each one sounded different with a voice of their own.

Nels lifted both hands. "It's just a theory. I don't have proof. Just... your magic acts strange. You're either a late bloomer, or there's some kind of—I don't know... block? Is that a thing?"

Jayce shrugged. She'd never studied the other abilities in depth and couldn't claim to understand how they worked.

A *late bloomer, indeed.*

She stared down at the ivy pattern on her left hand, a lump rising in her throat. "Sometimes I think the Three cursed me with this ability."

"The Three are good," Nels insisted. "They wouldn't curse you. This might not even be about you—maybe the magic itself is broken. Twisted somehow. Something dark enough to create the Plague King."

He paused. "Maybe you're meant to figure that out."

She let out another laugh, sharp and quiet, as tears pricked her eyes. "I'm not the one they want for that."

Silence filled the space again, Nels lingered on the far side of the bed, opening his mouth several times only to close it again, as if unsure how to keep the conversation going.

Jayce sighed and stood. "You can go see about that hot water pack now." A gentle dismissal, but it somehow created a barrier between them.

She waited for the sound of the door shutting tight before slipping behind the dressing screen. Damp fabric clung as she peeled off her blouse and skirt and hung them carefully. She hesitated between pulling on a nightgown or dry clothes—and opted for the latter.

Nels would be returning. Something about being seen in sleepwear felt... vulnerable.

Dressing quickly, her body warmed with motion and the comfort of dry fabric.

A knock came at the door.

She tugged her blouse into place and called, "Come in."

Nels stepped inside as she breezed out from behind the screen, adjusting the rounded collar of her shirt.

He eyed her outfit. "Are you going to sleep in that?"

Jayce flushed. "No." She didn't offer an explanation.

At the foot of the bed, Nels lifted the blankets and slid a floppy, hot-water-filled bottle beneath them, then laid the covers back down.

"Speaking of abilities," he said, as if he'd never left.

Jayce stiffened. She had just calmed down, if he dragged her back into that discussion, she might lose all semblance of peace.

“What do you think of what happened when the Head Dame showed up?” He raised one eyebrow in her direction.

“It—she’s interesting. Sav didn’t seem to like her. And there was this... energy. I couldn’t tell where it was coming from.”

“So you did feel something! I knew it!” Nels nearly toppled over in his excitement, catching himself with a hand on the blanket. He smoothed it out before straightening again.

“Perhaps,” Jayce said, hedging.

“Oh, no you don’t. You felt something. It was weird, right? Like the air was buzzing? I felt like I couldn’t move.”

“Yes! And the air got thicker. Someone was manipulating space or time or—”

“The people in it,” Nels cut in, snapping his fingers. “I’d bet all the rare gems in my collection that it came from Sav.”

“But I didn’t feel it until the headmistress entered the room,” Jayce countered.

“You’ve never seen Sav convince anyone of anything?” Nels raised his eyebrows. “Based on what you’ve told me, the man’s a professional charmer. What if he’s goddess-blessed?”

Jayce thought back over the past few weeks. She had seen Sav coax cooperation from the monks at the monastery, charm information from the grumpy innkeeper, even win favor with the queen herself—always with that handsome, easy smile.

She shook her head. "It never felt like this before today." She crossed to the bed and sat down on the long edge, staring at the wardrobe, thoughts churning.

"You have to admit Sav's hiding something from you," Nels said. "Possibly from his friends, too. They didn't seem to notice anything strange."

"*If* it is Sav," Jayce replied. "Wouldn't they have said something?"

"They all seemed to be accomplished magic-users. But if he's *that* powerful," he paused. "He might have them all under his influence."

She didn't want to believe that, but she couldn't argue any more that Sav was being forthright with her. More than ever, she wished she had been able to follow him to his meeting. She cursed the weakness and fear that had sent her running like a dog with its tail between its legs.

"I'm no scholar," Nels said. "but traveling with my family, I saw a lot of different magic. Mostly physical stuff. But there were healers, too. And people who could manipulate others with nothing more than their words."

"He's never used it on me," Jayce said.

At least, she didn't think he had. But how would she know?

Nels's brow creased. "What do you mean?"

"If his ability is to manipulate people, then he would've made me talk. But he never has. Even when it frustrated him, he respected that I couldn't." With the exception of his tantrum in Musport, but he had apologized for that. He hadn't used magic to try to make her tell him what he wanted to know.

"Or maybe you just don't remember," Nels pointed out. "Maybe the person being manipulated forgets the conversation entirely."

That.

That was the fear she couldn't admit aloud.

And yet—why was she still here, if he'd already gotten what he wanted?

"You could be right. I want you to be careful around him. I don't think he's being honest about what he wants from you. And I don't want you to get hurt."

Her heart thudded. Words failed her. No one had looked out for her like this since Javin, and that old insecurity rose up inside her. She couldn't stop Nels from protecting her, but part of her still believed he'd chosen the wrong person.

Nels crossed the room and sat beside her. The mattress dipped beneath his weight, and Jayce slid against him.

A surprise laugh escaped as his arm wrapped around to steady her.

She didn't intend to lean into him, but once she did, she didn't want to move. His arm felt like it belonged there.

Her gaze lifted. His face was closer than she'd expected. Their argument the previous turn surfaced uninvited, and guilt settled in behind her ribs. Even if he did act overprotective sometimes, she recognized his concern for her and knew she had spoken too harshly.

"I am really, truly glad you're here, Nels."

He blinked in surprise, seeming at a loss for words.

He still held her—and she didn't stop him. That thought alone knocked something loose inside her. Sav had made her feel this way, too. A comforting warmth, a desire to be closer, to discover where those feelings could take them.

The possibility that she cared for them both hit her like a warning bell, making her squirm.

"I wouldn't rather be anywhere else," Nels said as he released her. He tilted his head sideways. "Except maybe the mountains. Sitting on a nice, big pile of rocks."

The tension—or whatever existed between them—eased.

"You and your rocks," she said softly, fondness curling inside her.

He chuckled.

She hesitated. She didn't want to move, to break the fragile peace of the moment. But exhaustion dragged at her limbs and clouded her thoughts. She needed rest.

"Nels?"

"Hm?" He said, as if distracted.

"I think I'm going to go to bed. This turn has been... a lot."

"Of course."

He scooted away, and cool air filled the space between them. He hesitated a beat—then reached into his pocket.

"Before I go," he said, a little awkwardly, "I have something for you."

"Oh—no, you don't need to give me anything, I—"

"I insist. And it's nothing, anyway." He rummaged in his pocket and pulled out a palm-sized stone. Smooth, round, and gray, it looked like an ordinary river rock.

"It's a wishing stone, see?" He pointed out the white band that went all the way around the stone. "I've told this one to give you anything you want."

He held it out to her.

Jayce stared at the stone. He always showed up just when she needed him. Even when she didn't let him in.

They had known each other since they were kids—Nels drifting through Loshar with the merchant caravans during the Purple Bell Moon, his family always gone again by the scarlet of the Hunter's Moon.

Until one age, he stayed.

His parents had passed. He'd become an adult in a world that didn't wait for grief.

Her parents had invited him over often. And even after they'd succumbed to the plague, and her brother Javin didn't come home, Nels had still dropped by.

Every week.

Her house had felt too hollow, echoing with a life that no longer existed.

She hadn't been able to imagine making a new one with him. With anyone.

Why had she insisted on being so lonely?

A white band of quartz wrapped through the center of the stone. Was it just her imagination, or did it hum slightly where it touched her skin? It felt warm, as though it still carried Nels's touch.

She closed her fingers, a small smile tugging at the corner of her lips. "Thank you, Nels. It's lovely, but I'm not sure what good it can do."

"A wishing stone only works if you believe in it," he said. "And in yourself."

He said it with the kind of quiet confidence she'd never managed to feel.

She swallowed and glanced away. The weight of the turn—of the past few cycles—wrapped around her like a heavy fog.

"I'll be two doors down if you need anything. And I mean it, Jayce. Anything."

"Goodnight, Nels," she said with emphasis.

He nodded, though he lingered for another breath before stepping out and pulling the door closed behind him. The room fell silent, save for the distant murmur of voices down the hall and the faint patter of rain against the window.

Jayce exhaled slowly, letting the quiet settle into her bones. She rolled the wishing stone between her fingers, its smoothness steadying the churn of her thoughts.

At last, she set it on the nightstand, kicked off her boots, and sank onto the bed, pulling the covers over her. Her body ached with the kind of exhaustion that wasn't just physical, and she relished in the relaxing warmth of the hot water bottle at her feet. She didn't know what tomorrow would bring, but for tonight, at least, the world and all of its problems could wait.

Her eyes fluttered closed, then flew open as a whispered voice scratched against her mind.

The branches of the plant on the bedside table were *moving*. Delicate fronds stretched toward her, slow and deliberate.

She'd almost forgotten it was there, silent and watching like it knew her secrets.

Jayce tossed the covers off and snatched the potted plant. She swiftly shoved it into the wardrobe and shut the doors tight.

She dashed back to the bed and curled under the blankets.

The wardrobe doors rattled. A soft, persistent sound came through, like fingertips tapping from the inside. But the faint whisper had stopped.

Jayce grabbed the pillow and clasped it over her head to block everything out.

Sleep came in fits, twisted and shallow. Even in her dreams, her thoughts circled back to one question.

Why were all the plants in Enterea trying to speak to her? And more—could she trust a word they said?

CHAPTER EIGHT

JAYCE WOKE TO THE soft patter of rain against the window, the gray morning light filtering through the thin curtains. The quiet felt so heavy it could have been comforting. Her mind drafted in the haze of sleep, as though the events of the previous turn had been nothing but a strange dream.

A rapid knock jolted her awake. She sat up fast, the smooth wishing stone Nels had given her tumbling from her hand and landing on the blanket. She hadn't even realized she'd picked it up in her sleep.

"Jayce?" Nels's voice came muffled through the door.

She rubbed at her face, then frowned at the wardrobe door, slightly ajar with a single branch of the fern sticking out of it.

"Give me a moment!"

Jayce skirted the reaching branch—it was *definitely* reaching. What had gotten into the plants here?

She dressed as quickly as possible, her fingers fumbling on the clasps of the stiff green stay she wrapped around her waist. She swished her brown skirts, adjusted the cream-colored top, then ran a brush through her hair before braiding it with practiced fingers.

With the braid tied off and tossed over her shoulder, she stepped toward the door—only for it to swing open the moment her hand brushed the knob.

She yelped, stumbling back as Nels peeked through, sheepish and damp-haired, holding up a folded bit of parchment.

"Sorry," he said, leaning against the frame and raking a hand through hair that looked freshly washed.

"A girl needs time to get ready, Nels. I can't jump out of bed and toss on new clothes and call it good."

"Well, it was worth the wait," he said, eyeing her up and down before tugging at a loose strand from her braid.

Jayce flushed, tucking the hair behind her ear and clearing her throat. "What reason do you have for waking me like there's a fire in the building?"

Judging by the pale light outside, the seventh bell hadn't yet sounded, and Sav had arranged for her to be woken by the eighth. She could have slept a bit longer.

He brandished the parchment. "I came to wake you, hoping we could catch Sav before he crept off to wherever he's going to go today, and found this tucked in your doorframe."

Jayce reached for it. "Have you read it?"

Nels shook his head, brushing a few strands of damp hair from his eyes. "Nope. It's addressed to you. Looks like a woman's handwriting."

She turned it over and smiled wryly. "That's Sav's."

He gaped. "I *knew* there was something off about him. No man writes that neatly."

"He takes great pride in it," she said, unfolding the parchment. "Not everyone writes with barely legible chicken scratch like you."

Her eyes caught on the first word. Her name, scrawled in that beautiful swirling penmanship.

Jayce—

I should've brought you with me last night. You were right to be angry.

There's more going on than I was previously willing—or able—to say, and I didn't handle it the way I should have. If you're willing to chase the truth, even at great personal risk, meet me in the Lore Guild this morning.

Or, if you'd rather not get involved more deeply, you can head to the Mana Guild. I've arranged a turn full of lectures for you.

The choice is yours.

P.S. Come alone.

—Sav

She swallowed past the lump in her throat, sliding a second piece of paper out from behind the first. "He set us both up with classes."

Nels took it from her and scanned the page. "Look now, this is hardly fair. This morning is *Deciphering Crystalline Memories* and *Subterranean Vibrations*, followed up by a trip to the Arcane Guild archive! Do you know how many stone artifacts I could get my hands on?"

Her stomach lurched, like she'd missed a step on uneven ground. Why did this feel like a test? And why would Sav have left a note, rather than tell her himself?

The lectures sounded fascinating, but she wanted answers.

She shook herself. "What do you think he means by *great personal risk*?"

Nels frowned and scanned the letter again. "He could have been more clear, I think. But he's obviously trying not to say too much. Looks like our man Sav has gotten into some kind of situation where he can't speak freely."

He tilted the page, as if looking for hidden messages. "Could be as harmless as a secret club or as dangerous as a cult." He met her gaze, his blue eyes soulful. "What are you going to do?"

Jayce considered the papers in his hands. Meeting with him would give her a chance to confront him with the questions that had been building inside her since she'd arrived at the Guilds.

She squared her shoulders. "I have stolen from a monastery, witnessed a murder, been shot at, and imprisoned by the queen. I can't think of much that would be more dangerous than any of that."

His eyebrows rose. "You didn't tell me about getting shot at."

"I may have downplayed that encounter in my retelling," she replied, ducking her head. "I didn't want you to worry."

"Damn right I would have worried," he practically growled, resting his arm on the doorframe above her head, suddenly very close. Too close. "You aren't careful when it comes to that man. Everything involving him seems to put you in harm's way."

Her breath caught. The accusation that he was being a mother hen died on her lips.

"It turned out fine," she managed to squeak out. The swirl of emotion inside her couldn't have been more confusing. He was clearly acting jealous any time she was with Sav. She hated the way he expected her to stay out of danger just to keep him from worrying.

But she loved it, too. Loved that someone cared enough to want her safe.

He scanned her, one hand rising as if to touch her face. But then he sighed and stepped back, his arm falling to his side.

"I don't like that he's asked you to go alone." He shoved his hands into his pockets.

"He doesn't know you like I do. I promise, I'll tell you all about it."

"Unless he swears you to secrecy," Nels muttered, looking at his feet.

"Then I'll insist he tell you himself. I'm not having my best friend kept in the dark."

He gave her a quick, wry smile.

Jayce re-folded the note, hesitating before creasing it in half again, as if folding it tighter might make the message inside simpler, more manageable.

She slipped it into her pocket. "You know, you could come with me. The worst he can do is ask you to leave when we get there." Shrugging, she tried to act nonchalant.

"Do you want me to come? Because I'll go to those lectures, I'll sit here and be good and wait until you return. I will do whatever you say."

She hadn't known a pool of water could burn, but his eyes were doing exactly that. The intensity of his stare warmed her skin like sunlight, direct and unrelenting.

Jayce cleared her throat. "I want you to come."

Some part of her eased at the admission. As much as she wanted to prove herself capable, she truly did want him with her.

Relief broke across Nels's face in a wide grin. "But not on an empty stomach."

He offered her his arm, and she took it.

"All right. A quick breakfast. But no other delays."

Her stomach had already started sinking. How could she eat with that cryptic note—and the meeting with Sav—looming over her?

At the Common Hall, a buffet-style breakfast greeted them. They navigated around the bustle of students, and they came away with full plates—eggs and sausage for Jayce, a small mountain of fruit and muffins for Nels. They waved to Chef Roland, who appeared too busy to stop and chat as he ducked back to the kitchens. There was no sign of any of Sav's friends from the day before.

She barely tasted her food, nor did she hear whatever Nels prattled on about. She nodded and made sounds in the right places, but her thoughts were far away, on the Lore Guild and the man who waited there.

With their stomachs appeased, they crossed the grounds, a damp drizzle following them the entire way. The morning chill, coupled with her rising anxiety, left Jayce wishing for a cup of tea—whispers or not.

Unlike the chaotic Common Hall, the Lore Guild archives were quiet, even with students coming and going.

A sign she hadn't noticed the night before now caught her eye, written in delicate script:

No loudness. No running. No mayhem.

The familiar scents of parchment and lamp oil wafted around her, turning her stomach. She pressed her hand to it. Perhaps she shouldn't have eaten. Or maybe it was the memory—this was the exact spot she'd frozen last night, when the man with the cane had cornered her, claiming he knew her.

Nels nudged her gently. She blinked. She'd stopped in her tracks.

Students parted around them, shooting them irritated and curious looks.

"We should move," he murmured in her ear. He took her elbow and guided her toward a study area filled with plush chairs and couches. "Where to now?"

Digging Sav's letter out of her pocket, she read it again. "He doesn't say where to meet—just the Lore Guild." She frowned. "It's massive. You'd think he'd be more specific."

"Unless he is watching," Nels said, glancing around the busy room.

A passing woman hushed him. He dipped his head in apology, shoved his hands into his pockets, then raised his eyebrows at Jayce. "I feel like I'm not supposed to be here," he whispered.

"Me, too," she said, eyes sweeping the space.

A chair creaked nearby, and she startled. Only a student adjusting his seat.

Quills scratched. Pages turned. The hush of it all pressed in on her. She had the ridiculous urge to shout for Sav, if only to break the maddening silence.

But Sav wouldn't be out in the open.

A study room, maybe? Or upstairs?

She chose a corridor at random and started down it, walking as fast as she dared.

They passed a group of students clustered in a ring of chairs. All looked up at their pace, eyes wide.

Jayce selected another path between the shelves, Nels muttering behind her. Everything seemed too well lit, too busy. Where would one go for a private conversation?

"Surely he didn't mean for us to wander around until we found him," he whispered, breathless as he kept up.

Some side rooms opened into lecture halls with bookshelves, tables, and lecterns. Others were small—clearly meant for solo or group study.

She soon noticed notecards by some doors, listing who had reserved the room and for when.

"You take that side, I'll take this," she said. "We'll meet in the middle to say what we've found."

"I assume it's under his name?" Nels called as he sauntered off in the opposite direction.

He glanced at the bookshelf beside him, then paused, leaning in.

"They have books about everything, Jayce! Listen to this: *Grain, Fault, and Fracture: An Inquiry into the Soul of the Earth*. Fascinating."

"Stay focused," Jayce murmured, already at the third study room. Four more remained on her side, stretching into a dim, tucked-away corner of the library.

Eldrane. Dossel. Verrian. Each name disappointed her more than the last as she got closer and closer to the end of the row.

She glanced over her shoulder. No sign of Nels at the meeting point.

Her pulse quickened as she approached the final door. Her eyes caught the first letter on the placard.

K—

She almost turned away, but paused.

—eenstone.

Keenstone.

That was *her* name.

The door stood open just enough to reveal a flickering lantern light—but not enough to see if Sav was waiting inside.

"Nels!" she hissed, loud as she dared.

He returned at a trot.

She led him to the door and stepped through. Inside, a cozy study room waited: a table scattered with books, two stiff-backed chairs, and a single glowing lantern.

Sav was nowhere in sight.

Nels lingered in the doorway. "I thought he was going to meet you here?"

Jayce eyed the ceiling, the walls, trying not to let disappointment get to her. Perhaps Sav had left another note?

"Check under the table and chairs," she said.

He obliged, crouching to peer underneath.

Jayce leaned over the open book on the table. Lifting the cover, she noted the title *Selected Observations in Plant-Insect Symbiosis (Vol. III)*.

"Look at this," she said, angling the cover higher so the light caught it.

Nels stepped in and squinted at the cover. "Well, it's about plants. You think it's meant for you?"

Jayce bent to the desk.

Pinned beneath the book's edge was a small, folded note, its surface filled with precise, rectangular cutouts.

She picked it up and unfolded it, careful not to tear the delicate pieces.

"It's a cypher," Nels said, brightening. "Put it over the text."

"Which page, though?" Jayce muttered, eyeing the hole-filled sheet.

"Try both," he suggested.

She spread the cipher over the left-hand page. The words were a meaningless jumble of phrases about plant structures and elemental harmonies.

Jayce drew a slow breath, then shifted the cipher to the facing page.

This time, words snapped into place—scattered fragments aligning like they'd been written that way.

She read aloud:

"Follow the veins where stone gives way to root.
The path winds where secrets bloom in shade.
Ask the keeper of bees, where earth hums low—
The answer lies where the oldest roots grow."

Nels frowned. "What does that even mean? '*Veins where stone gives way to root*'? Sounds like a riddle."

"I think he means the Eldenreach Forest," Jayce said, hair falling into her face as she studied the message. "The veins could be tree roots breaking through the earth—'*where stone gives way.*'

"And the keeper of bees?" he asked, shifting uneasily.

The woman in the yellow dress she had seen during their ride to the Guilds flashed in her mind.

"There must be someone he wants us to find," she said, staring at the cipher until the words blurred and lost meaning.

"Who he wants *you* to find," Nels corrected, arms crossing again. "That riddle's so vague you could end up wandering the woods until you're old and gray. Or dead," he added.

Jayce pressed her lips together at the implication that Sav had meant to get her lost for some imaginary, nefarious reason.

She traced the words again.

"I think he means it as a challenge," she said softly, glancing back and up at Nels. "He has something to tell me, but I have to prove I'm worthy of it."

His blue eyes locked on her. "You shouldn't have to prove anything. You're already worthy. I don't like this, Jayce."

"I know. But I'm not going to sit around and wait for him to show up and explain himself."

He stepped back, dragging a hand through his hair until it stuck up in tufts. "So, how are you going to know where to go?"

"That's probably what the second book is for." Jayce slid a thin almanac from beneath the massive tome and flipped to the page marked with a ribbon.

A map of Enterea. Not especially helpful.

She swallowed past the dryness in her throat and reached for the cypher then placed it over the map.

"Which hole are we looking at? More than one overlaps a forest region," Nels said, peering over her shoulder.

"There's only one close enough to walk from the Guilds. And look—it lines up with the word *Keeper*, right here."

She shifted the cipher between the map and the other book a few more times, comparing alignments.

He groaned but ducked his head in reluctant agreement. "If we end up stung by bees or falling into some pit, I'm blaming you."

Jayce smiled faintly. "You could still make it to... what was it? *Crystalline Memories*?"

"I'm giving it up for you," he said, expression serious.

She hesitated, hand covering the cypher before she folded it and tucked it safely into her pocket alongside the wishing stone. The note's poetic cadence lingered in her mind.

"Let's go," she said, turning toward the door. "We've got a keeper of bees to find."

CHAPTER NINE

"REMIND ME AGAIN WHAT we're looking for?" Nels muttered, brushing a sodden branch out of his face.

The forest surrounding the Guilds was dense and sprawling, the kind of place where sunlight struggled to pierce the canopy even on clear days. Today, the soft drizzle had turned the undergrowth slick, leaves dripping with rain.

"That map of the Eldenreach Forest we looked at showed several promising areas. But that's why we packed a robust lunch. We might be out here a while," Jayce said.

"I like rocks, you know. But nature... not so much," Nels said, batting at another tree branch and sending water cascading down on Jayce's head.

"You could try coexisting. Make peace with it."

"Like you do?" His grin was a challenge.

She tugged on her leather gloves, making sure they were firmly in place. "That's different. My relationship with nature is... complicated."

Nels put his hands behind his head and stretched. "Can't you ask them where we're going? If anyone knows about a Keeper of Bees, it's got to be trees and flowers."

"Couldn't you ask your rocks?" she asked, moving forward again, if only so she didn't have to look at his smug expression anymore.

"Rocks don't care about bees. They just... know things. But not people things."

Before Jayce could answer, a buzzing sound reached her ears—a faint hum that stood out against the patter of rain. She slowed, straining to listen. "Do you hear that?"

They rounded several bends in the path, and the hum grew louder.

She pointed at the ground. "Those sure look like veins, don't you think?"

Thick tree roots crisscrossed over each other, the giants they belonged to looming in a half-circle, like sentinels guarding the gate to something sacred or secret.

Jayce turned, gazing upward in awe. "They're practically one tree. See the way their branches interweave?"

Nels joined her. "It's keeping the rain out pretty well. It's a wonder those flowers get anything to bloom with."

She looked where he pointed, finally noticing the carpet of blossoms. Tiny white, purple, blue, pink, and yellow buds filled the space between the massive roots, even growing over them in places.

"*The path winds where secrets bloom in shade*, Nels, that's it!"

"You lost me," he said, raising an eyebrow. He crossed his arms. "All I see are a bunch of tiny flowers."

"The flowers *are* the path."

She hopped onto the nearest flower-covered root, arms out for balance as she walked its winding length. At first, she'd assumed the blossoms grew at random—but they clustered in patches, almost like steppingstones laid out just for her.

They leapt across the root-filled clearing, ending at a point between two trees where branches formed a low arch.

Jayce passed through, and Nels followed, both of them coming out into a second, smaller clearing, like a cave made of tree trunks that grew so close it was like a wall of wood, their reaching branches twisting together to make a roof with a hole in the center that let the smoke from the crackling fire escape.

A plump, dark-skinned woman stood next to a low wooden table, a staff in one hand and a basket of honey-colored cakes in the other. The air around her swirled with bees, their movements slow and deliberate as though guided by an invisible hand.

She looked up and smiled, the kind of smile that felt like a sunrise. That bright smile faltered when her eyes landed on Nels.

"I was told there would only be one," she said, eyes narrowing.

"This is my friend Nels," Jayce replied. "Surely he can come with me?"

The woman crossed her arms over her chest. "Master Alighieri did not approve his presence. He will not be allowed to pass."

Jayce swallowed. "Where is Sav? Is he nearby? He could vouch for him." But he had told her to come alone, specifically excluding Nels.

Did she want to know what Sav had to say if he wouldn't say it in front of her friend?

The woman gave a little shrug, her amber eyes twinkling. "He may stay for the test, but you will part ways after. Do you accept?"

Jayce glanced at Nels.

"It's up to you," he said softly. "Don't let me hold you back."

That only made her feel worse. She had half a mind to waltz back out of that forest and give Sav a piece of her mind when she saw him next. But hungry curiosity yawned inside her. Wasn't this the point of coming to Enterea in the first place? To get answers?

"Fine. I agree," Jayce said, crossing her arms. She wouldn't be happy about it.

The woman smiled, showing her teeth. "You can call me Harobed."

Nels shifted. "Do you... live out here?"

"Sometimes," Harobed replied, rubbing the top of her staff, where a bee-shaped carving glistened. "You've done well to come this far. But distance isn't the only measure of readiness."

"Readiness? For what?" Jayce asked, her heart skipping. Sav had set this up as some kind of test, but they still didn't know why. Perhaps Harobed would tell them.

Harobed placed her basket on the table and picked up a small, plain box. "Bees guard the key to this box. All you need to do is retrieve the key, and you will have the answers you seek."

Jayce's mouth dried. She followed Harobed's smooth gesture toward the back of the clearing, where a massive yew tree spread its branches. Red berries glinted at her from among the needle-like branches.

The insects darted in and out between the branches, a swarm of them concentrated near a small hole in the trunk of the tree that seemed to be about the same height as her head.

She would either have to find something to stand on or reach inside without looking.

Her throat constricted as she recalled getting stung by the blister bees not so long ago. Sav had been there for that experience. Had he chosen this test specifically to bring that fear back up inside of her?

"You must be kidding," Nels said from behind her. "Even the calmest of bees won't tolerate an invasion of their hive."

"I know my bees. If she has control of her internal world, they will allow her to pass." Her golden eyes flashed, and her hand lowered.

Jayce hesitated. She could turn around. Leave the hive and the trees and the cryptic instructions. Go to the lectures like a proper guest and pretend she hadn't failed again.

But then Sav would know that she couldn't handle the intensity, the danger, the risk, and he would exclude her from his plans. Maybe even send her back to Loshar.

As uncomfortable as the past few weeks had been, she felt alive again. Important, wanted. She wasn't ready to give that up, to crawl back to her apothecary, return to the mundane life of meeting clients and testing remedies and dodging social invitations.

Starting this journey had woken her up. She couldn't give up, not yet.

Jayce stepped forward, her feet moving before her heart had decided she could do it. "I'll go first," she said.

Harobed inclined her head, the rope-like strands of her dark brown hair swinging in front of her face. "Take your time. Collect yourself. Any hint of discord in your soul will activate the bees' defenses, and you will fail."

A sharp breath escaped Nels.

She couldn't look at him. If she did, she would fall apart.

Squaring her shoulders, she walked forward, passing beneath the canopy of the yew.

The buzzing intensified. She shoved aside the warnings flaring through her mind and body, whispering a silent mantra: *I can do this. Stay calm. Be still.* Peace wasn't something she felt—it was something she had to project.

Jayce approached the trunk. A few feet away. An arm's length. Bees hummed around her head, not agitated, but curious.

She imagined them speaking to each other in their bee language, describing this giant being that approached. Perhaps they thought her a bear, coming to take their honey. Or perhaps a deer that would pass by without incident.

That was the image she placed in her mind. She was a deer. Harmless, passing by. As soon as she got the key.

She reached up, then noticed her leather glove. Washing honey off it would be a pain. But taking it off would expose her to the bees' stingers and the possibility of touching the tree itself.

Pulling her hand back, she tugged off the glove, and then shoved it into the pocket of her skirts.

"Jayce!" Nels's voice came as a whispered warning from behind her.

She ignored him, putting her hand up slowly toward the hole in the tree. Her breathing became ragged, and her eyes darted around, trying to follow the bees that had increased in number in the past few moments.

A cool touch slid down her neck, and she froze.

Yew. Fever, fear and weakness treat. Immortality if you drink tea from my fruit—

Yew was poisonous. Death would be the likely result of anyone drinking tea made from any part of the coniferous tree.

One of the spiked branches had worked its way down the collar of her shirt, finding her skin. Another tangled in her hair, and she reached up to tug it away, keeping her other hand in the hole.

The bees grew louder, several landing on the fingers she had pushed into the hole.

"Get the key!" Nels said, voice still hushed, but urgent.

She gritted her teeth and tried to channel calm amidst the irritated buzzing of the bees and the shock of cold working its way down the back of her shirt. She stopped trying to get the yew away from her and shoved her hand into the hive.

The volume of the yew's voice increased, the words becoming meaningless.

A vision flashed into her mind. Jayce saw branches moving in the wind, sap dripping, roots tangled deep below. The messages pulled at her, demanding her attention, dragging like invisible hooks against her thoughts. A freezing numbness covered her back.

Concentrate, she had to concentrate, but the yew screamed at her, and the cold pierced her so intensely she cried out.

The first sting came as a sharp, burning contrast to the cold. She yanked her hand out of the hole, scattering bees. Another stung her cheek, a third got her arm.

Panic overtook her. She bolted across the clearing, past Nels and Harobed, and dropped to the ground, arms over her head, bracing for the swarm's fury.

None came.

Her fingers, tangled in her hair now, were coated in sticky honey. She pulled them away from her head, glancing up to find Harobed hovering over her. Nels joined her, reaching out a hand to help Jayce up.

A ring of bees circled the top of Harobed's staff, flying in an unnatural, synchronized circle pattern.

Jayce got the feeling that they were the bees that had pursued her from their hive, and she trembled.

Harobed eyed her, but didn't speak, only turned and walked away, back toward the tree. She tilted her staff, muttering words Jayce couldn't quite hear. The bees circling her staff returned to the hive, and Harobed set her staff against the trunk. She bent down, scanning the ground, and plucked several things off the forest floor then placed them in an open hand.

She brought them back to Jayce, holding them up for her to see.

"Four. Four lives extinguished for your fear."

The little bee bodies rolled in her palm.

Pain throbbed through her.

"I didn't mean to kill them," Jayce said. As she met Harobed's eyes, she knew that to the Keeper of the Bees, it was a weak explanation. Unacceptable.

Harobed turned away, not speaking. But then, no words were needed.

She had failed.

Nels put an arm around Jayce. "You don't have to do this."

She shook his arm off. "Wait," she called out.

The beekeeper hesitated, back still to them.

"I want to try again," Jayce said.

"Return when you have more control," Harobed said.

Tears sprang to Jayce's eyes. Her breath came fast, and she forced it to deepen, to slow. "I can do it now," she insisted.

"She can," Nels said from beside her.

She glanced at him, grateful for his confidence in her. He smiled at her, nodding.

Harobed finally turned, looking imperious as she considered Jayce. "You may try once more. If you fail again, you will both be banned from my grove."

Jayce licked her lips. Her cheek and hand both pulsed with pain. She needed to get the stingers out, to treat the wounds and prevent infection.

"Do you have any salve for the stings?" she asked.

“After,” the keeper said, voice and expression hard. “To remind you what is at stake.”

Jayce closed her eyes. It would be harder to concentrate with the pain. But perhaps she could use it.

Nels’s hand rested on her arm. “I could go before you. Give you time to recuperate.”

She shook her head. No, she had to do it now, before courage failed her and good sense replaced her determination.

And yet, she hesitated, tempted to go back. Forget getting answers. She didn’t owe this to anyone. Not to Sav, to find out whatever secrets he withheld from her, not to the realm, to rid it of the Plague King.

No, deep down, the one she felt she owed was Javin.

What would he say if he were there?

If you want it, go for it.

She could almost hear the tone he used to say it in, too. He’d always been the more bold one between them. It matched his extra strength and speed, always pushing himself to go farther and faster.

But he had pushed her, too. He would tell her to chase the answers she wanted.

She walked forward with a steady stride, eyes fixed on the hole in the tree. She ducked around the yew’s branches, noting how they stirred with her passing, as if awakened by her presence.

Like the bloomvine. Like the fern. Like the dusk ivy.

No, she was in control. She hesitated an arm’s length away from the hive, then whirled around, looking up into the branches of the tree.

Sleep. I have a task to accomplish, and I won't have you distracting me. She sent the words to the tree, the same way she had asked for help from the willow and from the dusk ivy.

The yew's branches still bobbed, but it seemed a quieter sort of movement.

She clenched her right hand into a fist, the stickiness of the honey reminding her of her first attempt.

Sav thought she could do this. He wouldn't have given her the challenge otherwise.

She glanced over her shoulder, at Nels standing beside Harobed, watching. He believed in her, too. Had told her as much on several occasions.

But did she believe in herself?

As she reached inside herself to find the courage to move forward, her chest constricted so tightly she thought she might stop breathing. Almost as if she had hit a wall that existed inside her.

She pushed against it, but every push was answered with a surge of anxiety from within. If she broke through that barrier, what might wait on the other side?

"The Three help me," she whispered, like a prayer.

Rushing filled her senses as if in answer. Warmth spread through her chest, soft and persistent, like the faint glow of sunlight through heavy clouds, and the remaining seed of anxiety within her stilled.

A new whisper trickled into her senses, completely unlike the mumbled words of the yew. Jayce strained to make out the words, but either they were in a language she didn't understand or they were too quiet. Where had they come from? Nothing touched her, no plant reached for her.

Whatever it was, it felt large. Larger than the tree before her, larger even than the forest itself.

Despite her imperfections and failures, she had never stopped trying. To find a cure for the plague, to find evidence against Sir Dray, to pursue translation of the journal.

After all she had been through and done until now, she could face these bees, she could get that key.

She stepped forward, eyes on the hive.

Golden honey dripped from the hole, probably dragged out by her hand earlier. It glistened as it trailed down the trunk.

Jayce tore her eyes away from it. She would succeed, this time. She felt it in her heart, in the stillness of her soul, the warmth of a presence she couldn't identify still covering her in calm.

The bees moved around the hole in rhythmic, steady waves, flying in patterns that Jayce had never seen in nature. Almost as if they were hypnotized.

She swallowed hard, both thrilled and unnerved. This wasn't plant magic. It was something... more. And she had the feeling that this new voice was the one she was meant to hear. One she had avoided—or been kept from—hearing all her life.

Reaching slowly, her fingers parted through a ribbon of bees drifting past. Her breath caught in awe of the fact that they didn't swarm her, didn't sting or try to defend their hive.

Her hand brushed the honey-laden comb that made up the hive's walls, and her hands brushed the cool edge of the key Harobed had promised. She pulled it free, taking it from the hive.

Its bronze surface gleamed like the wings of the bees that guarded it.

She left the shade of the yew and held the key out in front of her. A surge of delight filled her, relief and joy almost choking her, and she laughed out loud. She looked from Harobed to Nels, who looked at her as if he'd just seen his first sunrise.

"You found it!" His face erupted into the brightest smile.

Harobed inclined her head. "Well done," she said.

Jayce held the key out to her, but instead of taking it, Harobed picked up the small white box from before and held it out toward her.

Nels hesitated, glancing over at Jayce. He held the key out to her.

She felt the outline of the key in her hand. It seemed so ordinary.

Except for what it had cost to earn.

She had been ready to give up, until something—or someone—had answered her plea to the Three.

Perhaps within that new voice lay the truth she had sought her whole life. The answer to mastering her power over plants, and with it, how to defeat the Plague King.

CHAPTER TEN

JAYCE PUSHED THE TINY bronze key into the lock and twisted. It moved smoothly, clicking with success as the key stopped.

Harobed opened the lid, revealing another folded piece of parchment resting inside.

Jayce drew it out, hesitating before unfolding it.

"You have proven your ability to control your inner state," Harobed said, her amber eyes glinting. "Well done." She set the box to the side and picked up her staff, its golden top gleaming in the dim afternoon light beneath the trees.

Holding her breath, Jayce unfolded the paper and scanned the single line there. Nels peered over her shoulder.

"Follow the bees? Didn't we already do that?"

The breath whooshed out of Jayce. The single line of scrawled text did, indeed, say *follow the bees*. Nothing else, not even a signature. What was Sav getting at?

She looked to Harobed. "What do we do next?"

"*He* will return to the Guilds," Harobed said sternly. "Master Alighieri will be angry if I let him go with you uninvited."

Nels put his hands up. "Got it. No following Jayce. If I hurry, I can catch the end of my *Subterranean Vibrations* lecture."

He smiled, and anyone else might have thought he was taking the rejection well, but Jayce knew him. Beneath that calm exterior, he worried about her and about Sav's true intentions. If he thought he could get away with it, he would follow her in secret.

His eyes said as much as they landed on her, and she tried to convey through her own gaze that all would be well.

"Before you get any ideas," Harobed intoned, a slight amusement in her voice. "The bees will not tolerate unwanted followers."

Nels winced, as if that had been exactly his thought, and Jayce put a hand on her hip, shaking her head at him.

He opened his arms. "In case I never see you again," he said with a wink.

She rolled her eyes, but stepped forward and let him wrap his arms around her. She returned the embrace, taking in his familiar pine and leather scent. She wished, not for the first time, that he could come with her. That Sav had trusted him, included him. Was it possible Sav saw Nels as competition for her affection and had excluded him as a way to get closer to her?

She pushed away that thought. What nonsense. Sav was a reasonable man. He wouldn't stoop so low.

"At the first sign that he's doing anything shady, you wrap him up in vines and hang him from the trees," Nels said, leaning back to look at her.

"I can handle him," Jayce said. "I'll be back before you know it. And you can tell me all about your field trip."

She tugged herself reluctantly out of his arms and waved. He walked backward almost the entire length of the clearing, until he stumbled and was forced to turn around so he could safely navigate his way back to the Guilds.

Jayce watched until she couldn't see his tall form anymore through the trees.

"Now," Harobed said, "You will follow the bees."

She swirled her staff in the air, the gesture attracting a small swarm. She thrust it forward, and bees streamed out from it like a ribbon, passing Jayce and hovering in a line pointing out of the clearing.

"You will need the key again." She bent down to retrieve it from the box. It passed from her hand to Jayce's, still sticky with honey.

Her glove was still in her pocket, Jace realized. She would have to wash before she put it back on.

She adjusted her grip on the key. "What will I find there?"

Harobed leaned forward, her expression softening. "Someone is waiting for you. You can trust him."

A chill ran down Jayce's spine, though the air was warm. She didn't need to ask who it would be. She had so many questions only Sav could answer.

Harobed held out something small and wooden. Jayce took it, turning the lidded, circular container.

"For the stings," the bee woman said softly.

"I'm sorry about them. About the bees."

Harobed smiled sadly. "They accepted the possibility of sacrifice. Remember that next time; it might be your friends' lives you risk."

Jayce's chest hollowed out, and her eyes burned. She nodded, unable to say anything in reply.

Harobed gestured with her staff. "Don't keep the bees waiting. They aren't a patient lot."

"Thank you," Jayce said.

The bees led her to an ivy-covered wall that, by all appearances, was a dead-end. Her humming travel companions flew away the moment she reached the wall, leaving them in the middle of a forest that she wasn't sure she could find their way out of on her own. At least not without using her powers, and she wasn't keen on that at the moment.

Every direction she turned, the trees blurred into sameness—trunk after trunk stretching toward the clouded sky, indifferent to her presence.

Thunder rumbled close behind a sudden flash of lightning, and wind stirred the canopy overhead, shaking loose a shiver of leaves. Shadows thickened at the base of every tree, pooling like ink, and the silence that followed clung to her skin like damp wool.

Goosebumps rose with the hairs on Jayce's arms, and she rubbed at them, staring at ivy swaying against the stone wall.

What could this place be? It didn't look like any sort of building she was familiar with. Ruins, perhaps, but they seemed to have been well-kept or repaired.

Walking along the length of the wall, she used one gloved hand to move aside thick swaths of ivy vines.

She trusted Sav. Or at least, she thought she could. He had challenged that trust every moment since arriving in Enterea. Surely, he had his reasons.

She pocketed the key and checked her gloves. The last thing she needed was the ivy murmuring in her ears while she searched for a keyhole.

Several feet down the stretch of wall, she parted the vines and found a wooden door. Its shiny, new surface didn't match the crumbling stone of the wall around it. Could this be the right place?

Her eyes landed on the shape of a bee that looked as if it had been burned into the surface of the door.

A shiver of anticipation went through her, and her fingers fumbled as she took out the key. She stared at it and that bee on the door.

He had made her go through all of that—the cipher, the bees—for what purpose she still didn't know.

Her good sense screamed at her to leave this place and run back to her room at the ambry.

But she was here for answers. Answers about the man with the cane who claimed to know her. Answers about the magic Sav wasn't supposed to have. And answers about what they were *really* doing here.

The key turned easily in the lock, and the door opened, flickering torchlight spilling outward.

A figure stood in the short corridor beyond the door. The stone walls and dirt floors cast in shadow from several lit torches created an air of tension that sent a wave of dread through her, until the figure spoke.

"I was starting to wonder if you would come," Sav said, his golden curls highlighted by the torchlight. His smile was warm. "I never should have doubted."

Jayce put her hands on her hips, irritation rising. He presumed she would just go along with this? After he had left her cryptic notes and made her decipher codes, and undergo a test involving *bees* of all things? Not to mention making her leave Nels behind.

She walked forward, jabbing a finger into his chest. "You-you self-important fungus!" She stumbled over the ridiculous insult, the first thing that had popped into her head as she faced him. "You couldn't just come to my room and tell me whatever all this is about? All the secrecy, denial, and dancing around my questions. I've *had* it!"

Sav blinked in surprise. He grabbed her hand, still pressed against his chest and lowered it. He took her in, pausing on the areas of her arm and face where the bee stings had swollen but improved somewhat after using Harobed's salve.

"Perhaps I've gone about this the wrong way—" Sav began.

"Perhaps? *Perhaps*?" Jayce let the anger flow through her. She sensed her magic stirring without her asking it to. "You let me believe you were nothing more than a *historian*. And yet you have all this money—"

"Um, Jayce—" Sav started.

She raised her finger. "Don't interrupt me. You have all this money, and everyone, including the Head Dame, does whatever you say. You act like you're some kind of king. You use whoever you want and don't care about the consequences."

"Are you done?"

She hadn't gotten to the man with the cane, but that didn't seem important at the moment. Not the way Sav looked at her, with an infuriatingly tender sort of expression that didn't fit how she'd expect him to look after what she said.

"First, maybe we should close the door. Unless you intend to bring those with you." He pointed.

Jayce turned and found several ivy vines reaching through the doorway toward her. She batted at them. "Plants have been acting *strange* since I got here," she said. "Then again, so have you."

Sav reached past her and pulled the door shut slowly. The vines retracted just before it closed on them, leaving them in a corridor lit only by the single torch on the wall.

He withdrew his arm but stayed close to her, as if he wanted to touch her but didn't dare. "What you've seen of me before now... the charming, carefree historian... it's a mask. One that is easy to wear, because it is who I am with all the responsibility stripped away."

His light blue eyes searched hers. "I need you to know that while I may not have told you the truth, I haven't outright lied to you. I told you what you needed to know so you would trust me. Once I got the information I wanted from you, I planned to vanish from your life. But it seems the Three have had other plans for us. For you."

Jayce gaped at him. What Nels had said all along was true—Sav had intended to use her and leave her behind. What did he want now that she was here?

"I know you must be angry and wondering if all I've said and been is a lie." He took her hand in his, and despite her anger, her heart beat faster and her face felt hot, her body responding to his touch.

"You deserve answers to every question you have. And I will answer them, Jayce. Trust me for a bit longer. Please?" His tone went up in a pleading tone, and his eyebrows raised over widened, puppy eyes.

Jayce snorted. Frustration filled her, mostly at herself for the curiosity and desire that made her want to hear him out. Despite everything, that quiet voice inside her that helped her sense right from wrong, safety from danger, still trusted him.

"Everything will be clear soon. But first, I must warn you... my warning of danger was entirely serious. What you hear could get you imprisoned if we're caught. It will possibly ruin your reputation, and your career. Are you willing to take that risk?"

Jayce swallowed hard. Answers waited on the other side of this choice. If she said no now, they'd vanish—and with them, her chance to do something that mattered. Turning back meant returning to the mainland, to Loshar, to a plain and simple life she'd already outgrown. She could never be content in her apothecary again. Not while the plague still spread unchecked across the realm.

"I've already been imprisoned with you," she said wryly. "And I followed you here, didn't I? Sav, if I haven't made it perfectly clear, I'm going to find answers. I won't let anyone stop me. Not some silly decree, not any self-important blue-eyed men."

He cracked a smile, glancing at the ground. "You are a force of nature, Jayce Keenstone. I think you're exactly what we need here."

The compliment made heat rise in her cheeks. How did he manage to take her from frustrated to flattered in a matter of moments?

The easy curve of his mouth vanished, tension tightening around his eyes. "Before I take you back, do you swear that you will never reveal what you see and hear to anyone?" He emphasized the last word.

Jayce knew who he meant, but she had to ask anyway. "I can't leave Nels in the dark, Sav. He should be here with me."

Sav lowered his head. "I wanted him here. I promise I did. But what you're about to hear... we must limit who we let in, for their safety as well as ours."

Jayce shook her head. "I won't lie to him."

"I'm not asking you to," Sav assured her, his expression earnest in the torchlight. "But the others with me... they needed convincing to allow you to come and outright refused Nels because none of us know him. If things go well today, you can invite him yourself."

It didn't sit right with her to make a promise about something she hadn't yet heard, or the idea that she might be asked to keep things from Nels, but what other choice did she have? It came down to whether she trusted Sav and how much she wanted to be part of whatever he was doing.

"I agree," Jayce said, shuddering in the cool touch of the breeze that drifted past.

"Good," Sav said. He took a torch from its sconce and faced one of the corridors. "Come meet the others."

Despite her brave words, her palms were sweaty. She didn't know what to expect, and the mystery of it had her mind seeking all the possibilities. Sav would keep her safe, she was certain of that, but there was an element of danger about this whole thing, danger that he perhaps couldn't predict or prevent. He had mentioned as much in the note on her door.

They made several turns, and Jayce tried to mentally keep track of them, but she eventually lost count, and the order of lefts and rights got all muddled up. He passed multiple doors in varying states of decay, clearly unused, before he stopped in front of one that must have been recently replaced, the same carving of a bee in the center as the one at the ivy wall.

Sav placed the torch in a bracket outside the door and knocked a distinct pattern that was echoed from the other side, and then the door swung open to reveal a well-furnished sitting area filled with lanterns and plush chairs and a large rug, as if they had entered a common area back at the Guilds rather than a secret meeting room in the middle of the forest.

She gaped at the bookshelves on the walls. Not all of them were filled. In fact, most of them were less than half-stocked with volumes. There was a table at the front of the room, with an enormous map sprawled out on it, and a drawing board hung on the wall, freshly erased.

Bentley waved from a chair to her left, a friendly expression on his round face.

Next to him, Yamalda glanced at her, face a mask of calm.

Corbin tossed the hair and lifted two fingers in greeting.

And lastly, sitting farthest from her, Fiametta stroked the rat resting in her lap. She didn't meet Jayce's eyes. The beads in her hair clacked as she inclined her head.

"What is this place?" Jayce asked.

"Welcome to our literary rebellion," Sav said, grin wide. He took her by the shoulders, steering her to the left side of the room. "We've gathered every source we can find on the plague that the queen doesn't have locked away in the Draigh Monastery and the basements of the palace."

Jayce gaped. "You're gathering forbidden books? About the plague? If the queen got word..." It would be the monastery all over again, except multiplied. And a lifetime sentence in the Hobhorn salt mines. "This is dangerous."

"So is ignorance," he replied. Then, with a small smile, "The right information is worth the sacrifice."

Jayce wondered what he had sacrificed to obtain the volumes lining the shelves before her. There were so *many*.

"What he's not admitting," Yamalda said, "Is that he's recorded many of these volumes. Transcripts from interviews with people he tracked down from before the plague, and the early days."

"May I?" she asked, gesturing at the book.

"Go ahead."

She lifted the slim volume off the shelf and opened it to a random page. Sketches of moribund greeted her, surrounded by writing. Observations about the moribund, how they moved, whether they could see or smell...

Thinking about the monsters the plague created from those who perished with the sickness made her stomach churn. She flipped the pages, every single one filled.

"Who did you interview?"

Sav shrugged. "Anyone who had something to say about the plague, the moribund, the Plague King, the war. King Reginald and Queen Lyra," he added, almost as an afterthought. No, not an afterthought. To gauge her reaction.

Jayce placed the book back on the shelf and clamped her arms around herself, turning to face the others. "You're all part of this?" she asked. "Gathering information?"

"We don't all have the same role," Yamalda said. "Sav is the main one gathering information. But there are others, spread across the realm. They send information and we compile it."

"But… why?" Jayce asked, reaching out to touch a leather-bound volume. Sure enough, it had Sav's name embossed on the cover, but no title. Only markings that told her it was the fourth volume in a set.

Sav approached her, standing close. He pushed his hands into his pockets. "Because knowledge belongs in the hands of the people. And I have reason to believe our monarchy is hiding more than we know. That they are responsible for the plague and are perhaps withholding the cure." His expression darkened.

"But the king died," Jayce blurted. "He died before the plague started."

Sav spread his hands. "Precisely what they want you to think. After all, if it was revealed that they sought this power to end the war, and then that power got out of hand and was killing the people of the land, there would be riots. Neldor would fall into chaos."

A chill went down Jayce's spine. She relaxed her hands that had cramped from clenching. "What proof do you have?" she asked, forcing steel into her voice.

Sav's gaze pierced hers, his crystalline blue eyes earnest. "What proof do *you* have that I'm lying? You've seen and heard enough to know what I'm saying could be the truth."

Jayce's thoughts flashed to her time in the palace, before she'd met Sav. When Javin was still alive, and they had been taken before the queen and her counselors, trained and tested and told what to do. Their failure to destroy the Plague King.

The thing that stood out most was the decree the queen had made as soon as they had returned. That only qualified individuals would seek out a cure. That all written information about the plague would be turned in and kept in the stewardship of the queen.

Queen Lyra Ennisi-Donovanu had clearly not wanted to freely share information about the plague or the being suspected to have caused it. What reasons could she have? Perhaps hiding the truth about what—or who—had created the problem in the first place?

Jayce didn't have enough pieces to figure out how any of it was connected to her, to Dagric Wortcunning's journal, to the letter signed by L.A.—the person who had paid Sir Dray to create a false, even toxic, remedy for the plague.

Could the queen really have betrayed her people?

She didn't share any of this out loud. She brought her eyes up slowly to meet Sav's. "What are you planning to do with all of this?"

"We plan to challenge the queen to release information about the plague."

"And if she refuses?" Jayce asked, her throat dry.

"If she refuses," Yamalda spat, "We will put someone on the throne who cares about the people. Someone who will tell the truth and not hide behind pretty songs and promises."

"Someone with claim on the throne," Bentley added.

"But there's no heir," Jayce blurted. "King Reginald and Queen Lyra never had children."

Corbin's smirk held a glint of something unreadable. "That's what they want people to think."

Fiametta straightened, her attention suddenly pulled away from the rat on her shoulder. "There are rumors, but no one has come forward."

Jayce glanced around the circle. No one else seemed to have anything to add. Could there really be a legitimate heir?

"Heir or not, our first goal is to convince the queen to reveal the truth about the plague to the people," Sav said.

"Then... what do you need me for?" she asked.

"So few have seen the Plague King in person, and none of them have been willing to talk, or they've *conveniently* passed before we could meet," Sav said, perching atop the armrest of Corbin's chair, eyes locked on her.

The implication of the intentional murder of those who had witnessed the Plague King with their own eyes sent a shiver down Jayce's spine. Would she have been next had she not left Loshar when she did?

"You're our eyewitness, Jayce," he said softly. "Not only to the Plague King, but if Queen Lyra commanded you to not tell anyone what you saw, that's evidence we can use for our cause. For truth."

"And you brought me here..."

"To protect you," Bentley piped up, his brown-eyed gaze earnest, sincere.

"I thought we came to have Dagric's journal translated," Jayce stammered.

"We did," Sav soothed. "It will fit right into the collection we have. And Fiametta has something that will help you tell us what you saw. A tonic."

The woman sat up straighter, beads clicking again. She gazed toward Jayce with a stoic expression, and Jayce remembered that she was partially blind.

Sav continued. "One of her specialties is a truth tonic. We think taking it would allow you to circumvent your trauma response, to finally speak about what happened when you went to the Hobhorn. It has to be made fresh, so I had to bring you to her."

Jayce licked her lips. She swallowed past the lump forming in her throat, glancing from Sav to Fiametta to Sav again. She wished Nels were beside her, so she could take his hand and gain strength from it.

More questions and thoughts than ever milled around in Jayce's mind. Were there people following her, who wanted to silence her? Could the man with the cane be one of them?

"You met the queen. Why didn't you say anything to her then?" The words felt as brittle as dry leaves crackling underfoot.

"The more evidence we have before we confront her, the better. Your story is key, Jayce. I just know it will fill so many of the gaps we have," Sav replied.

"And if I agree to take this tonic... what part would I play after?"

Sav spread his hands. "If you choose, you could stay with us. Be part of this literary rebellion, dedicated to making sure Neldor knows the truth. Once the knowledge is widespread again, perhaps we can focus on finding a cure. With our resources, perhaps you'll be the one to finally succeed."

Jayce licked her lips. It sounded promising. She had little confidence she could find a cure on her own. But with access to the information Queen Lyra had hidden away, to funds for materials and research, perhaps she stood a chance. Perhaps they all did.

She forced herself to breathe. She hadn't come this far to turn back. If she could relive the memories, face them, and give Sav what he needed—maybe the tragedy of her past could mean something.

"I'll do it," she said, breathless. "I'll take the truth tonic."

Her heart pounded like a warning. Reckless. Maybe even foolish. But she needed answers.

She didn't know if she believed in Sav's rebellion—not yet. What she believed in was his desire to help the people of Neldor.

That fragile trust was all she had.

And for now, it would have to be enough.

CHAPTER ELEVEN

THE SALTY TANG OF the ocean filled Jayce's nostrils as she followed Fiametta through the crowded market in Starfall. A morning breeze played around them, carrying the sounds of several different languages.

Fiametta, with her long, dark dreadlocks swaying and beads clicking rhythmically, moved with purpose through the maze of stalls. Jayce struggled to keep up. Between exhaustion from the events of the past two days and overwhelm at the vibrant, bustling market, she felt like she could use a nap, and the turn had only just begun.

Add to that the guilt she felt at dodging Nels the previous evening, turning in early to avoid his inevitable questions. She wasn't certain what she could tell him or what she thought about most of it. Maybe she could tell him about the truth tonic. Would he tell her not to take it?

She paused at a break in between the houses, stalls, and shops, and spotted the ocean, its water sparkling such a bright blue that it hurt her eyes.

"I assumed we would be foraging for the ingredients?" Jayce said, her voice barely audible above the din of haggling merchants and excited shoppers. She was relieved not to be among the trees this morning, but the location had surprised her.

Fiametta paused, her gaze sweeping over a stall overflowing with shimmering powders and dried herbs. "Starfall has a thriving market, and we can likely find what we need here. Why would I spend all turn in the forest when I can buy it?"

Jayce fell into step beside the woman, unsure how to continue the conversation. She had imagined meeting another person who had skills with plants would make friendship easy, or at least give them a lot to talk about, but Fiametta had been silent the entire wagon ride, with Bentley carrying most of the conversation. Now that he was gone, an uncomfortable tension filled the space between them, emphasized by the enthusiastic chatter of the market.

"So... how long have you known Sav?" Jayce asked.

"Three ages," Fiametta said shortly.

Jayce waited for her to expound, dodging around a group of young women giggling over the jewelry they held up to their clothes and tried on their wrists. Fiametta remained silent, and Jayce blew a stream of air from her lips. She would have to keep trying.

"Do you like teaching? Sav said you are a Dame at the Guilds,"

"It's a recent promotion. My first lectures will be next age, assuming the Guilds are still standing by then." Her dry, disinterested tone made Jayce wonder if she might be joking, but she couldn't quite tell.

Commotion started somewhere in the crowd ahead, and people jostled to make room, pushing back into Jayce and separating her from Fiametta.

Jayce nervously grasped at her satchel, wishing she were taller as she scanned the crowd to find out what had caused the disturbance. She spotted Fiametta across the street, but the people were packed too tight to allow Jayce to pass.

"Unclean! He's unclean!" A woman with frizzy yellow hair screeched, pointing at a man cowering in a cleared area of the street. He tried to dash away, but the crowd blocked his exit.

The hair on Jayce's neck rose. The murmur of the crowd had a dark, frightened undertone, one that reminded her of ages in Loshar when everyone was on edge, watching for evidence of the plague, and especially moribund.

Jayce wished she had her final glass sphere. She had brought it with her, but it remained tucked away in her luggage. She hadn't thought to bring it to the market, not when Enterea had done such a thorough job keeping the plague—and the moribund—at bay. She had felt safe here, but now she regretted letting her guard down.

Jayce craned her neck and stood on tiptoes, but just as she caught a good view, she was knocked off balance by two men in uniform shoving their way forward.

"Officers, let us through," one of them shouted.

Jayce took advantage of the path they'd created, finally able to reach Fiametta.

"What's going on?" she asked.

"The shopkeeper has likely spotted a symptom of the plague on the man. It's rare to happen so publicly these days, but it does happen. Poor bloke." Fiametta shook her head.

Jayce relaxed, taking her hand off the sphere. "What will they do with him?"

"They will quarantine him and attempt to cure him. They will fail, and he will die."

The man shrieked and thrashed as the officers donned gloves and some sort of face covering and grasped the man by the arms, dragging him off. The crowd obliged, parting far wider than they needed for them to pass.

Fiametta glanced sidelong at Jayce. "How do they handle the plague where you are from?"

"I'm from the capital. In the beginning, we did not implement safety measures soon enough, and the plague spread like wildfire. The queen came down harshly, using the military to trap people in their homes, marking houses with quarantine marks and refusing to let even the healthy people out. Some starved before they could prove they were well." Jayce licked her lips, her entire body shuddering with the memory. Her eyes unfocused, and it was as if she were back there, huddled alone in her house with her brother, terrified to go out lest someone accuse them of being sick.

And then they'd been collected by a man from the queen's council. She didn't remember his name or really even his face, but she remembered his earnestness as he'd explained that there was a connection between twins born in a certain season of the moon and defeating the being known as the Plague King, thought to be the source of the plague.

They'd been trained, their powers tested, and then they'd been taken before the Plague King with barely a semblance of a plan, and her brother...

Fiametta leaned in. "Are you all right?"

Jayce shook her head. The woman hadn't asked for the whole story of her past. She'd wanted to know what they did now.

"I'm sorry, I said more than I needed to and didn't even give you what you asked for. The people revolted and once the moribund numbers decreased, the queen relaxed the restrictions. Curfews are in place, and households still get put under quarantine if someone shows symptoms, but healthy individuals can quarantine in rooms made for the purpose, and if they don't fall ill, they are allowed to leave."

"I've heard of these moribund," Fiametta said. "The sick, transformed into creatures without will, with intent to spread the infection, yes?"

"Yes. Don't you have them here?" Jayce asked.

"I have heard rumors, but none of them substantiated. Perhaps further inland, beyond the borders, in the larger cities..." Fiametta trailed off, eyes scanning the crowd.

Jayce followed her gaze, and her eyes landed on a man moving fast toward them, pushing people out of his way.

Fiametta grabbed Jayce's arm and moved through the crowd so quickly, Jayce had to jog to avoid being dragged.

She darted down a side street, looped back around, and zig-zagged until she stopped as suddenly as she'd begun, still looking through the crowd as if watching for someone.

Too out of breath to inquire why Fiametta had gone madly running about, Jayce bent over and focused on easing the burning in her lungs.

Jayce straightened. “Who was that?” She asked when she could finally speak.

Fiametta shook her head, beads clacking. “We know someone in the Guilds suspects us, but we do not know who. I keep telling Sav we need to move the center of our operations to the mainland, but he says it isn’t time yet.”

Movement darted up Fiametta’s arm, and Jayce stifled a yelp. It was only Mortimer, Fiametta’s pet rat. He nibbled at Fiametta’s earlobe, and the woman leaned in, as if listening to the rat.

Jayce rubbed her temples. Between the sick man getting apprehended and Fiametta’s paranoia, the stress-filled morning was getting to her. Her stomach rolled, feeling sick. Or perhaps she needed something to eat. She placed her hand over her abdomen, wishing she were anywhere but this crowded street filled with strangers.

“I have taxed you past your strength,” Fiametta observed, looking her up and down.

“No, I’m certain I’ll be well once I get something to eat. I missed breakfast.”

“I forget most people eat before noon,” Fiametta said, her tone amused. “I know a good stall. Come.”

This time she moved much more slowly, checking to be sure Jayce could follow.

Jayce wished she could close her eyes, feeling the world spin as dozens of faces moved past, shouts from the merchants filled the air, and too many colors and sights and scents swirled around her. She wanted to take it in and appreciate it, but her body betrayed her with its stress-induced weakness.

She focused, instead, on the back of Fiametta's blouse and her swinging dreadlocks, and on breathing in and out in a steady rhythm to keep from passing out in the middle of the Starfall marketplace.

Fortunately, Fiametta soon halted in front of a stand where a woman fried long tubes of meat on a dark-colored slab of rock.

Jayce sniffed the air, and her mouth watered.

"Two please, Ignia," Fiametta said, placing two coins down on a ledge.

The woman swept her short red hair from her eyes and grasped the coins, glancing at Fiametta and grinning. "I've told you to call me Iggy. Everyone else does."

"It isn't your given name. Why would I change it?"

Ignia laughed brightly and tossed the meat tubes expertly with the two-pronged fork she wielded. "It's meant to show affection. Like if I called you Fi."

"I would wonder if you recalled my real name. Or if you were too lazy to be bothered with the pronunciation."

"You've been in Enterea for seven ages. Are you still not used to our strange customs?" Ignia asked.

"No, I simply do not like this one." Fiametta bared her teeth in a grin at the fiery-haired woman. From the sound of things, they knew each other well.

Ignia grinned back and grabbed two smooth wooden sticks. She used them to pick up the steaming hot meat and thread it on.

Jayce gasped. If she'd tried that, her fingers would be blistered.

Ignia winked and handed her one of the sticks, then offered the other to Fiametta. "Who's your friend?"

"I have recently become acquainted with her. This is Jayce Keenstone, one of Savage's newest charges."

"That man collects people like others collect rocks."

"I have a friend who collects rocks," Jayce blurted. "He's here, too."

Ignia raised an eyebrow. "I'd love to meet him. I like rocks, too." The woman gestured at the stone slab.

"How is it hot?" Jayce asked, feeling flustered at trying to follow the exchange.

Ignia wiggled her fingers. "Magic."

Fiametta rolled her eyes. "Ignia can call the heat out of the certain stones. Did I explain that right?"

"Exactly! It's not fire, like a lot of people think. I can't do anything with wood or light up a room. But give me a rock that used to be liquid fire, and I can make it remember being hot… Does that make sense?"

"So your name, Ignia… that's not your real name, is it?" Jayce said, realizing that while Fiametta had sounded so affronted at the idea of using the woman's nickname, she'd actually been using it all along.

Ignia gestured at Fiametta. "See, she gets it."

"A nickname of a nickname is simply ridiculous," Fiametta said around a bite of the meat. She gestured at Jayce. "Try the sausage. It's the best you'll ever have."

She eyed the speared meat, then took a tentative bite. It burned her mouth a little, but the spices flooded her senses, and her eyes rolled back into her head. "That's delicious!" she said.

"My father is a butcher, and his father. We've developed this recipe over generations and guard it closely," Ignia replied.

Jayce took another bite, this time with curiosity. The plant voices rolled across her tongue, a dozen very faint whispers vying for attention in her mind. She closed her eyes.

"Rosemary, brindleweed, thyme, marjoram, garlic, emberwort, and shadowpepper," Jayce said, opening her eyes.

Ignia blinked at her, nearly dropping the meat fork. "You got all that from just a bite? Fi, who is this woman?"

"Do not call me Fi." Fiametta said, her tone flat. She grasped Jayce's arm. "We must be going."

"Wait, I—" Ignia started.

Jayce stumbled after her, the warm spice of Ignia's sausage still lingering on her tongue. The sudden shift made her stomach twist again—not from hunger this time.

"What did I do wrong?"

"You drew attention to yourself. People will remember you. When they remember you, those following can find out more about you. Then they have the advantage, because they know you, but you don't know them."

Fiametta slowed her pace and released Jayce. They walked in silence for a time, Fiametta stopping at a few different stalls, scanning over dried roots and leaves and powders.

Jayce grew more and more irritated as they walked. This woman had brought her here to ask her questions, but so far, all she'd done was buy her sausage and berate her. She didn't even trust Jayce with the knowledge of what plant they were looking for, when she seemed to know plenty about Jayce's powers and something of her past and career as an apothecary.

Jayce tightened her grip on her satchel, the irritation bubbling up with every step. The ocean breeze and heat of the sun felt oppressive under Fiametta's brisk pace and cryptic attitude. It was one thing to be questioned about her abilities—she was used to that—but Fiametta's tone carried an edge of condescension that set Jayce's teeth on edge.

Fiametta stopped at a stall where a gap-toothed woman worked at a mortar, grinding bright orange flower petals into powder.

Fiametta scanned the offerings, then reached toward a pile of shriveled gray roots. "Here we are," she said, her voice infuriatingly calm as she plucked one from the pile.

Jayce crossed her arms, planting herself a few paces away. "Care to share what you've found?"

Fiametta glanced back, her dark eyes sharp. "Patience, Speaker."

Jayce froze. "What did you call me?"

Fiametta sorted through a pile of roots, bringing each one close to her face before setting it down. Perhaps she needed help selecting one with her limited vision, but Jayce couldn't bring herself to offer. Not when the woman had just used the same term the bloomvine had when Jayce first arrived here.

"In my culture," Fiametta began, "Those who can hear the voice of inanimate things are called speakers. Your friend would be a speaker for rocks, Ignia is a speaker of fire. You are a speaker of plants, are you not?"

"I... I suppose. I'm not very good at it, though. I don't understand them half the time."

Fiametta exchanged coins for the root she had selected before tucking it into her satchel. “That’s the problem, isn’t it? You don’t know. You’ve spent your life running from what you are, pretending your powers are nothing more than a convenient trick for making potions. You don’t even trust yourself enough to listen properly.”

Jayce blinked, caught off guard. “That’s not true. I-I’ve studied for ages trying to understand.”

“And that’s why you wear gloves. You’re afraid to find out what you can really do?”

Tears sprang to Jayce’s eyes, and she clenched her hands into fists. “You have no idea what I’ve been through, how difficult it is just to get through a turn with every plant I touch whispering its lies and vanities to me, even when I eat. What do you know about my powers?”

Jayce’s raised voice drew curious eyes. *Let them look.*

Fiametta glanced every which way, then moved around the stall, gesturing for Jayce to follow her. She walked down two more and turned onto a street that led from the market.

Jayce’s instinct was to bolt. Ask Bentley to take her back to the Guilds, retreat to her room, maybe find Nels and let him make her feel better the way he always could.

But Fiametta’s words dug their claws in. *You’re afraid. You’re afraid.*

She was tired of being afraid, and she had come to Enterea for answers. So she moved forward, meeting Fiametta in the cool shade between buildings.

“Savage told me about you. About your struggle with your powers, the trauma of your past. He wanted me to help.” Fiametta’s brow furrowed. Her voice was quieter now, but it carried the same weight. "You have talent, Jayce, but you've buried it under so much fear I'm surprised you can hear anything at all."

"I've been told my whole life that if I didn't control my ability, it would consume me. You want to know why I wear gloves?" Jayce held up her hands. "Because if I don't, the whispers threaten to consume my mind, and touching them makes my skin as cold as ice." She yanked off her left glove and held up her hand, revealing the swirling brown lines left by the dusk ivy when she had faced Dray. "A plant did this. I held it for mere minutes, and it marked me."

"Curious," Fiametta said, leaning in to get a closer look.

"You try living like that without fear. Everything I eat, grow, touch talks back to me."

"And yet you chose a career as an apothecary? Most would run from such a gift." Fiametta's dark eyebrows raised, and she straightened, still staring at Jayce's hand.

"I wanted to control it, not let it control me," Jayce replied, repeating the words her mother had told her over and over again in her youth.

Fiametta shifted her stance, folding her arms over her chest. "Do you know what it is I do?"

"You work with poisons, right? And cures?" Jayce said, feeling suddenly off-balance, like the world was beginning to tilt.

"Yes. My powers allow me to sense poisons and how to cure them. But this heightened sense gives me another advantage. I can sense when the energy of a person's ability is blocked. Usually the cause is emotional, but it seems with you, it is two-fold. When I touch you, I feel stagnation. Imagine there is a dam inside you, holding that power back."

Jayce frowned. "A dam? What do you mean?" Her voice wavered, a mix of skepticism and dread.

Fiametta turned back to face her, the beads in her hair clinking softly. "A block like that is only placed in the most extreme of circumstances. A few people hold magic that can suppress others' abilities. They are meant to keep the individual safe, or to keep others safe from them."

Jayce's hands tightened around the strap of her satchel, her breath catching as a memory surfaced—her mother's hands on her shoulders, her stern voice warning her not to touch the plants too often.

A time when the plants were her friends and didn't burn her with cold, when she was very small.

"M-my mother taught me not to use my magic too often," Jayce stammered. "She's the one who told me I needed to control my powers. She gave me my gloves, and..."

A headache came on, and Jayce's brow furrowed in concentration. She put a hand to her head, trying to bring forward the memory her mind was screaming for her to remember.

Mortimer crept down Fiametta's arm, nose pointed at Jayce as he sniffed the air. It unsettled her for some reason. What could the rat sense?

He scampered back up to Fiametta's shoulder and snuffled around in the hair near the woman's ear.

It's just a rat, Jayce tried to reassure herself.

Fiametta continued, her voice sounding far away. "Did your mother take you to see anyone? Someone who promised to reduce your abilities, to make them more manageable?"

A *stern man with spectacles*. His face was blurry—she couldn't have been more than four or five ages old.

Her mother had spoken at length with the man, holding Jayce to her side with an iron grip to keep her from exploring the room's many temptations—bottles and jars and shiny metal tools on the shelves surrounding the room. Jayce remembered the way they gleamed and wanting to touch them but trying hard to be good. She didn't recall anything the adults said, but she had climbed up into an armchair, bouncing her legs on the cushioned seat until the man placed a hand on her chest and told her to be still.

A hard, firm, pinching sensation pierced Jayce's consciousness and she cried out, falling to the street holding her chest. Something throbbed there, an echoed memory of pain.

Fiametta dropped to her knees on the cobblestones beside her, arm around her shoulders. "You feel it now, don't you?" she asked in a hushed voice.

Jayce nodded. Now that she knew it existed, her magic beat against it like a bird trying to escape a cage.

Her mother had paid that man to lock away Jayce's full abilities.

But why? What had frightened her so much that she would limit her daughter in such a way?

"We will not be able to utilize the truth tonic with this block in place. It could be inhibiting things other than your magic, such as memories. I suggest removing it before we proceed."

Jayce swallowed hard, the weight of the past pressing against her ribs. "How do I remove it?"

Fiametta's dark eyes held hers, steady and unflinching. "You have to decide if you want it fixed, first. There's power in you, Jayce, and power changes things. If you open yourself to it, you will not be able to remain the same."

Jayce pressed a hand to the tight ache in her chest, focusing on filling her lungs so she didn't pass out on the street. She closed her eyes, wishing she could block out sound and sensation—just long enough to reach the place inside that felt sealed off.

Could it be true? Had her magic really been suppressed?

Maybe her mother had done it to protect her. Had she believed that Jayce couldn't handle her own power?

Jayce couldn't imagine living the rest of her life leaving part of herself locked away. And she was tired of being protected. Of being underestimated.

Especially by herself. And if there was any hope of ending this plague, she needed to understand and use her magic. All of it.

She loosed a breath and faced Fiametta, shoulders squared.

"Tell me what I have to do."

CHAPTER TWELVE

JAYCE GAZED AROUND THE grounds of the Ivory Guilds without focus. The trip back from Starfall seemed to have taken but a moment, so consumed was she with thoughts about the block inside her.

Fiametta let her off in front of the ambry, promising that once she had finished putting the truth tonic together, she would return and introduce Jayce to the head of the Mana Guild, an expert in magical maladies of all kinds, and someone she thought could help Jayce break through the barrier inside of her in a controlled and safe manner.

Jayce still couldn't believe she hadn't noticed it sooner. She'd lived all twenty-six ages of her life with part of her magic cut off. No wonder using it was so uncomfortable. She should have felt relieved that she would soon get answers, but she felt more numbed by the shock than anything.

She moved to open the door to her hall, and hesitated. Nels might not be around. He might have gone to a lecture. But if he was here, waiting for her, he would confront her about avoiding him. About what had happened yesterday and where she had been this morning.

Facing him weighed on her like a boulder on her chest. She turned away from the doors.

Maybe a walk in the fresh air would help her sort out her feelings.

She trusted Nels. That wasn't the problem. And she *could* talk to him.

But if she opened up, everything might come spilling out, and then he'd see the truth. How broken she really felt. How little she matched the ideal he probably held in his mind.

The turn felt cool, evidence of the warm, Purple Bell Moon season shifting to the cooler Hunter's Moon. Soon, the leaves would change and fall, and the earth would go to sleep.

She let her mind drift away from confusion and guilt, watching squirrels chatter and play in the branches of nearby trees as she wandered.

Her feet carried her to the Warrior Guild. The building was smaller than the others but made up for it with impressive grounds containing several massive training fields partitioned off with fences. Students sparred, climbed, and trained in a variety of fighting methods. Sweaty and shouting, they were a lively group that jarred Jayce from her stupor, and she moved up to one fence to watch the archers.

Five men and women lined up, each one practicing on their own and shooting at different times. They had runners who fetched their arrows after they ran out.

Jayce had little skill in any fighting technique. She hadn't taken to it the way Javin had, with his added physical abilities. But she admired those who honed themselves to become one with their weapons.

She leaned against the fence, basking in the warmth of the sun as it shone through the parted clouds above. It heated her back and hair as she watched the archers, not caring about the time that passed, letting all her worries fall away.

One by one, they finished their training and left the field, leaving it empty. Jayce woke, as if out of a trance. Her stomach felt pinched and empty, and she realized she had never had lunch.

As she turned away from the training area, a man walked onto the field, bow in one hand, a quiver slung over his shoulder.

It was Sav. He hadn't noticed her standing there, watching, or he might have called out to her. She didn't call to him, instead watching silently as he set up, stretched his shoulders and arms, rolled up his shirt sleeves, and then aimed at the target.

He seemed like a different man than the one she had met. Or perhaps she simply had a different view of him, now that she knew the secret he had kept. This was the rebel, a man who trained his body as well as his mind. His arrows found their mark every time, striking the inner rings of the targets and even the bullseye multiple times. He moved back, increasing the distance, and his accuracy remained.

Quietly, Jayce moved closer, until she stood behind him, her breath catching when he drew back, and the motion emphasized the muscles in his back and shoulders.

Sav lowered his bow and turned, looking at her in surprise. He ran a hand through his sweaty blond curls, making them wild, and grinned.

For a moment, she could forget the block on her magic, the rebellion, the plague, and fall into his sparkling blue eyes, relishing the way she felt like she was the only one in the world with him.

He jogged closer. "You could have said something. I would've shot better knowing you were there." He seemed more relaxed, as if shooting had calmed some strain in him.

"I would have distracted you. Besides, you shot wonderfully," she said around the lump that had formed in her throat. She tucked her hair behind one ear, suddenly uncertain what to say.

"So, how was your—" Jayce started.

"How was collecting herbs with—" Sav burst out, then looked embarrassed. "You first, then."

"No, you," Jayce replied.

Sav gave her an exasperated look, tilting his head in a way that made her heart beat faster. "As a gentleman, I insist."

She rubbed at her right eyebrow, then caught herself and stopped. "I only meant to ask about your morning."

Sav bent down near a small pile of items by the fence, pulled out a towel and wiped at his face and neck. "Corbin, Yamalda, and I worked on sending out messages and erasing evidence of our passage to the place you found last night."

Jayce blinked, tearing her eyes away from his arms. There was something suspicious about his casual tone, as if he didn't want her to ask more questions.

Sav put the towel back in his pack and straightened. "You know, now that I think about it, you could help with that. If you're up for it. Make the paths grow over again. We try to take different routes, but sometimes they start to look less like game trails and more like paths. If that happens, curious individuals might wander in and find more than they bargained for."

She didn't miss the veiled threat, and she wondered at it. What would they do to someone who came across the hideout uninvited?

"I-I could try," Jayce stammered.

"All right, then. How was the market with Fiametta? She didn't scare you away, did she?" he asked, chuckling.

"We found things to talk about," Jayce said, still not sure how much she wanted to get into the details. Would Fiametta tell him if she didn't? That thought made her squirm.

"We ran into a friend of hers. Ignia?"

Sav's eyes lit up. "Did you try her sausage?"

Jayce couldn't help but laugh at his eager expression. "Yes, I did. And it was marvelous." *And then Fiametta went all cryptic and told me I have a block on my magic, and I can't stop thinking about it, and I'm scared.*

She stared at Sav, not saying any of those things. She wanted to tell him, wanted things to feel easy between them, the way it had all those weeks ago while traveling to Musport.

But he had gone to meet the translator without her. She still hadn't heard what had happened there. And he had kept such massive secrets from her, like the rebellion. There was more. There had to be. But she didn't know what to focus on or how to fix this feeling that there were too many secrets between them for it to ever feel easy again.

Sav didn't seem to notice her angst. He unstrung his bow, prattling on about Ignia's sausages and other food that Jayce needed to try while she was in Enterea.

"Why didn't you tell me about the rebellion?" Jayce blurted.

Sav froze, glancing from side to side to check for passersby. He came closer, until the only thing between them was the fence.

She waited to feel the energy ripple through the air like it had on their first turn here, to catch him in the act of trying to manipulate her with whatever power he might have.

All she sensed was the wind, watching as it rifled playfully through Sav's curled hair and moved on.

"There are more lives than just mine at stake in this," he said, low and serious.

A shiver went up Jayce's spine. A normal reaction to the heaviness of his voice, the closeness of his breath. No trace of magic in the words.

"Who you've met so far… they're my inner circle. They've been like my family here at the Guilds. There are so many more, spread all across the realm. Every new person we bring in is another potential person who could betray us. I wanted to tell you. I did. But I needed my friends to approve of you first."

Jayce swallowed past her tightened throat. She understood that part. "But why me and not Nels?"

Sav blew air through his lips. "That wasn't my decision. Yamalda, in particular, didn't like the look of him. Bentley is all for it. Corbin will take convincing. Fiametta will most likely go with what I say."

"She seems... stiff," Jayce said.

"She is. I think it's her culture. Laughter is largely considered rude there, frivolity is a waste of time and resources. I like to think we've helped change that for her, but..." He shrugged. "Who knows. She is brilliant at detecting poisons, and she's close to the Head Dame—"

He clamped his mouth shut and straightened, looking around with sudden interest at the empty training grounds.

Had he shared more than he meant to?

Jayce's eyes narrowed, but she didn't ask him about it. Fiametta would be one to watch, then. Perhaps they all were.

"Look, I want things to feel... right between us," he said at last.

"I want that, too!" Jayce said, heat rising in her cheeks.

He stared at her, then took a sharp breath in. His hand reached out, sweeping her hair behind her ear. He held her gaze, blue eyes searching hers as if he had a thousand things to say but didn't know how.

Jayce swallowed. What was that feeling twisting her gut into knots, tightening her chest, making her want to lean forward and embrace him?

Nothing in his manner indicated an attempt to manipulate her. And there'd been no trace of that strange magic that made her feel compliant and empty-headed at dinner the turn she had arrived.

Either he had told the truth and didn't have powers, or he at least didn't use them with her.

She cursed the fence between them and that there was no graceful way to reach out and touch him.

"Fiametta... she says there's something inside me that needs to be... repaired." She bit her lip, regretting the way the words broke the spell between them.

"Oh?" Sav asked, leaning back slightly, crossing his arms.

"She called it a dam—something holding my magic back. Probably put there as a child. I have... memories of it happening. She thinks the head of the Mana Guild can help. I'm seeing her later."

"That is fantastic news. I knew Fiametta would be good for you."

Jayce didn't know if she would go that far. But she enjoyed the sensation of something loosening in her chest. Whatever existed between them, it could be resolved. If she opened herself to him, and he did the same...

She opened her mouth, prepared to tell him about the man with the cane who she had seen everywhere since arriving.

Sav spoke before she could. "Are you hungry? We could implore Chef Roland for some fare."

"Famished, thanks for asking," Nels said, walking up with a wide grin on his face.

Jayce wished he hadn't interrupted, then felt guilty for thinking it.

The two men looked at her expectantly, and she blinked rapidly, worried she'd missed something one of them had said to her. Both of them standing in front of her made her tongue seize up.

"Let's go, then," Sav finally said, breaking the awkward pause. He slung his bag over his shoulder and carried his bow in one hand, offering his other arm to Jayce.

Nels offered his arm at the same time, and all Jayce could do was laugh nervously and take both.

Muscles flexed in Nels's bicep and forearm, and she recalled seeing him, straining as he held back the rockslide. He didn't train with weapons, but he hiked mountains and hauled stone regularly. What would it feel like if he picked her up?

A sudden thought nearly stopped her in her tracks, and it was only fear of looking like a fool that kept her moving.

They couldn't *both* have feelings for her, could they? Did she have feelings for each of *them*? By the Three, this was the last thing she needed to be worrying about with the plague, the rebellion, and her magic block.

She glanced between the two men, trying to give them equal attention and feeling like a fish out of water. She'd rarely had the attention of any man, except the flirtations from Nels that she'd never recognized and Dray's unwelcome advances. Had she been so oblivious?

To be fair, her adult life until now had been a series of traumatic events. From dealing with her magic, to the plague and her parents dying, to Javin, to defeating Dray, to now.

When life settles down, I can think about romance, she reassured herself as they stepped into the seating area in the courtyard.

The private, covered eating area from last time was taken, so Sav sat them down at a table along a vine-covered wall.

"Will you be all right here, Jayce?" he asked, setting his pack and bow down in an empty chair nearest the wall.

"I'll fend off the ivy," Nels said, plopping himself down.

Jayce sat across from Sav and next to Nels.

Sav leaned back in his chair, a relaxed smile on his face, while Nels traced patterns on the table with a finger, his energy quieter but no less present. Tension thrummed under the surface, like a thread wound too tight, and Jayce struggled to think of how to continue the conversation and keep things light.

Fortunately, just then the server arrived, offering a distraction as menus were placed in front of them. Sav flipped his open immediately, rattling off suggestions. "The chicken is to die for. The beef stew here is excellent. And they make a spiced cider that's perfect for this season."

Nels didn't even glance at the menu. "I'll have whatever Jayce is having."

Jayce blinked, caught off guard. "Oh, um, I haven't decided yet."

"Take your time," Sav said, but his tone held a lightness that made her feel rushed all the same.

Jayce skimmed the options, her thoughts straying despite her best efforts. Warmth emanated from Nels at her side, and their elbows kept brushing.

She ordered fish, and the server vanished with their choices, leaving the three of them in a silence that felt anything but comfortable.

"So, how was your meeting with the translator?" Nels began, his tone casual but his gaze direct.

Sav's smile faltered for a fraction of a second. His gaze flicked to Jayce. "It went well. He looked over the journal and agreed to spend some time on it as he's able."

"When do you see him next?" Nels asked.

Jayce felt like dying. He was interrogating Sav for her, and no doubt because she hadn't told him about the previous night, but did he have to do it so forcefully?

"We're due to meet in a few days. I'll be certain to update you both."

Nels leaned back in his chair, sighing. "You know, I am so, so curious what could be so important—so *secretive*—that you had to get Jayce on her own to talk about it. I mean, I've only saved your life, what, three times now? What does it take to be considered for Sav's inner circle? Or perhaps it's just that I don't have her pretty looks?"

"Nels!" Jayce hissed, a pit opening in her gut. She couldn't look at Sav.

Nels's gaze lingered on her, as if expecting her to come to his defense.

He dug this hole himself. Though perhaps she had contributed by not telling him everything sooner.

Chair legs scraped across brick as Nels pushed away from the table and stalked across the patio, to an area where no one sat.

"I'm sorry," Jayce said to Sav, eyes on Nels. "I'll talk to him."

The ivy grew more thickly in this area, and the added shade felt cool. She flexed her hands as she approached Nels, who paced with his back to her.

"Nels?" she took a shaky breath in. Every part of her trembled. "Why are you acting this way?"

His steps halted, facing away from her. His shoulders lifted in a shrug. "Tell me you wouldn't do the same if I started hanging out with someone you thought wasn't good for me."

He turned to face her, eyes searching hers expectantly. What did he want from her? She wasn't going to agree with him.

"I happen to trust Sav. I've said that before, but you won't leave it alone. It's like... it's like you don't trust *me*."

Jayce glanced around the patio, noticing their server making her way to their table, arms loaded with plates. She swallowed, trying not to think about the spectacle they were making, standing where everyone could see. She wished this conversation were happening back at the ambry, in the Eldenreach, anywhere but here.

"I can't trust you when it comes to Sav," Nels admitted. "He makes you reckless, asks you to keep things from the people who care about you—"

Anger rose in Jayce. "That's what this is about? Nels, it's been half a day. Are you so impatient and needy that you have to know everything the moment it happens? I've been trying to figure out what I can tell you without betraying their trust. It hasn't been easy for me, either."

His arms relaxed by his sides as his blue eyes searched hers. His expression seemed to alternate between hurt and yearning. His throat bobbed. "Have you... decided? What you can tell me?"

Jayce made a split decision. Sav hadn't said to keep this secret, and it wouldn't reveal anything about the literary rebellion. But perhaps it would be enough for Nels. "They're asking me to take a truth tonic."

Nels's brows furrowed. "A truth tonic? Why?"

She waved her hand, the gesture far more casual than she felt. "It's supposed to get past the trauma response I have whenever he asks about... it."

"I know talking about it is hard for you. But do you really need to be drugged?"

She gave him an exasperated look. "It's not like that."

He shook his head. "You're deluding yourself again. See, this is what I'm talking about. When Sav asks you to do something, you do it. You're not being logical about this. I mean, do you even know the possible side effects?"

The words felt like bricks. She was usually good about researching things like that. Her livelihood, after all. In the heat of the moment, she had agreed to take the tonic without even considering the implications. But she wasn't the only one acting without sense here.

"I'm not being logical? What about you? I turned you down in Loshar, and you still followed me across the ocean like some lovesick pup. You didn't even ask if I wanted you to come."

The words burned her throat as they left, and she immediately wished she could take them back. She stepped out of his reach. Her cheeks burned. Their voices had risen to the point that people stared at them, and she couldn't bear the scrutiny. His or theirs.

His hardened expression melted, replaced by softness and hurt. "If you wanted to be alone with Sav, you should have said as much. I never would have come."

"Nels, that's not—" She cut herself off, frustrated. Couldn't he see how jealous he was acting? "I wanted you to be here, but now I'm not sure it was the best choice. If you can't trust Sav, if you can't trust me, then maybe you should go back to the mainland."

Nels lifted a hand and opened his mouth but stopped himself.

Jayce's skin prickled, and her eyes stung. The lump in her throat wouldn't move so she could ask him what he meant. He wouldn't really leave... would he?

He walked forward, passing her, headed toward the exit.

She turned to watch him go, and he halted before looking back over his shoulder. Those eyes, as blue-gray as a deep mountain lake, lingered on her, as if taking her in for the last time.

"Promise me you'll be careful. Trust your instincts... and maybe mine, too. Because I..." He stopped, as if gathering himself before he said, "I came here for a reason. And it wasn't for the lectures."

The words struck her like a blow. Her mind raced, but words died on her lips. None of them seemed right.

With a quiet shake of his head, he walked away, the space between them stretching with every step.

Jayce stood rooted to the spot, staring after Nels at the empty arched entrance to the courtyard.

She hated how the air felt with her words lingering there. *Perhaps you should go home.*

Pointed. Barbed. Thrown like weapons in the face of someone who had long been her friend. The one person who had been there for her through everything. The last person who knew her brother.

She clamped down on the sob that tried to escape her throat, covering her mouth with one hand, holding her abdomen with the other as if she could hold herself together.

A soft touch on her shoulder made her turn, facing the ivy growing on the trellis around the courtyard. No one stood there, and it wasn't until the ivy whispered that she realized the plant had grown toward her again, touching her cheek with a gentle tendril.

As we cling to the oak, your heart clings to him, Speaker.

Grabbing the vine, she ripped it off her shoulder, then rubbed her cheek to rid herself of its cold touch.

The broken vine fell at her feet. She stared at it as its leaves went limp and lifeless. What else had she torn that might never be recovered?

CHAPTER THIRTEEN

AUDITORY AND VISUAL HALLUCINATIONS. *Violent mood swings. Heart palpitations. Chest pain. Heart stopping. Headaches. Nausea. Stomach pain...*

The list of side effects for an infusion of glassroot—the main ingredient in all seven of the truth serums or tonics she had found in the Mana Guild library—went on for two paragraphs. The section ended with *death*.

Jayce stared at that period after the last word, chewing on her lip and rubbing her right eyebrow until both hurt. She sat up and sketched the notes in the book of notes she kept on all the plants she encountered.

Glassroot had a lot of nicknames. Truth finder. Truth teller. Tonguebreaker. Mindsplitter.

Those last two worried her.

The seventh bell rang, and Jayce quickly made a sketch of the root, taking it from a second book sprawled open on the table before her.

In her haste, quill ink came out too thick at the bottom of the drawing and made it look sloppy. She blew on the extra ink, willing it to dry. She capped the ink and her quill, then tossed both in her satchel.

Closing the other books, she picked them up in a stack with her open journal on top and balanced the load all the way to the desk at the front of the library.

"Thank you very much," she said to the stern-faced library steward, sliding the books toward her.

"Oh wait!"

She snatched her journal back, thumb smudging the still-drying ink. She grimaced, then raced from the library. Her meeting with the Head of the Mana Guild was meant to be happening *now*, and she had to get across the vast building to the front doors, where she had agreed to meet Fiametta.

The tall woman looked surprised when Jayce burst through the doors, out of breath and bent-double with exertion. She stroked the rat sitting in her hand, the evening sunbeams highlighting the light and dark patches of vitiligo skin on her arms and face.

"I was doing research," Jayce said, trying to decide whether or not to share precisely what she had been studying. And then the realization struck her that Fiametta's power was in *poisons*. She was a Dame of the Mana Guild. She knew that long list of side effects and had still recommended Jayce take the tonic.

Did that mean she intended to poison Jayce? Or that she was one of the few who could prepare and administer a properly made tincture?

Sav trusted her, even including her in his inner circle. But he had also said she was close to the Head Dame, who hadn't seemed fond of Sav. Did that mean Fiametta worked for both sides? And if so, which was she loyal to?

"You look as if you're seeing spirits. Are you drunk? Did someone get you into smoking the strong grass?" Fiametta pushed herself off the pillar, Mortimer skittering up her arm. She looked down her nose, looking imperious and disapproving.

"No, I have *not* been smoking," Jayce said. "I was merely... thinking."

When she didn't expound, Fiametta made a sort of low-pitched sound from the back of her throat, the kind one made to sound polite when they were actually disinterested.

"Dame Febris will meet us in the atrium. Come." Fiametta took off at her brisk, long-legged pace.

Their boots clicked against the polished marble floor, evening light streaming through high windows that cast rainbows on the walls and floor.

Jayce felt small here, even more so as Fiametta led her toward a plant-filled, glass-encased sitting area where a tall, imposing woman stood waiting.

Dame Febris was taller than Fiametta, her long robes a soft green trimmed with shimmering gold thread that complimented her light olive-colored skin. Her graying hair was pulled back into a severe twist, but her intelligent eyes softened as they landed on Jayce.

“So this is the speaker you’ve brought me,” she said, her voice soothing.

Jayce bristled at the title but forced herself to nod in greeting. “It’s just Jayce, Dame Febris.”

The woman smiled faintly, gesturing for her to sit on a cushioned bench nearby. “Names are powerful things, child, but we’ll start where you’re comfortable. Please, sit.”

Fiametta remained standing, her arms crossed as she leaned against a living tree growing up through a hole in the floor. Mortimer still perched on her shoulder, his tiny black eyes gleaming.

Jayce sat, her palms damp against the soft fabric of her skirt. The broad, frond-like leaves of a nearby velris palm brushed her shoulder, and despite the fact it only touched her blouse, she felt the slightest chill and shrank away from it.

Dame Febris lowered herself into a chair opposite Jayce, studying her. “Fiametta tells me you’ve struggled with your magic—discomfort when using your ability and hearing voices from the plants you contact. Is that correct?”

Jayce nodded hesitantly. “Yes, I’ve always felt like… like my ability should work like anyone else’s. I should be able to use it without getting cold, without being driven mad by the indiscernible whispers.”

“If your ability was solely in plant magic, I would indeed be concerned. But I suspect there is more to you than meets the eye.” Dame Febris reached a hand toward Jayce. “May I connect with your heart center? It will only take a moment, and it will be painless.”

“Yes,” Jayce said, breathless with shock.

Fiametta had already told her she had a block containing her true abilities, but Jayce still hadn't thought it might be something other than plant magic. She'd heard plants talk her entire life. How could her magic be anything else?

She sat up straighter, pushing her hair behind her shoulders and leaning in to meet Dame Febris's outstretched hand.

Jayce felt a light pressure on her chest, but otherwise nothing.

"Fiametta is correct. There is a block on your abilities—a significant one," Dame Febris said.

Jayce's stomach tightened. "Can you remove it?" she asked quietly.

Dame Febris's eyes dimmed, and she looked apologetic. "No. Sometimes our wounds are not merely physical but emotional and spiritual in nature. I can only do so much for spiritual maladies. I suspect you are goddess-touched. This block is deeply rooted. Whoever placed it on you was skilled and thorough."

Goddess-touched. What could that mean? Did Dame Febris mean she had somehow been gifted directly from the Three?

"I-I've never taken a pilgrimage. I was born with my abilities," Jayce stammered.

"The Three sometimes touch infants directly. Those they wish to give a greater call in life. And when humankind interferes with that bond, it can have unintended, even dangerous consequences. It will get worse before it gets better, I'm afraid."

"Then I must break through this barrier on my own?" Jayce's heart sank, her fingers curling into fists in her lap.

The older woman stood, her movements fluid and deliberate. "You're stronger than you think, Jayce. You wouldn't have come this far otherwise." She turned to Fiametta, who straightened under her gaze. "Take her to the temple grounds and introduce her to Keeper Solmere."

Fiametta inclined her head. "Of course, Dame Febris."

Jayce stood slowly, her legs shaky beneath her. As Fiametta led her toward the courtyard, she glanced back at Dame Febris, who watched her with an expression she couldn't quite read—part curiosity, part expectation.

The weight of it followed Jayce out of the Mana Guild. Her worship of the Three had been more of an acknowledgement and the occasional whispered prayer, but she'd been far from devout. What if the block was a punishment for not seeking them more intently?

The temple crouched in the Mana Guild's shadow, half-swallowed by ivy and the tall wall that surrounded it.

Jayce gasped as the garden revealed itself beyond the arched gate. Neatly trimmed hedges carved a labyrinthine path through beds of late-blooming flowers and serene stone statues, their features softened by time. The air was rich with the fading sweetness of the season's end. But what truly stole her breath was the prismvine. It draped the walls, twisted up pillars, and threaded through the shrubs like living starlight. Its blue and violet leaves shimmered with an inner glow, refracting the sunlight in fractured rainbows that made the whole garden feel less like a place and more like a vision—fragile, luminous, and holy.

The hushed atmosphere closed in on Jayce, and she felt like a trespasser on the sacred grounds.

Ahead, the temple stood, small yet breathtaking. Arches cradled glowing stained-glass windows, each depicting one of the Three in vibrant, swirling colors. She even spotted one depicting Thengroth the necromancer, the first true evil the Three had faced. Her father used to spin tales of the Three around a communal campfire during festivals in their small village outside Loshar.

A cool breeze whispered through the courtyard, carrying the faint scent of incense, as if the temple exhaled a sigh of welcome.

Fiametta dropped to one knee suddenly, bowing her head. "Keeper Solmere is a Warden of the Wind. That's his greeting. Pay your respects."

Jayce had never been inside a Temple of the Three, and the only person she had ever knelt for was the Queen of Neldor. But she obeyed without question, bowing her head and feeling a bit silly as the breeze circled her several times, lifting her hair and clothes as if curious and questioning. Then, the small wind left as abruptly as it had come, and the air hung with stillness.

"We are accepted. Rise and follow," Fiametta said, barely waiting for Jayce to get to her feet as she strode toward the temple entrance.

They entered the temple, where the quiet was almost deafening. Jayce's boots thudded on the stone floor as her eyes traveled upward to the vaulted ceiling. Faint sunlight poured through the stained glass, casting fractured rainbows across the central altar surrounded by countless flickering candles.

"Welcome," a gentle voice murmured.

Jayce turned to see the Keeper of the Three. His white hair hung long and straight past his shoulders, and his wizened face held a serene expression as grounding as the earthy scent of the temple's incense. Despite the solemnity of everything around them, the Keeper's eyes seemed to twinkle with reassurance, and Jayce's shoulders relaxed, at ease by his calming presence.

"What can I do for you young ladies this turn?" the Keeper asked.

Fiametta bowed. "Keeper Solmere, I have brought a seeker of truth to you. We were sent by Dame Febris to ask for guidance on healing what seems to be a block on her abilities. This is Jayce Keenstone of Loshar."

His green eyes lit up as he stepped closer. "Ah! Loshar. My childhood home still stands there. It is good to see someone else who hails from my homeland. I am Orwen Solmere, guardian of the temple and Keeper of the Three. Well met." He bowed, rather than extending a hand for her to shake.

Jayce inclined her head, still uncertain what the protocol was in greeting a religious leader in a Temple of the Three. "Well met, Keeper."

"And it is as she said? A block on your magic, spiritual in nature?" he inquired.

"The Head of the Mana Guild—Dame Febris—said she couldn't heal it, so it must not be physical or emotional. She said..." Jayce swallowed, trying to moisten her dry mouth with her tongue. "She said that I may have been touched by the Three. Only, I can't see how that would be, as I've never walked the path of a pilgrim."

"I'm sure she explained infants are sometimes touched by the Three. Sometimes they hand-pick their disciples for special purposes. If that is what happened to you, and someone sealed your powers, it must have caused you much difficulty over the ages."

"I-yes," Jayce said, nearly choking on the words. Tears sprang to her eyes. It explained so much of the trouble she'd had with using her magic, she hardly dared believe that by talking to this man she could resolve it.

She sniffed loudly, and the Keeper produced a handkerchief, offering it to her.

Jayce took it gratefully, blowing her nose. It sounded far too loud in the echoing chamber of the temple.

"You seem... uncertain," he said, stepping closer. "That's natural. What we do here demands trust and courage. But I can assure you of two truths: the Three are caring and benevolent. They do not seek your destruction, nor your discomfort. But you'll find that surrendering to the process often yields answers you didn't know you were seeking."

Jayce nodded. She didn't trust herself to speak and clutched the handkerchief to her chest, finding strength in the silken fabric.

The Keeper gestured toward the central altar. "Here, we can create a bridge—not just to the Three, but to the truth buried within yourself. It is a rare gift, one that only the Three can bestow. If you are healed this turn, it will not be my doing, but Theirs. Perhaps one, or more, of them will hear your plea."

Jayce blinked to clear her eyes and gazed at the altar. "I... I don't know what to say. I have never done anything to warrant their attention or deserve a gift like this."

Keeper Solmere's smile was warm. "Child, they would give it to you just for asking. If your heart and intent are pure, they will know."

The truth of his words settled inside her, a deeper part of her simply knowing that all would be right.

"Kneel here, and we will begin. Fiametta, stand outside, and if anyone passes, let them know there is a ceremony in process."

Fiametta bowed and left. Jayce hardly knew the woman, but she wished she could have stayed. It felt strange to be in the temple alone with the Keeper. She didn't feel unsafe, but she did feel exposed.

She lowered herself onto the cushion before the altar, the weight of the moment pressing against her ribs like a too-tight bodice. Flickering candlelight softened the edges of the chamber, casting long shadows across the polished stone floor that met the rainbow light of the stained-glass depictions of the Three.

Keeper Solmere moved with practiced ease, his robes rustling as he arranged three objects before her—a copper disc, a bundle of dried herbs, and a slender shard of bone, each placed within the intricate carvings inlaid into the altar's surface.

"These are the elements of the Three," Keeper Solmere murmured. "Copper for truth, herb for healing, bone for sacrifice. They will anchor you as you seek your answers."

Jayce took a deep breath, gripping her skirts with her hands at her sides. She wasn't entirely sure what he meant, but she was committed. She would follow through with this.

The Keeper struck a match and lit a narrow stick of incense, delicate curls of smoke rising to join the haze above. The scent—earthy and rich, with a sharp undertone—coiled in Jayce's lungs, and she relaxed further, closing her eyes and breathing.

A low hum filled the chamber as Keeper Solmere chanted in a language she didn't know.

"Close your eyes," Solmere instructed. "Breathe deep. Let the Three find you."

Jayce obeyed. The first inhale was shallow, the second deeper. On the third, something shifted. The light behind her eyelids brightened as if the sun had risen inside the chamber. A tingling sensation traced her skin, and when she opened her eyes, the room had transformed.

The colors around her pulsed with a vibrancy that made her heart stutter. The gold embroidery on Solmere's robes gleamed too brightly, the candle flames stretched taller than they should, and even the incense smoke moved with an unnatural grace, curling in purposeful patterns.

Patterns not unlike those on her left hand. She raised it, noting the similarities and wondering at the meaning of it. Her ears picked up every sound, including those she never would have noticed with her usual mortal hearing—the rustling of the Keeper's robes, the distant crackling of wax melting down the candles, even the near-imperceptible scrape of stone as cool air shifted against the temple walls.

Then came the voices.

Three distinct female whispers brushed against her consciousness. Familiar and strange all at once. She could not understand what they said, though she strained with all her senses.

Keeper Solmere's voice reached her through the haze. "Speak your plea, Jayce Keenstone. Let the Three hear your heart."

Jayce closed her eyes again, the whispers of the goddesses weaving around her like strands of ivy. She had come this far. There was no turning back now.

She exhaled, bracing herself.

And she spoke.

CHAPTER FOURTEEN

"WHY HAVE YOU LET this happen?"

She didn't plan the words. They poured out of her almost by force, as if the arcane energies of the room demanded them. *Let them hear your heart.* She squeezed her eyes shut, overwhelmed by the tide of emotion welling inside her.

Her heart held far more anger than she'd realized. Here they were, three goddesses that most of the people of her land revered, prayed to, depended on. They had let the Plague King rule for seven ages, allowing people to get sick, to die. And they hadn't provided a cure.

What were they doing, if not protecting their devout from this sickness? Protecting *her*?

Her fists shook, pressing against the side of the altar. She hadn't even realized she'd clenched her hands. Tears fell hot against her cheeks, like twin rivers.

"Where have you been?" the words tore from her throat, echoing through the church. From her peripheral, Jayce thought she saw Keeper Solmere step back.

We sent you.

The voices surfaced in her mind, and Jayce gasped, eyes flying open. Pressing darkness encroached on the altar. The temple walls and stained-glass windows and rainbow light—all gone. The only thing she could see was the altar right in front of her, with three of the tallest candles blazing taller than they should have on their own. In the flames, she could just make out three feminine figures.

Her breath left her in her awe, and her fingers unwound from their fists, coming to rest on the altar, bumping the three items: the copper disk, the bone shard, and the herb bundle.

The latter whispered as she touched it, mostly garbled gibberish, perhaps words meant only for the divinity before her, but one word stood out among the rest.

Speaker.

"What do you mean?" she said, her voice coming out small and quiet, muffled somehow in this cocoon of candlelight and darkness.

You were chosen. Born at a time when heavens aligned and we could reach across the distance and bless you. A twin soul, strong enough to accept the fate that would come. Speaker of the Well.

Jayce's brow furrowed. She tried to think when she'd ever heard of a well, and the old stories, the ones her father used to tell, surfaced in her mind.

"The Well? *The* Well?" The one where these goddesses had been made? She knew the story. But the name and location of the Well had long been forgotten, perhaps protected from those who would use it for ill, as the necromancer had.

The Well of Origin, the Three pronounced. Their images flickered in the candle flames, and Jayce had the distinct impression they couldn't hold this form for long.

"I don't know what you want from me, but there's this block on my magic."

Yes. We can sense it.

"Did you place it there? Can you remove it?"

We did not place it. We can remove it, but there will be a cost.

"What cost?" Jayce asked, rushing. She had so many questions, too many. So much information was spinning around in her mind, but she didn't want to waste this chance.

You must come to the Well. We cannot remove it here. The Essence is too weak.

Essence? What was that? Jayce shook her head, adjusting her position on the cushion. Her folded legs were falling asleep.

"Where is the Well?"

A pause, heavy and humming, pressed down around her. The candlelight flickered, their flames stretching impossibly high, distorting the shadows of the three figures until they were unrecognizable.

The Well lies where the first breath of magic was drawn. Where the first oath was spoken. Go to the Silver Moon Woods in Thorgor. From there, let the plants guide you.

Jayce swallowed, frustration clawing at the back of her throat. Thorgor was in the southern part of the mainland and took several days' journey on horseback from Loshar. It would be weeks, if not cycles, before she could go to the Well of Origin and have this block removed.

"Is there nothing you can do now?" she asked, desperate for some measure of hope that her magic might be normal, that she might have answers in the midst of all the confusion of the past several days.

We will leave you with a parting gift, Speaker.

A sharp pulse rang through her skull, like a ripple through still water. Jayce gasped, doubling over as a sudden pressure built behind her ribs. Her fingers dug into the altar, knuckles white, as an aching warmth unfurled inside her.

The words were distant, submerged beneath the roar of her own pulse. Heat lanced through her chest, cracking through her bones like lightning seeking purchase in the earth.

She *felt* it. The block—splintering.

Not gone. Not yet. But fractured.

Jayce gasped as her senses flared. The temple walls blurred, the air around her warping as if space had been stretched thin. She felt everything for a moment—the pulse of life in the candles, the age-old hum of the stones beneath her, the haggard breathing of the Keeper standing near.

Then the world snapped back into place, and Jayce slumped forward, catching herself on the altar, scattering the totems laid before her. Her breath came in ragged gasps, her body trembling as if she had run for miles.

The flames flared brighter for a moment, the figures within them turning as if to look at Jayce. Before she could glimpse their faces, the figures vanished with an audible cracking sound.

The goddesses were gone.

Silence pressed in on her, thick and smothering.

A warm, steadying hand landed on her shoulder.

"You are still with us." Keeper Solmere's voice was gentle, his palm firm against her back as she slowly righted herself.

Jayce swallowed, her throat raw. "I—I think so."

Solmere crouched beside her, pressing a metal cup into her hands. She hadn't even noticed him retrieving it. The water was cool, grounding, though her grip felt weak as she held onto the smooth pewter surface.

"What happened?" she murmured, her voice quieter now, as if speaking too loudly might shatter the moment.

Solmere regarded her with knowing eyes. "I was hoping you could tell me. What did you see?"

Jayce pressed her lips together and shook her head. "I-I don't know, exactly. Were they really here?"

Solmere's eyes gleamed with tears. He folded his hands inside his robes and looked at the altar with a far-off expression. "I have been in Their direct presence only once before. During my own pilgrimage. I would recognize them anywhere."

He smiled, beaming at the memory, then focusing on her. "Some experiences are too sacred to share. I would encourage you to hold these things in your heart until the time feels right to share them."

Jayce forced herself to take another breath, her head still spinning. She didn't feel different, not in any way she could describe. But she knew—something had shifted inside her.

And the goddesses' words still echoed in her mind.

We will leave you with a parting gift, Speaker.

She set the empty cup aside, pressing a hand to her chest, half-expecting to feel the crack the goddesses had made within her. But there was nothing—just the steady drum of her heartbeat, more restless than ever with the excitement she'd just had.

Solmere offered his hand, and Jayce took it, letting him pull her upright.

"Take care of your heart, Jayce Keenstone," he said, watching her carefully. "Your power is only part of the journey. It is your heart that will decide your true course."

Jayce nodded, uncertain but grateful. She took one final glance at the altar, at the copper disc, the herb bundle, and the bone shard. Her mind scrambled to grasp hold of some detail there, to make sense of the significance of it, but no sensible ideas took purchase.

She thanked Solmere, and she left the temple, feeling lopsided, like she'd forgotten to put on a shoe that morning.

Both shoes clacked against the stone, reminding her of reality, and she emerged from the temple into evening air, already cooling in the deep shadows of the Mana Guild building towering beside the temple.

Fiametta wandered in the gardens, murmuring softly to the rat on her shoulder, navigating the twisting spiral path despite her partial blindness.

She looked up, as if noticing Jayce's observation, but didn't speak, and Jayce was grateful. She still needed time to ground herself.

Everything *looked* the same.

The sky stretched above her, deep violet streaked with the last embers of sunset. Birds flew past, calling out in their evening songs, and Jayce felt as if she were back home in Loshar, listening to the fading notes of the Queen's Evening Song.

Her heart lifted, and she reveled in the beautiful moment, knowing that when she did finally return to her apothecary, nothing would be the same as it once had.

CHAPTER FIFTEEN

JAYCE STOOD IN FRONT of the mirror in her room, clutching a note she hadn't yet written. The blank parchment crumpled at the corners where her fingers curled around it.

She'd tried to talk to Nels the night before. Knocked once. Waited. Knocked again. He hadn't responded, despite the hour still being early. She couldn't believe he had truly left to go back home without her.

But when knocking on his door that morning had yielded similar results, she knew he was either sick, avoiding her, or he had followed through on his threat to leave.

She smoothed the paper on her chest and frowned at it. If he hid in his room, she thought a note might give her a chance to apologize, but she couldn't think of anything to say.

Her wardrobe doors rattled. She sighed loudly and crossed the room, tossing the useless parchment onto her bed. Standing before the wardrobe, her hands rested on the doorknobs. She should take the plant to the front desk and tell them she couldn't tolerate it. They could find another room to keep it in, one where it would at least get sun.

Keeping it locked in the wardrobe was cruel.

She flung the doors open and bent to grab the pot of the fern with a swift motion.

Its delicate fronds wrapped around her arms, curling around her like a toddler grabbing onto its mother.

We do not bloom like others. We uncurl, slow and silent. But still—we grow. The fern whispered.

More nonsense. She would be glad to be rid of it. The Three could keep their Well, their power. She wanted none of it.

She gritted her teeth and hefted the fern pot higher up on her hip, reaching for the door with one fern-covered hand.

Why do you pull back when the light touches you?

Jayce paused. It was speaking to her, she realized. Not spouting nonsense. Her heart had responded to its words, pulse picking up pace as she considered what it said.

It was standing there, at the door to her room, she realized she barely felt the cold of the fern.

You fear you are too much. But we are never too much for the ground that holds us.

She nearly dropped the fern in shock. Instead, she turned away from the door and sat on the bed, staring down into the feathery fronds of the plant in her lap. It slowly relaxed its grip on her arms, fronds springing up and stroking her face.

It wasn't comfortable, but she wasn't *cold.* Goosebumps still surfaced on her skin, and the markings on her left arm itched something terrible, but she didn't feel the freezing burn of the plant's touch.

Was this the gift the Three had given her?

She leaned into the fern's touch, laughing at the fronds on her face, and that laughter turned to tears, then sobs so violent she had to move the plant to the bed and let the emotion move through her.

Relief and fear, in equal parts. Because what if breaking through the barrier inside of her removed all the discomfort she had dealt with her whole life? What if using her powers became *easy*? But also, what if she never made it to the Well? Or what if she did, and she was expected to do something great in the name of the Three?

She wasn't cut out for greatness. Her brother had been, and he was gone.

She emptied herself out, and when the tears slowed to quiet sniffles and hollowness ached in her chest, she found herself wanting Nels.

His warmth beside her. His smile on her. His arms around her. She would pound his door down if she had to. He couldn't hide from her forever, and she owed him an apology.

She washed her face quickly at the wash basin, then headed for the door. She turned the knob, pulled open the door with force, and strode right into Savage Alighieri.

Sputtering, apologizing, limbs flailing, Jayce and Sav worked to untangle themselves and stepped apart.

"What are you doing here?" Jayce asked, straightening her blouse.

Sav coughed into his hand. "I came to invite you to a meeting. I realized I've been too cryptic and distant lately, and I thought inviting you to come with me would help repair some of the damage I've done."

He extended a hand toward her, blue eyes beseeching. "Jayce, would you accompany me this morning?"

Jayce swallowed. She glanced from Sav's offered hand, down the hall, toward Nels's door.

Sav followed her gaze. "We could invite him, too. The others would be upset, but I'll take the brunt of it."

"Really?" Hope surged for a moment, then died. Too late. The gesture came too late. She shook her head. "He won't answer the door. If he's even there. I haven't seen him since yesterday."

Sav frowned. "I wouldn't have expected him to actually leave. Come on, I'll try."

Nels didn't respond to Sav's pounding on his door, nor the friendly jibes he passed through the wood.

Sav strode back to Jayce, hands in his pockets, shaking his head. "He's either stubborn, gone deaf, or he isn't in. Let's head out, and we ask Bentley if he's seen him."

He held out his arm, and Jayce took it, taking a deep breath and blowing air out her lips. She tried to convince herself that Nels would show up eventually. He was probably sorting his feelings out alone somewhere. Maybe communing with the rocks he loved so dearly.

That thought made her smile, lifting her heart somewhat.

"You aren't wearing your gloves," Sav noted.

Jayce glanced down. He was right—she had forgotten to put them on. She didn't even have them in her pocket. She could picture the spot she had left them, on the small desk in her room.

She had no explanation for him. Her experience with the Three sat close to her heart, still too recent to share. How to explain something so... other? When she still didn't understand it herself?

"I guess I forgot," she said.

Sav didn't comment, and they walked out of the ambry in an easy silence.

That same silence accompanied them across the Guild grounds and into the Eldenreach forest. Sav led her on a different path than she'd taken before, one she assumed was much more direct.

She remembered what Sav had said about the path, and with a rush of courage, reached out to a tree she passed. Like the fern, the tree's bark didn't bite her fingers with cold the way it usually would have. She smiled and sent a thought to the tree.

Cover our passing.

She shivered at its wordless response, glancing over her shoulder to see if anything had happened.

The slightest bit of movement from the lower plants as they grew, creeping outward and upward to cover their trail, and she smiled.

Sav stopped. "What did you do?"

"What you asked me to do," Jayce said. "I'm covering our tracks."

He looked at her like he was seeing something sacred. "You are incredible."

A thrill went through her at the praise. He had always complimented her. Did it make her blind to his faults because he was so nice to her? His tone and expression seemed genuine.

"The roots did all the work," she said.

"They wouldn't have listened to me," Sav said with a laugh.

The path wound around and around, weaving back and forth, taking them over a fallen tree and a small, burbling brook, both of which Sav helped her over.

The stone wall and the bee door became visible through the trees, the same as before. Sav unlocked the door with a bee key exactly like the one Jayce had in her pocket. She figured carrying it around with her would be safer than trying to find a hiding spot for it back at the ambry.

He led her down the damp, dark, and musty interior of the tunnel with a flickering torch for light. And when he opened the door to the main room at last, it felt like walking into another world.

Jayce breathed deep, taking it in. The warm lantern light, plush chairs and rugs, the partially filled bookcases, and the people.

Fiametta fed Mortimer tiny bits of cheese and crackers. Corbin brooded, arms crossed over his chest. Next to him, Yamalda fidgeted with a dagger, chatting with Bentley.

It felt so different from just a turn ago. She still didn't know these people well, but she felt like she understood them better. And she *felt* better, with the symptoms of using her magic slightly improved, and a full night's sleep under her belt.

The only thing missing was Nels.

She approached Bentley at the center table, the surrounding armchairs pulled close for easy access to the fruit bowls provided there. He was hunched over a plate of fruit, nodding along to whatever Yamalada was saying.

The warrior noticed Jayce waiting and paused her own line of conversation to let her speak.

"Have you seen Nels?" Jayce asked, tucking her hair behind her ears.

Bentley paused mid-bite, gesturing with a finger for her to wait a moment while he chewed. He swallowed, then, "Yes, I did. The evening prior."

Her heart sank.

"He asked about passage to Starfall, and I told him I could take him this morning on my first run." He went in for another bite of a pink-fleshed melon.

Jayce would have been tempted to try some if the thought of Nels leaving hadn't made her stomach turn. She put a hand over it, as if that would curb the nausea.

"And... did you? Take him, I mean?"

Bentley seemed to finally take in her face, as if realizing what it might mean to her if Nels had left.

"Oh! No. He didn't show up at the pickup point. I assumed he had changed his mind. He hasn't been by to see you?"

Jayce shook her head, her throat tight and her eyes burning. Not gone... but still avoiding her. She supposed she deserved it after the way she had acted.

"Thank you, Bentley," she said.

"We will keep our eyes out for him," Sav reassured her, taking a seat in a sage-green armchair that matched the vest he wore. He picked a piece of melon from the tray and held it out to her.

She accepted, knowing she needed to eat. She had skipped breakfast to be here, after all. She took a bite. Whispers glazed across her tongue, but it was surprising how easy they were to bear without the cold. Instead, a strange numbing sensation flooded her mouth the more she chewed. Still uncomfortable, but not nearly as bad.

She ate one piece, then another, and another.

Sav stared at her. “I don’t think I’ve ever seen you eat that much fruit in one sitting. Isn’t it... uncomfortable?”

Jayce picked up a napkin and wiped her face. She had never enjoyed fruit so much. She glanced at Fiametta, but the woman only stroked her rat, not looking at Jayce.

She wouldn’t say anything about their excursion, leaving it to Jayce to decide how much she wanted to share.

“I saw Dame Febris yesterday, and she recommended I meet with Keeper Solmere. He... it...” She swallowed, struggling to find the words. “I feel better now. A little. If I want to recover, I need to go back to the mainland. To Thorgor.”

Sav’s posture stiffened, and he suddenly became absorbed in his plate of fruit.

“What could possibly be in Thorgor? It’s a swamp,” Corbin asked incredulously.

“There’s a Well...” Jayce began.

“*The* Well? From the legends of the Three?” Sav asked.

“I think so,” Jayce stammered, caught off guard by his sudden interest.

Corbin’s expression turned from doubtful to awed. “Imagine if you actually found it... No one ever has, you know. Not and lived.”

"That isn't true," Sav started, and he launched into a gleeful debate about some enchanter or another from three centuries prior.

Corbin countered with references to another, more recent scholar of the Guilds who had exposed the enchanter's false claims by cross-referencing several ancient texts describing the Well.

Jayce only half-listened as she thought about the Well and tried not to feel sorry about Nels's absence. She sat on a mauve armchair between Bentley and Sav while she ate another piece of fruit, a strawberry this time.

Eventually, Sav raised two hands, palms forward, in surrender.

He cleared his throat, and chatter around the rest of the room died down, everyone's eyes turning to him.

"I have an update for everyone," Sav said.

Jayce straightened. It had to be about the translation. It had been several days, after all.

"Tonight is the annual Ivory Concord, a dinner held to raise funding for the Guilds."

Her hope fell. A party? What did that have to do with anything?

"From Jayce's findings about the person who funded and likely directed Sir Dray's efforts to create a false remedy for the plague, we can presume they are wealthy and connected. Exactly the kind of person who would attend this event." His blue eyes shone as he looked around the table, the intensity holding them all rapt at attention.

Yamalda raised her hand. "I assume you want to infiltrate the party, but how will any of us know who we're looking for?"

"Ah, yes," Sav said, adjusting his seat. "Actually, no infiltration is necessary. Being a baron has its uses. I am allowed one guest, and I will take Jayce. The rest of you will break into the Head Dame's offices and find evidence that she is in contact with this person. Their initials are L.A."

He smiled at her, and Jayce was glad she was sitting down, for her stomach did a flip flop, and her knees felt weak. She almost didn't care that he'd assumed, rather than asked if she would attend.

She suddenly thought of the man with the cane. He had looked well-dressed enough to be a member of higher society. Would he be at the party? She should tell Sav about him, warn him that this man might approach her.

She opened her mouth, but Sav cut in.

"You'll need something appropriate to wear. That won't do for blending in, I'm afraid."

Jayce glanced down at her simple blouse, corset, and skirt, one of the two outfits she'd brought with her. She had nothing that would suit a high-society fundraiser.

"This is all I have," she stammered.

Sav waived a hand. "Never mind that. It's only unfortunate we have such short notice. Fiametta, you can handle that, right?"

Fiametta snorted, barely glancing up from feeding Mortimer. "Absolutely not. I'll stick to my poisons."

Yamalda perked up. "I'll take her. Yvla will kill me for giving her a client on such short notice, but she owes me."

Sav clapped his hands, rubbing them together. "Perfect. Jayce, Yamalda will take you dress shopping."

Jayce blinked at the short-haired, knife-wielding woman.

Yamalda grinned. "Don't worry, Jayce. I'll find you something stunning."

Jayce suddenly wasn't sure if she should be reassured or terrified.

Corbin coughed into his fist, failing to hide his amusement. "Be careful, Jayce. Yamalda's idea of *stunning* might involve knives."

"Oh, it definitely involves knives," she said, her grin growing wider. She leaned forward, resting her elbows on the table. "Jokes aside, you might not regret a knife or two. You'll need to be able to look out for yourself at that dinner. Walking in with Sav means walking into a room full of people who'd like to hurt him, and the easiest way would be through you."

A chill ran down Jayce's spine. She hadn't considered that Sav had made enemies.

Sav's lips were drawn into a thin line, and he looked pale. "They might be exaggerating the danger, but it's still present. Will you take the risk, Jayce, and attend the Concord with me?"

His expression, in addition to her own concerns about the man with the cane, made her wish she knew how to use a knife.

She looked at her ungloved hands, at the whorls left from the dusky ivy on one side and the smooth skin on the other. She wanted to find Nels and leave the Guilds. Return to the mainland and Loshar, spend time recuperating and researching the Well. She supposed it would be a pilgrimage of sorts, if she ever got the courage up to actually take it.

She could say no. They would understand. Maybe even expect it. But then she would still be the woman who hid in her apothecary. Who let fear of the past hold her back.

Looking around at the five pairs of eyes all staring at her, waiting for her decision, she found herself searching for a pair of lake-blue eyes. What would Nels say if he were there?

She put her hand in her pocket, touching the smooth wishing stone he had given her what felt like ages ago.

I told it to give you anything you want.

If she could wish for anything right now, it would be for Nels to be here. For him to forgive her, and for things to go back to the way they were.

But things would never be the same, and only she could decide what she wanted, and what risks she was willing to take.

"I'll do it," she said, resolve coiling inside her.

Finding the Well would have to wait. The Ivory Guilds still had secrets, and she wasn't leaving until she uncovered the truth.

CHAPTER SIXTEEN

THE SEAMSTRESS'S SHOP SMELLED of fresh linen and roses, the warm glow of afternoon light spilling across bolts of fabric in every shade imaginable. Yamalda strode in and greeted her sister—Yvla—with an affectionate slap on the shoulder.

"Jayce, this is Yvla. She's the reason I didn't look like a complete disaster when I first arrived at the Guilds."

Yvla grimaced. "Must you be so rough? You were trained in refined social arts, as I was."

Yvla shared Yamalda's silvery-white hair and narrow, pixie facial structure, but the similarities ended there.

Where Yamalda carried herself with the ease of a trained fighter, always ready for action, Yvla was poised and graceful as a dancer. She kept her hair long, the curls pinned neatly around her head.

She gave Jayce a measured once-over before offering a warm, knowing smile.

"Shopping for the Concord?" Yvla guessed, already reaching for swaths of elegant fabric. "I assume this is because of Loreman Alighieri?"

Jayce flushed. "How did you know I'm attending with Sav?"

Yvla held up several small swatches to Jayce's face. She let out a small laugh, shaking her head. "That man is an experience."

Yamalda snorted. "That's one way to put it."

"I think blue," Yvla muttered. "We don't have time to create a custom gown, but I have a few finished gowns in the back we could adjust. I'll fetch them; you wait here."

Jayce watched her go, then turned to find Yamalda's green-eyed gaze already on her, assessing.

That look made Jayce's stomach twist. What was the warrior thinking?

"So… how long have you known Sav?"

Yamalda smirked, leaning against the front counter. "Longer than any of the others. I was his first sparring partner, first friend, first love. Well, first everything, I suppose."

Jayce's cheeks heated at the implication in Yamalda's words. She hadn't even been *kissed* yet, much less… anything else. That's what happened when one made a hermit of themselves for their formative adult ages.

Yamalda continued. "He was different back then—figuring out who he was, carrying the weight of a past he rarely talks about. He had a lot of fire. He still does."

Jayce gave a nervous laugh. "I'm glad someone else noticed."

Yamalda didn't even crack a smile.

Jayce fidgeted. How long could finding a few dresses take?

"He seems pretty besotted with you, now. How long has it been? A single turn?"

"Almost two," Jayce said, clearing her throat. She glanced out the window, watching people pass on the street, growing uncomfortable beneath Yamalda's weighing stare.

Something clattered to the floor, making Jayce jump. A spool of thread rolled across the floor, landing at her feet.

She bent to pick it up and held it out to Yamalda.

The woman didn't reach for it, crossing her arms over her chest and glancing at the doorway Yvla had disappeared through.

"You know what my job is in this whole, grand scheme? Bentley is our transport and has connections, Corbin has powerful magic... Do you know why Sav keeps me around?'

Jayce shook her head, not knowing what to say.

Yamalda ran her hand along the counter, riddled with spools, scissors, fabric, and buttons. "Because I'm the most loyal friend he has. He knows I'll always have his back, that I'll take out the danger before it ever reaches him. Before he knows about it, even."

She picked up a pair of scissors and snipped them together, the metal making a soft snicking sound in the silence of the shop.

"What's your purpose, Jayce? Why did you come to the Guilds?"

The warrior stalked toward her, scissors still in hand, until Jayce was forced to back up against a dress form that nearly toppled over.

"I-I don't know. He needs my story, but I haven't told it yet. I can't tell it yet."

Nose-to-nose, Yamalda stared her down. "If you ask me, you're dragging this out as long as you can, trying to get close to him. Close enough to take his money or betray him. Either way, you don't belong here. So follow your rock friend and leave the Guilds before I'm forced to take more drastic action."

Jayce's fingers tightened around the spool. She considered whether it would make a good weapon or at least distract the woman if she threw it at her face.

"I simply couldn't decide between blue and purple. You have such lovely brown hair, and pink would also do nicely, I—Yamalda!" Yvla came bustling back in, arms full of fluffy, sparkling dresses.

Yamalda spun around, putting the scissors behind her back. "Yes, sister dear?"

Yvla narrowed her eyes. "Make yourself useful and fetch the measuring tape from the counter, if you please."

Yamalda obeyed, trading the tape for the scissors so subtly her sister didn't notice.

Yvla draped a deep purple gown in front of Jayce. "I remember when Yamalda was courting Sav. Don't let her fool you—that man was single-minded. I'm surprised he remembered to talk to her, much less do anything romantic."

"Sav can be *very* romantic when he wants to be. You're still salty that he didn't pursue you." Yamalda snorted and moved away from the counter, taking Jayce in. "Go back to the lighter one that looks like a waterfall."

Jayce's heart rate still hadn't come down. Why was Yamalda threatening her one moment and pretending to care what sort of dress she wore the next?

Yvla tossed the other two dresses to Yamalda, who caught them deftly.

"Change into this," Yvla insisted, holding up the lightest blue gown. "There's a curtained dressing area over there."

Jayce took the dress and went the direction the seamstress had pointed. The gown was made of a flowy, light blue fabric that glittered ominously in the sunlight coming through the shop window.

What's your purpose, Jayce? Why did you come to the Guilds? Yamalda's words, and her haunting, green-eyed gaze, followed her to the dressing area. She drew the heavy curtain across the entrance and started to change.

She managed to do up the first few buttons but couldn't get to the ones at her mid-back.

"Um, I need some help," she called, sweating with the warmth of the small dressing room.

The curtain covering the room yanked open, and Yamalda slid inside.

Jayce's skin prickled with fear. She tried to focus on breathing as she felt Yamalda's fingers fumble at her back.

"Yamalda, where are my scissors? They were here a moment ago," Yvla called out.

Jayce's back stiffened. Her breath seemed too loud, the space too small.

"They're next to the bolt of jade fabric," Yamalda called.

"Thank you," her sister trilled.

Jayce's shoulders slumped with relief.

“Straighten up. I can’t get these buttons,” Yamalda muttered.

Tense silence filled the small space. Jayce couldn’t stand it. The itchiness of the gown, the moments passing, wondering if Yamalda would say something or just stab her and be done with it.

“I’m told I come off... strong sometimes,” Yamalda began, finishing the buttons near Jayce’s neck. “But if you knew what I knew... you would be protective of him, too.”

Jayce turned as she finished, staring the warrior down. “I didn’t come here to hurt him. He’s my friend, and I want to help. You really should ask more questions before you threaten people.”

Yamalda barked a laugh. “Yeah, I’ve been told that, too. By Sav, in fact.” She rubbed the back of her neck, having the decency to look embarrassed. “Sav trusts too easily and takes risks like he has nothing to lose. He’s one of the most brilliant, and simultaneously idiotic, people I’ve ever met. I’m afraid that one of these days his lack of awareness is going to get him in a lot of trouble.”

It already had. Jayce had seen it at the Draigh Monastery. Even before that, when he met her. He often seemed to act before thinking things through, but he cared deeply about the people around him.

“I think... I think we just have to trust him. And do our best to help him,” Jayce replied. She looked down at the pale blue fabric, gathering it in her hands. It shimmered like still water, nearly matching the color of Sav’s light-colored eyes. Had the dressmaker done that on purpose, knowing they were a pair?

“Hey, are you going to be all right?”

Jayce looked up, a grin creeping onto her face. "Probably. As long as no one threatens me with sewing scissors."

Yamalda looked horrified, flushing again. "You *cannot* tell Sav I did that."

"Ladies," Yvla sang from the other side of the curtain. "Do I need to send in a search party?"

"Just finishing up!" Yamalda shouted.

Jayce cleared her throat. "I understand why you did it. You care about him; you want him to be safe. I'm an unknown, and that's frightening. I came here to find answers. About the journal, the plague, and if I'm being honest, about Sav. He's kept things from me—like all of you, and his true intentions. He broke me out of a dark place that I'd kept myself in for too long, and I feel like I need to do something to repay him. Even if it means taking the truth tonic and reliving memories I wish I could forget."

Yamalda nodded, then put a hand on her shoulder. "Then I'm glad you're here, Jayce. Sav could use more friends he can trust."

The warrior's blond hair fell into her eyes as she leaned in closer, her hand sliding up to Jayce's neck and tightening as it pulled her in. "I will be watching you," she said in a forced whisper. "Not because I don't like you or trust you. But because if you betray him, I'll make sure you answer for it."

Jayce nodded frantically, and Yamalda released her.

"Blue suits you, by the way."

Then she vanished through the curtain before Jayce could respond.

She rubbed her neck as she straightened. What to make of that woman? Warm one minute, burning with cold fury the next. What had Sav done to deserve such loyalty?

Shaking out the dress, Jayce drew in a long breath and emerged. The sparkles in the gown caught the late morning sun streaming in through the shop windows and sent tiny dots of light scattering across the shop wall and ceiling.

She had to hold the swaths of fabric up off the floor so she could walk.

"She'll need taller shoes," Yvla muttered.

Jayce straightened her posture, adjusting the folds of her dress with shaking hands. Her heart thundered. She didn't look Yamalda's way, not even as the woman handed the tape over with a casual flick of her wrist.

"Thank you," Yvla said primly, then turned to Jayce with a dazzling smile. "Let's see what we're working with."

She began circling Jayce with the tape, calling out measurements in a quick rhythm and noting them on a slate.

Jayce tried to focus on the numbers, on the pinpricks and fabric, but she could still feel the heat of Yamalda's breath from moments before.

The dress shop bell rang, and a group of distressed girls rushed in, immediately banishing the tense atmosphere in the room.

"Yvla, do you have any gowns left? We've checked *everywhere*!" one young woman moaned.

Yvla gave Yamalda an exasperated look, then smiled at Jayce and shooed her off to change.

One of the girls caught sight of Jayce and squealed so loudly Jayce thought she'd hurt herself. She froze when the girl pointed at her.

"Oh, look at her! She's stunning. I want something exactly like that."

Yvla tsked. "You know my rule, Jenna, no dress in the same color and style at the same event. Come now, we will find you something else. That pale blue would wash you out terribly. Jayce, I'll have your gown delivered this afternoon."

Jayce stepped behind the curtain again, managing to get enough buttons undone by herself to peel off the gown with care and hang it gently on the provided hook. The glittering fabric swayed as if reluctant to be left behind.

Her hands shook.

Yamalda had pressed her hard. But she seemed to have accepted her. For now.

She changed quickly, smoothed her hair, and checked her reflection once in the narrow mirror beside the curtain.

Somehow, her exchange with Yamalda made her feel more ready for what was coming. She wasn't the same shrinking violet of a person she had been before meeting Sav.

She had faced danger, and had survived.

She had met new people, and they accepted her into their circle.

She had communed with the Three, and had emerged with a gift.

She still didn't know exactly who she was becoming, but she wasn't hiding anymore. And tonight, she would face the danger again, this time dressed in glitter and lace.

CHAPTER SEVENTEEN

"YOU LOOK STUNNING TONIGHT. Yvla outdid herself," Sav said, complementing her for the third time since he'd picked her up at her room in the ambry.

He led her toward the Guild Hall, a building that he had explained contained mainly offices for the administration, but also a ballroom where the Concord would be held.

Banners with each of the Guild symbols emblazoned on them flapped in the wind, hanging in front of the pillars. Flower bushes in ornate pots lined the stairs, and a rich purple rug had been rolled out from the top of the stairs, leading inside.

She felt like a gangly, awkward youth at her first festival dance. She'd rarely been asked and even more rarely said yes. In fact, she could only remember dancing with Nels once, both of them tripping and laughing more than dancing. He'd sworn off dancing forever after crushing both of her feet and knocking them into at least two other couples.

The memory made her smile, and she found herself looking for him as they approached the building, despite the fact she knew he wouldn't be there. Where was he hiding himself? Perhaps in his room, or perhaps he'd found another corner of the Guilds to hide out in.

Sav presented their invitation at the door, speaking in a low voice to the attendant, whom he somehow managed to make laugh, and then they were in. He took her down a wide corridor and up the stairs to a ballroom on the top floor.

Jayce had to remind herself to keep her mouth closed and not stare too open-eyed at the overwhelming amount of luxury and opulent beauty that had been prepared for the Ivory Concord.

Golden chandeliers hung like captured stars from the high-vaulted ceiling, casting their warm glow over the glittering gowns and crisp formalwear of the gathered nobility. Music floated above the murmur of conversation, a soft, elegant waltz played by a small ensemble tucked near an ornately decorated fountain. The scent of jasmine and beeswax polish filled the air, mingling with the sharper tang of expensive perfumes and the cloying richness of roasted meats displayed along a grand banquet table.

Jayce adjusted her gloves, smoothing them over her fingers as if the silk could anchor her to something solid. This was a world far removed from her own.

She should have been enjoying herself. A younger version of her, one untouched by the weight of her past and recent secrets, might have stood in awe at the wealth and wonder around her.

Beside her, Sav was perfectly at ease. He had been made for this, it seemed, slipping through the crowd with the confidence of a man who belonged. He greeted nobles with a warm smile, his polished charm effortless. He would introduce her, praising her work as an apothecary in Loshar, and people seemed impressed at her charity, as they called it.

It was hardly a charity to work for money, but these people had so much money they could hardly fathom the kind of life she had been living, neck-deep in debt and dependent on the daily work to keep her alive and out of the hands of wicked men like Dray.

Sav's voice broke through her thoughts. "You look tense. Drop your shoulders."

Jayce exhaled through her nose, forcing her shoulders to relax. "It's harder than I thought. Standing and talking. Responding to introductions and niceties."

"It gets easier the more you do it. But not more pleasant. These people all have their own agenda. They spend the entire conversation assessing whether you could be valuable to them or not. It is exhausting. We can take a break if you like."

He gestured to the side, his arm sweeping around behind her as if to steer her somewhere, but he froze as someone approached.

He looked so different, Jayce almost didn't recognize him. Clean-shaven and dressed in a navy-blue silk vest over a flowing ivory shirt, Nels looked the part of a wealthy gentleman. He could have been a trade merchant, a luxury jeweler, a gem dealer. His floor-length pants were dark blue as well, and a pair of polished black shoes completed the look.

But his eyes were the same, and they were fixed on her, deep blue and unwavering. He stopped a few feet from them and inclined his head politely.

"Good evening," he said smoothly. "I don't believe we've had the pleasure."

As if they were strangers. But beneath his serious expression, Jayce thought she caught a gleam of amusement. What sort of game was he playing? And how was he *here*? And why?

She hesitated for only a second before following his lead and bobbing into a shallow curtsey. "No, I don't believe we have."

"Nels Martin," he introduced himself, offering his hand. "And you are?"

"Jayce Keenstone," she replied breathlessly, slipping her hand into his. His grip was warm and firm, grounding her for the briefest of moments.

"A pleasure," Nels said, his eyes sparkling. "Would you do me the honor of a dance later?"

Sav placed a hand at the small of Jayce's back. "I'm afraid she already has an escort for the evening." His tone held a veiled warning.

You aren't supposed to be here. Why are you here?

Nels arched a brow, unconcerned. "Ah, but the night is young." He flicked his gaze back to Jayce, his blue eyes like pools of deep water, concentrated only on her. "I hope to see you on the dance floor."

With that, he stepped away, disappearing back into the crowd.

"Well, we found him," Sav said, not sounding amused. "Though how he got into such an exclusive party is beyond me. Are you all right, seeing him?"

"Yes, I'm all right," she replied, only half-aware of what Sav was saying as she peered through the crowd after Nels.

She swallowed, unsure what to make of the tension she felt coiling between the two men. She wanted to feel comforted by Nels's presence, and in a way, she did. But she also felt unsettled. He hadn't seemed surprised to find them there, so he had to have come to see her. Perhaps Bentley had told him where they would be. But he hadn't insisted on being included in their plans, nor had he pushed hard to be alone with her.

Had he intended to make her feel unsteady so she would mess up her role? Or was he giving her space to do what she came to do, appearing only to let her know he supported her?

She wished she knew which it was, and she wanted nothing more than to run after him and demand answers, demand he hear her apology and let an easy friendship return between them.

But she had a purpose here, and it was not yet complete.

She brushed hair from her eyes, noticing with a glance that Sav still stared at her.

"Do you think L.A. is a man or a woman?" she asked, hoping to steer Sav away from the topic of Nels before he brought it up.

Sav sighed and glanced around the room, rubbing his temple. "I had heard the Head Dame had a special guest from Loshar tonight. I'd like to find out who it is. Keep your eyes open. Perhaps you will recognize them."

Jayce wanted to point out that she hadn't frequented Queen Lyra's court in several ages, and even then, she hadn't been part of parties like this, but she had a feeling it wouldn't do any good.

As they worked their way around the room, Jayce kept her eye on Head Dame Tsega. The woman's bright red hair was visible from anywhere. Paired with the glittering, elegant dress she wore, the woman was like a magnet. Always surrounded by people, but Jayce didn't glimpse the man with the cane among them.

She suddenly felt lightheaded, a buzz of strange energy pulsing through the space. It was either the heat of the room or someone was using magic. She put a hand to her head.

"You're doing well," Sav murmured, passing her a glass of a sparkly, pale pink liquid in a tall glass.

"Thank you," Jayce said. She sipped cautiously at the pink drink, making a face when the bubbles tickled the inside of her nose. It tasted sweet. The whispers of whatever plant the drink came from were garbled and impossible to understand.

She still hadn't decided if she liked it or not but decided a few more sips wouldn't hurt. As she drank, the tight coil of nerves in her chest unwound.

"Go easy, it can muddle your senses," Sav said, putting an arm around her and steering her toward another group of attendees. "I forgot you wouldn't have had roselight before."

"Roselight?" Jayce replied, staring into the sparkling liquid in her glass. She felt the urge to keep drinking, almost irresistible. It worried her, and with her nerves she would end up drinking the entire thing without noticing. "Perhaps I should drink something less... enticing."

"Yes, perhaps that's best." Sav took her glass and put it on the nearest tray, held by a server for the purpose. He found another with a full tray of drinks and picked out a clear bubbling one. "Try this."

A drink had never tasted *dry* to Jayce before, but this one somehow managed it. The bubbles of the fizzy water danced on her tongue and made the inside of her nose itched. It tasted slightly sour, but otherwise had no flavor, and she didn't hear any whispers when she drank it, and her head cleared.

"Most people add fruit juice to it, but I figured you'd prefer without," Sav said.

"Not for the taste, certainly. But it's nice not to have my drink talking back to me," Jayce said, trying to sound grateful. Why would anyone drink something like this?

Casual talk and tasting the new drinks had distracted her from their purpose: to discover if anyone with the initials L.A. was in attendance, and whether or not they had anything to do with Sir Dray, Dagric Wortcunning, and the poisonous noxbrosia mixture.

Jayce's eyes flickered through the crowd. It was hard to imagine that somewhere among the swirl of silk and satin, there was someone who might hold the key to unraveling the mystery of L.A.

A chime rang through the room, and a wave of silence passed over the crowd.

“Welcome, all, to the Ivory Concord!” The Head Dame stood on a stand at the front of the room. Applause broke out at her words, and people moved closer, crowding in.

Sav led Jayce to a place near a pillar behind everyone else.

She leaned against the stone pillar, putting a hand to her head. She had only had a few sips of the Roselight. Why did she feel like the room was spinning. Sucking in air, she concentrated on the Head Dame, only hearing half the words.

“… to your donations, the Guilds will…”

Sav leaned in from behind her, whispering in her ear. “Do you see anyone we should talk to next?”

Jayce licked her lips and tried to reply, but her attention was inexplicably drawn forward, to where Head Dame Tsega stood with her arms outstretched, looking over the hushed crowd.

“Thank you. Now that I have your full attention,” she flashed a smile. “I would like to announce that there is a new member on the board of directors for the Ivory Guilds. Please welcome Lord and Wardsman, Leth Alend!”

The roar that filled Jayce’s ears didn’t come from the crowd alone as she watched the man approach the stand.

All she could hear above the clapping and cheering was the click of his ebony cane on the marble floor.

Click. Click. Click.

He faced the crowd, running a hand through his gray hair and straightening his maroon jacket before leaning on his cane and addressing the crowd.

“Thank you, thank you. I am honored to be here tonight, to be among friends and fellow alumni of this prestigious institution." His iron gaze swept through the crowd, as if searching.

Jayce turned to hide on the other side of the pillar, and ran into Sav, who took one look at her face and pulled her behind the pillar with him.

"What is it? Who did you see?"

She shook her head. She couldn't get the words out. Did Sav not feel it? The magic sweeping through the room like a pack of hounds on the hunt?

"It's all right. Breathe," Sav said, gesturing to encourage the motion.

She forced herself to do it, gulping down air. Pain had blossomed in her sternum, like something was stuck there. She took a sip of the awful, dry drink in her hand and coughed, nearly choking.

Sav took it from her and set it on the banquet table behind him. "Enough of that. Just focus on getting air, for now. Do we need to step out?"

Jayce shook her head. She could do this, she just needed a moment. And for that energy to stop swirling through her mind. She shook her head, willing the sensation to go away.

"Do you feel that?" she asked Sav.

"Hm?" His eyes were fixed on the Head Dame and the man with the cane—what had his name been?

She couldn't remember. Why couldn't she remember? Panic blossomed again, and she was back to focusing her breath.

Sav didn't have magic. Without it, he probably wouldn't recognize it even if he could sense it.

"Someone... is using... magic," she gasped out.

Sav barely glanced at her, eyes fixed on the front.

She stared at him, then out at the rest of the crowd. All of them had their eyes fixed on the front. She felt the magic pushing against her will, urging her to look. *Pay attention. The Head Dame is speaking*, it seemed to say.

She plugged her ears and hummed to herself, trying to block it out. The pressure in her head eased. She tugged on Sav's arm and showed him the posture to take, praying he would get the message.

He shrugged her off. "Just a minute. The Head Dame is speaking."

A chill went through her. Whoever the magic belonged to, they were using it to force the entire room to pay attention to the Head Dame's speech, and that of her special guest, the man with the cane.

She hunkered down next to the pillar, hunching her shoulders and keeping her ears tightly plugged.

Applause broke out, and someone shook her shoulder.

"Jayce? Jayce, are you all right?"

She looked up into Sav's clear, blue eyes. Lucid blue eyes, no longer enraptured with the Head Dame.

She released her ears hesitantly, then stood, realizing she'd somehow ended up in a crouch.

"What happened?" she asked.

"They're opening a new Guild campus on the mainland," Sav said with unfeigned enthusiasm. "This is what we've been waiting for, Jayce! We can open a second operation there at last, with the resources of the Guilds available to us. It's wonderful news!"

She tried to smile, but the expression didn't feel right on her face. Her gut had tightened in warning.

"Sav, you didn't feel it? Someone was manipulating you. They were doing it to all of us."

He laughed, then looked at her with disbelief. "The entire room? No one has that much power."

"That man—the Head Dame's special guest—can you remember his name?"

"Sure. It's—" He broke off, confusion passing over his face. "Huh, that's funny. I heard him say it, and I swear I remember it, but when I go to tell you, it vanishes."

His brow furrowed, and then his posture shifted, becoming stiffer, more alert. "I'll be right back. Stay here."

She didn't want to stay alone, but she didn't trust herself to walk straight in this state, either.

She nodded. "I'm going to get some food."

"I'll meet you at the table, then." He shot her a quick smile, then straightened his jacket and strode confidently toward the group.

Jayce made her way to the central table, mind still spinning. The table was filled with a lavish spread of fruit and vegetables, roasted meats, and desserts. Perhaps eating something would soothe the tight, nauseated feeling in her stomach.

She took a plate and as she reached for a cluster of grapes, a voice—low and polite—drifted to her from behind her.

"Enjoying the party?"

She dropped the grapes on the table. The purple orbs burst apart and scattered, some bouncing and rolling across the floor.

It was him. The man with the cane. One of the queen's counselors. Why couldn't she recall his name?

"I'm sorry, I don't—" she began.

"I must apologize for our earlier encounter." He interrupted, swirling the drink in his hand. "It must have been so confusing to be approached abruptly and without an introduction like that. Quite rude of me."

Jayce put a hand to her chest, willing her heart rate to slow. She felt very much like a rabbit cornered by a wolf. She forced a polite smile. "Do I know you?"

The man nodded, then took a slow sip of his drink before saying, far too casually, "I knew a boy once. Looked quite a bit like you."

The words sent a cold blade of unease through her spine. Jayce stiffened, her grip tightening on the empty plate. She swallowed, trying to keep her voice even. "Are you from Loshar?"

His gaze flickered over her face, as if cataloging every detail. "Yes, I am. Now, what was his name? Javin, wasn't it?"

Jayce's heart stopped.

The Head Dame's guest was said to be from Loshar. She licked her lips, wishing she'd had something to drink after that awful fizzy water.

"I didn't catch your name?" The words floated out of her mouth. The heat of the room pressed in around her, the light of the chandeliers glaring, the scent of jasmine and roasted meats turning cloying in her nostrils. She forced herself to breathe, to keep her expression neutral.

If this was L.A., and he knew who her brother was, then he knew who she was, and he would know she had gotten Sir Dray sent to the mines. There was no telling how he might react when confronted with the person who had muddled in his plans.

Where was Sav?

She tried to peer around the man's large form, but he stepped over, forcing her to look at him.

"What I'm wondering," the man continued, ignoring her question. "Is how you came to be here, and how after all this time, you've managed to get yourself so deeply involved in things that don't concern you."

She set the plate down on the table, picking up her skirts and turning to move past the man. "I'm sorry, I think you must be mistaken."

The man's hand shot out and grabbed her elbow, holding her just tight enough to keep her rooted in place. "Am I?" His voice was soft, almost thoughtful, and his eyes searched hers. "No, you're her. You're the other twin. I would recognize your mind anywhere."

Shock went through her like a wave. Her heart seemed to skip several beats, and she could not move anything except her eyes. She tried to come out of the paralysis, to breathe and remind herself that she was safe in this room full of people, and there was no reason really why this man, of all people, would cause such a response in her.

Except... except she *knew* him. Why, then, could she not remember his name?

Nels appeared. Smooth as ever, he swept in beside Jayce, his hand settling at her waist. "I haven't had the pleasure," he said to the man.

The man grunted and spun away, fleeing at as brisk of a pace as his limping gait would allow.

Sav approached swiftly, his expression hard. He took Jayce's arm and pulled her away from Nels. "You aren't supposed to be here."

"Good thing I was. That man was harassing her," Nels said, voice rising.

"You need to leave," Sav growled.

"If Jayce wants me to leave, she'll say so."

Both men looked at her.

Jayce could hardly follow the conversation, much less add to it. Her eyes had tracked the man with the cane until he vanished into the crowd. Her mind spun, putting the jumbled pieces together. She knew who he was. She just needed to remember his name...

Her tongue loosened, and the name fell from her lips before her mind had a chance to catch up to the implications of it.

"Leth Alland."

"What did you say?" Nels asked.

"L.A.," Sav murmured, loosening his grip on her arm.

Jayce sagged, then fell to her knees, holding her chest as the place where she'd felt the block on her magic pulsed with waves of spear-like pain.

The man with the cane was Leth Alland.

And she remembered him.

CHAPTER EIGHTEEN

SHE REMEMBERED HIM AS one of the queen's counselors, watching from the sidelines as her powers—and her brother's—were tested.

But she recognized him as someone else, too.

He was the man her parents had paid to repress her goddess-given powers. The block inside her seemed to reach for him, responding to the presence of its creator.

Sav helped her up. He said something to Nels about getting her a drink of water, and Nels left.

Sav muttered instructions in her ear as they walked. *Look up. Smile. Walk this way. We're just getting some air.*

That last one he said out loud to a concerned couple who approached asking if they could help.

Jayce saw it all through a blur, and everything sounded as if she were underwater. She focused on getting enough air.

She suddenly wanted Nels to come back. She needed him there, to feel his touch, hear his voice.

But none of the faces they passed were his.

They left the stuffy, lavish ballroom behind and emerged onto one of the balconies. Two potted rose bushes on either side of the entrance writhed as she passed, thorny branches reaching for her.

Jayce shrieked and yanked herself out of Sav's arms. She stopped at the edge of the balcony, whirling around and gripping the stone ledge with all her might, leaning as far away from the plants as she could.

She drew in air, but her breaths were too shallow. She couldn't get enough. Her vision fuzzed. Sav's concerned face floated in front of her, his mouth moving.

Jayce put a hand to her head and forced herself to take in air. Her chest throbbed at her sternum. Was this an effect of the "gift" the Three had given her in the temple?

Sav shut the windowed double doors, muffling the sounds of the music and chattering guests.

The rose bushes had stilled. She watched them carefully, but they didn't so much as trail a vine toward her. Had they reacted to her emotional state somehow? And had Sav seen? What did he think?

The cool night air touched her sweat-slickened skin. She shivered, wrapping her arms around herself. At some point while they were in the Grand Hall night had fallen, and now, silver moonlight colored the stone balcony.

She inhaled deeply, filling her lungs with the crisp air. It did little to steady her racing heart, but the terrifying blur of memories faded to the back of her mind, slipping out of the grasp of her conscious memory once more. She tried to hold on to the details, but every time she caught something, panic rose again, and soon enough, it was all she could do to breathe and hold on to the railing.

Sav stood beside her, his usual effortless charm subdued, concern threading his voice. “Are you all right?”

Jayce closed her eyes. No, she wasn’t all right. She’d had her heart cracked open and her world turned upside down in the space of a single turn. Every turn since coming to the Ivory Guilds had held more secrets and too few answers.

He waited, showing again that enormous patience of his. Caring? Or calculating? She couldn’t tell with him.

Her heart slowed, and her lungs loosened. She sucked in the rose-scented evening air.

Sav cleared his throat. “What happened in there?”

Jayce shook her head. If she tried to talk about what that man had said to her, she would go into a panic again.

Sav sighed and rubbed his forehead. “Fiametta said the tonic should be finished tomorrow. Perhaps you’ll be able to tell me then.”

She stared down at her dress, glittering like it was made of moonbeams and stars. Its serene beauty didn’t match the turmoil inside her, like waves of the sea if they could boil and writhe.

She opened her mouth thrice to speak, and closed it each time. What could she say? She was an apothecary. She could heal others, but not herself. It had been two ages since Javin left her, and she still couldn’t talk about it.

“I’m sorry,” she hated the words as they came out of her mouth. Apologies didn’t help Sav, or the rebellion, or her.

"If you just try a little harder, you might be able to—" Sav reached for her, then paused at her expression of disbelief, and his hand dropped.

"Try harder? What do you think I've been doing all this time?" Jayce's voice climbed higher, cutting through the peaceful evening.

"Then what do you want? I paid your life debt—is that not enough? Or is there something else you've been after all along?" Sav turned to face her, face hard and angry.

"For someone who promised to never hold that against me, you've done it twice now," she snapped, whirling away from him. Nels had been right. Not that Sav wasn't worthy of her trust. But that she had been blinded by his charm. She *liked* him, and that made her do things that ended up putting her in danger. Like coming to the Concord, essentially bait for those who wished her ill. She had served herself up to Leth Alend on a platter.

"I-I didn't mean to," he stammered.

"Then stop treating my breakdowns as something that inconveniences you. I promise they inconvenience me, too."

He approached from behind her, a hand touching her shoulder. "Jayce," he said softly.

She shuddered, hating that his touch elicited anything from her. She spun around to face him. He was too close. Far too close and gazing at her with those apologetic blue eyes, his expression both sincere and desperate.

She shoved past him, crossing to the other end of the balcony, dress clenched in her fists as she lifted it so she could walk easier.

"Why are you angry with me?" Sav asked, not moving toward her. "I've given you everything I thought you needed. I've included you when you asked, I—"

"I had to ask, Sav," she said, dropping her dress and pressing her hands into her eyes. "You see people as a means to an end. Your end. You act considerate and charming, but it's an act. You said you were wearing a mask, and I think you forget to take it off with the people closest to you."

She let her hands fall away, hanging limply at her sides. Staring at him, she took him in.

His shoulders had slumped, and his expression was open, head tilting to one side as he looked at her with pity.

No, not pity. Sorrow.

"That's how you feel about me? That I'm using people? That I'm... using you?" He ran his hand through his curls, glancing from her to the windowed doors and back again.

"Yes," she said. She felt emptier now. The pain in her chest still throbbed, but dully. She could address it later. For now... Sav needed to hear this from her.

"I will always be grateful that you paid off my life debt. But you treat me like an investment, or a project, rather than a person. And if that's how it will be, then I will pay you back. Every djewl."

"I don't want you to pay me back," Sav said, sounding exasperated. He ran his hand through his hair again and paced several steps away from her, then turned back and approached her.

She backed up a step, involuntarily, and he halted a few feet away.

"Tell me what I can do to fix... this." He gestured between them, his expression eager.

"I don't even feel like I know who you are anymore. I'm not sure I ever did. You're a historian and a baron, an archer and the leader of a rebellion. But who is Sav?" She held his gaze, as if the truth would emerge from it.

He searched her eyes. "Are you certain you want to know? Once I tell you... your opinion of me could forever change."

"I want the truth," Jayce replied, heart thudding against her ribcage.

He stepped in fast, grabbing her hand. She let him pull her aside, backing toward the far edge of the balcony—still in view of the glass doors, but not centered.

They were closer to the rose bushes than she wanted to be, but they didn't writhe as they had before.

Sav closed his eyes, his shoulders moving as he breathed deep and let it out quickly. His eyelids flew open, revealing bright blue orbs intent on her and filled with an anxious sort of energy that made it seem as if he cared that what he said didn't drive her away.

"I am the heir to the throne of Neldor," he said, each word deliberate and heavy.

He brought his other arm up to grip hers and caging her into the new reality he'd presented. He searched her eyes, an edge of panic in his gaze, like he feared she wouldn't believe him.

Jayce's lips parted. Of all the things she'd expected him to say, that hadn't been one of them. A thousand questions poured into her mind, but only two fell from her lips. "Then Alighieri isn't your surname? You're not a baron?"

"I didn't have a last name as a child. When I asked about my family, I was told they had all died in a fire. Their names were never given to me. But every year as long as I could recall, a man would visit. He dressed in simple traveling clothes and claimed to work for the queen, looking for promising young men who could serve in the realm one day."

Jayce barely dared to breathe. She had known he kept secrets for as long as she'd known him. But this? Heir to the throne? It was difficult to believe.

Sav's gaze grew distant, and his grip on her arms slackened, but didn't fall away. "He would ask about my studies and encourage me to do better. He called himself Roderic. Roderic Aligheiri. Between visits, he wrote letters. I grew to think of him like a father and daydreamed about him revealing the secret to me and taking me away. Not that I wasn't well-cared-for, but I was lonely and longing to know where I had come from.

"The visits stopped when things with the southern lands grew tense. I lived in the north, and whispers of war reached me before his next letter confirming it. He apologized for not being able to come for my eighteenth year, saying he was obligated to fight for Neldor, but he promised to try the following year."

His thumbs brushed across her skin, and he stared down at their linked arms. "By then, I had started to suspect I was being kept in the dark for a reason. I sensed a scandal was being covered up, and when I was granted permission to attend the Ivory Guilds the following year, I took full advantage of the records in the libraries, researching the name Aligheiri. I discovered the noble family bearing it had died out decades before, and in the tales I read, I found the story of a man who had a child with his mistress and was forced to send the child away so there might be no obstruction to a legitimate heir's claim on the family lands and titles."

"Roderic Aligheiri," Jayce replied, breathless. Her heart squeezed at the desperate beauty of a father trying to send his son a message the only way he could, and the son who had discovered the truth and taken on the false last name, all he had of his father.

Sav nodded. "Yes. This man visiting me had chosen the name deliberately, a message for me, should I ever seek to know the truth. After that, I discovered a painting hanging in the Head Dame's offices, an image of the same man who had visited me my entire life. King Reginald Donovanu. The painting confirmed it in my heart, but then word came of the king's death."

He cut off, his voice hoarse with emotion, and his hands fell away from her arms. Somehow, with the moonlight on his curls and that expression on his face, he looked like an entirely different man.

"And your mother?" Jayce asked, gripping her elbows. Her dress rustled as she shifted.

"I couldn't find anything about her at the Guilds, but when I went to Loshar, I planned to get my hands on the census records for the year I was presumed to be born. I found out they were being kept at the Draigh Monastery, in the restricted area."

Her heart raced, realization clicking into place. "The book you tore the pages from. It was the census." He had told her it had information about the Plague King's prophecy.

Another lie. A distraction. Because he hadn't trusted her with the truth, a truth he was still solidifying in his own heart and mind.

Sav shoved his hands into his pockets and ducked his head. "Yes, it was. I panicked when I heard the monks coming, knowing I would likely never get to return to that room, never get a straight answer about the identity of my mother and confirm that of my father. So I tore out the pages I thought most likely to have information on my birth."

"And what did you find?" Jayce asked, hands gripping her skirts.

He lifted his head, his expression soft. "Her name was—is—Mireth. I don't know whether she lives or not. She doesn't seem to be anyone of significance in history. I haven't found a single other mention of her name or family anywhere. But I'll keep looking until I know for certain whether she lives."

His throat bobbed, and he approached Jayce again, reaching his hands out to her. "The record also confirmed King Reginald is my father. I have since spent every moment trying to uncover the truth of what happened to him when he went to Thorgor—straight into enemy territory—in search of the sacred Well of Origin and never returned. Those who went with him claim they were attacked by opposing forces who killed him and took his body. The other side, of course, claims they had nothing to do with his disappearance. I believe Queen Lyra knows the truth."

The son of a king. Jayce thought she could see it—something in the way he held himself, the confidence he exuded, the way he connected with people. The reason she had thought he was the one wielding the manipulation magic since they came to Enterea.

Instead, he had been practicing to take his father's place.

She studied his face, looking for evidence of truth or lie. Her heart told her to believe him, but her head...

"There's little proof of what you've said. I could easily refuse to believe you. The illegitimate son of a king thought dead, and no one to corroborate your identity... it's convenient, to say the least. It would be easier to believe that you are a rogue who has somehow come by—or stolen—an absurd amount of money and set yourself up to be a savior of the realm."

Jayce spoke as if to herself, out loud, the way she sometimes did when working out the ratios for a complicated tonic.

Sav's head lifted, and his blue eyes caught hers, filled with shining, unshed tears. "But you *do* believe me," he whispered.

She pulled a breath in, hesitating to make sure she meant the words before she said them.

"I do."

Sav stilled. He was close enough she noticed his breathing grew more shallow, as if he was afraid to startle her if he so much as sneezed.

Something moved out of the corner of her eye, but when she glanced at the glass doors, she only saw people moving in the distant room, none of them close to the doors or paying them any attention.

"Ever since I met you, I wanted to tell you. But my head told me I couldn't trust you, even though my heart..." His voice trailed off.

Jayce's heart galloped in anticipation of what he was about to say. She couldn't even think, much less predict what might come out of his mouth next. He had already revealed the most startling truth, hadn't he?

Sav moved closer, taking her hands in his, stroking over her fingers with his thumbs as he stared into her eyes, as if searching for something in them. Permission?

"Jayce," Sav said, his voice more raw than before. "I've felt lost these last few days. Keeping this from you, trying to convince the others to let you in... not knowing... how you felt. If you feel the same way that I do."

Her breath caught.

His eyes sparkled in the moonlight like clear crystals.

She had the thought that she should put more distance between them, but Sav's hand reached up and ghosted along the side of her face, tracing the curve of her jaw with the barest touch and drawing her face back to him.

He leaned in with an intention she instinctively understood. Curiosity betrayed her, and she tilted her face upward, giving him the permission he needed.

He cupped his hand behind her head and pulled her into him. He kissed her like he had something to prove—like he was unraveling, like she was the only real thing left in a world built on shadows and whispered deals and whatever secrets he kept.

The warm weight of his lips on hers only lasted a moment before he broke away.

Jayce stepped back. She needed time to process, to understand what she was feeling. Anxiety and wonder thrummed through her.

Sav stood still as a statue, hands flexing at his sides, and he gazed at her as if he were keeping himself from pulling her in for another kiss.

A kiss she knew she didn't want.

She pressed a hand to her stomach, hollowed out with guilt and relief—because her heart had finally stopped wavering.

"Sav, I—"

A figure standing on the other side of the balcony doors caught her eye. She turned her head to look fully and found a familiar face.

Nels.

The golden light from the ballroom cast him in sharp relief against the glass, highlighting every tense line of his posture. Something flickered across his face: shock, or perhaps disbelief. His lips parted slightly, and for a moment, she thought he might barge through the doors, shout at Sav, even challenge him outright—the kind of thing a jealous man might do when he saw another with the woman he loved.

Instead, he turned sharply on his heel and strode away without looking back.

The moment hit her like a spark to dry kindling. Had she been wrong about how he felt? She'd accused him of jealousy often enough, yet in the moment that counted, he hadn't shown any.

Sav cleared his throat. "I shouldn't have assumed—"

"No, it's my fault," Jayce murmured, still staring at the place Nels had been standing. The warmth of the ballroom felt distant now, his absence sharper than any presence, leaving only the fading imprint of his expression burned into her mind.

"Jayce—" Sav began.

"I need to go," she blurted.

Sav's hand lifted, as if he might reach for her, but he didn't try to stop her.

Jayce pushed through the doors, holding her dress clear from her feet so she could walk fast. Should she follow Nels? Try to find him and explain?

The thought sent tremors through her. Because no matter what she said, Nels had seen what happened.

And she had no idea how to face him after this.

CHAPTER NINETEEN

EVERY FACE THAT STARED at Jayce in the Grand Hall was a stranger's, and she raced through the party dodging guests with concerned and curious expressions until she burst through the entrance to the building.

Nels was gone.

She slowed to a walk, disappointment crowding inside her with guilt and dampening the urgency to find him, to explain.

The Guild protectors on either side of the doors watched her movements, but didn't inquire after her.

The Ivory Guilds spread before her, each building in the distance standing sentinel. She hadn't realized she could see them all from here. Even the spire of the temple behind the Mana Guild could be seen.

Jayce removed the beaded slippers she wore, then hiked up her dress and started toward the ambry. Perhaps she would find Nels there, and she could explain what had happened with Sav. As well as the truths she had learned, and about what had happened at the Temple of the Three, and the discovery of Leth Alend and what he had done to her.

Her heart and throat both ached. She hadn't realized how much had happened without Nels, and how much she wanted to share it all with him, to hear what he had to say and what advice he would give.

Nels did not answer her knocks on his door. Jayce's fingers splayed out on the wooden surface, and she pressed her forehead against it. She thought she heard the slightest shuffle of movement from inside, but it could have been her imagination. She thought of a dozen things to say to try to entice him, but so much had happened between them recently, she didn't think any of it would help.

"Nels?" She tried, once, but he didn't come to the door.

She had to get out of this dress.

Her room was pitch dark, and she fumbled to get a lantern lit so she could change. The poofy vastness of her evening gown didn't help matters, and she nearly knocked over the fern where she had left it on her bed, and then struck the table with her hip, no doubt bruising it, before she finally managed to strike the flint and illuminate her room.

Jayce dressed down to her shift and pulled out the pins holding her hair, then flopped onto the bed, all energy gone and yet somehow far too alert to sleep.

She touched her lips, remembering Sav's kiss. From hearing others talk about kissing, she had expected butterflies to erupt, for her stomach to fill with warmth, to be swept away with passion and excitement. She had thought she would *feel* something.

But it had been a press of his lips, and then nothing.

The build-up she'd felt the past few weeks seemed to have been more tied to the newness of it all—a new person, new places, new feelings.

But not love. Not even a flicker.

Laying in the dark, with her fingers on her lips, she wondered what kissing Nels would be like.

Her heart immediately jumped, and everything warmed at once, so much so that she sat bolt upright and walked to the wash basin to splash her face.

She stared at her darkened reflection in the mirror.

How long had it been Nels?

How long had she pushed away her feelings for him?

She felt like a fool believing him when he insisted that he didn't think of her that way, that he'd only offered to marry her to save her from Dray's threats.

He had followed her across the *ocean.*

And she had muddled it all up, not knowing her own feelings, telling him to leave, kissing another man.

Jayce flopped back onto the bed and shut her eyes.

She'd been alone so much of her adult life, too consumed with the deaths of her family, and finding a cure for the plague, to socialize the way her peers did. She'd considered what it would be like to find someone and settle down, but her life debt had always gotten in the way.

She had let it get in the way.

There was always something getting in the way. Her debt was gone, but her past loomed darker than ever. Giving all of herself to someone meant she had to have herself intact to give. To do that, she would have to heal.

And healing meant speaking the truth of what had happened out loud.

Could the truth tonic really help with that? If she took it, would it bring the dark and frightened parts of her into the light at last?

She eventually did fall into a fitful sleep, grateful for a wool blanket rather than a linen so she slept in fitful, but blissful, silence.

Weak sunlight filtered through the trees as Jayce lifted her head from the leaf-littered ground and peered around in confusion. She was in a forest clearing where many trees gathered tightly around a pond at the center.

The trees' whispers reached her without her even touching them.

She wakes. The Speaker wakes. The Speaker has come.

Beneath their voices, another, smaller voice chanted the same words, and Jayce's cheek felt numb, tingling with cold. She reached up and peeled a leaf off her skin, wiping vigorously to get any remnants off.

Speaker? Why did they call her Speaker? She didn't speak for anyone or anything. She could barely speak for herself.

Standing, she caught sight of a glimmer in the pond. The light spread across the water's glass-like surface, a moving image rippling to life.

Sav, bound and shouting as he was dragged away, his hair askew, a bloody lip showing he'd been fighting.

An enemy at the Guilds? Who would treat him in such a way? After attending the ball, Jayce could believe that just about anyone there might want an advantage over him, especially if they caught wind of the rebellion.

A chill shivered down her spine. She watched the image repeat itself, Sav yelling, being dragged. Was this a vision? And if so, who might have sent it?

A tickling sensation started in Jayce's ankles, and she glanced down to find a creeping sort of vine snaking its way up her legs. She stumbled back, trying to shake it off, but it tightened its grip and pulled her down to the ground, dragging her toward the pond.

See. See. See. See. It chanted senselessly.

"I saw! I understand! Sav is in trouble! Please, stop!" Jayce shrieked, fingers grasping at nothing but leaves and loose soil as her feet touched the water and she was dragged into the water.

Kicking did nothing against the plant's incredible strength. Bubbles of air left Jayce's mouth, and she knew that she would perish here. She opened her eyes one last time and realized the vision surrounded her.

Sav on one side, shouting, struggling against the grips of the faceless men that held him. And on the other side, Jayce caught sight of red hair, a long purple dress, a cold and calculating stare, and the feeling that she could not escape, no matter how she tried.

Jayce woke bolt upright, her entire right arm numb. She tried to shake it, but something held her tight in its grip, and she panicked, yanking hard and kicking her feet until something heavy crashed to the floor, breaking.

The potted fern writhed in a mass on the floor, vines stretching toward her like the tentacles of a sea creature from the legends.

Jayce yanked at the plant tendrils and rolled away from it across the bed, sliding off the side and falling onto the floor.

The room went silent.

She crawled around the bed, cautiously peering around at the plant on the ground amidst shards of broken pottery, barely visible in her moonlit room.

Why had the plant attacked her? Had it somehow sent her the vision?

She gazed at her arm, the imprint of fern leaves patterned faintly across her skin.

The fern had left its mark, the twin to the swirls on her left arm.

Jayce sat back, her head and heart both pounding. She had only managed to relax a moment before a knock came at the door.

It was not a gentle knock—more of a rapid staccato demanding entrance.

"Guild protection, entry required."

Jayce blinked blearily for a moment, still stunned after her encounter with the fern, but she pulled herself up using the bed for support and stumbled to the door, opening it to the serious faces of two Guild protectors.

Behind them, Sav's door stood open across the hall, the room trashed. Papers, clothes, books, and other items were strewn about, as if someone had gone through it all in a hurry.

Her thoughts went to Sav and her dream. "What happened? Is everything all right?" She realized too late that she stood in only her shift and hastily angled her body behind the door.

Another door opened down the corridor and Nels's familiar voice wafted toward her.

"Evening, gentlemen. Or should I say good morning? Not sure the socially correct response when one is dragged from bed on the early side of midnight."

Relief flooded her at the sight of him. She tried to catch his eye, but he stayed focused on the Guild protectors, expression wary, determined.

"You need to come with us," one of them said to Jayce, ignoring Nels.

Jayce forced her attention back to the two men. "Allow me to dress," she insisted.

They looked at each other, then nodded.

Jayce retreated, trying to hear what Nels said to them through the closed door, but their voices didn't quite come through over her struggling attempts to get dressed.

She skipped the corset, hastily tugged her blouse into her skirt before tugging on her stockings and tying her ankle-high boots. Hair went into a quick braid, and she grabbed a shawl to fend off the night's chill. Last, she pulled on a pair of leather gloves.

Thoughts rushed like a river through her mind. What could this be about? All she had done was attend the party last night.

Then she remembered the other part of Sav's plan. While he had been with her trying to discover the identity of Head Dame Tsega's special guest at the Ivory Concord, Corbin,

Yamalda, and Bentley had been going through Head Dame Tsega's offices to look for evidence connecting her to the same.

Had one of them been caught? Did they know about Sav, his true identity? Would they question her?

Her mouth went dry with panic, and then her eyes landed on a white-banded stone sitting on the table holding the wash basin across her bed. Nels's wishing stone.

I've told this one to give you anything you ask for, he'd said.

Such a small and simple stone couldn't do much of anything for her current situation, but having it with her would make her feel better. Perhaps she could borrow some of Nels's confidence.

She slipped the stone into her pocket, squared her shoulders, and left her room.

Sweat broke out on Jayce's brow the moment she stepped into the corridor. She tugged anxiously at her gloves, hoping the Guild protectors didn't notice her nerves.

She had never been interrogated before. Could she withhold sensitive information? Could she *lie* to protect Sav? And did he deserve it?

The Guild protectors with her joined four more outside, two of which stood on either side of Nels.

Had he gotten himself in trouble?

Jayce moved toward him but was blocked by the Guild protectors with her, and although they didn't speak, she understood: they wouldn't be allowed to speak or be near one another.

The march across the Guild grounds was quick but cold. Despite her shawl, Jayce felt chilled to the bone. They were led, as she expected, to the building that held the main hall and the Head Dame's offices, through corridors with lanterns lit but turned down so low Jayce could barely see.

The Guild protectors halted outside a mahogany door and knocked loudly.

A small, squirrel-like woman answered, her voice too quiet for Jayce to make out what she said, and then she gestured to Jayce and Nels, motioned behind her, and opened the door.

"There's a room for each of them," the woman said softly, wringing her hands together. "The Head Dame wants them separated. She's with the leader now."

That has to be Sav, Jayce thought, blood running cold. What would he tell her to do right now, if he were there?

She locked eyes with Nels before they were taken in opposite directions, and she thought she saw warning in his eyes.

Was that "tell them nothing" or "look out for yourself?"

They put her in a small, almost closet-like room with only two chairs and a table with a single lit lantern sitting upon it. The Guild protectors didn't enter the room, instead they shut the door behind her and left her alone.

Jayce paced for a while, hand going to her pocket and rubbing the wishing stone. If she had a wish, what would it be? To not be here? For everyone to be safe? For the Head Dame to forget whatever it was she was accusing them of?

Sav had a terrible habit of sneaking around where he didn't belong. Why had she let herself get caught up in it? First the Draigh Monastery, now this. If only she could let all this mystery about the journal and the Plague King go and return to her cozy, quiet life at the apothecary.

Quiet, but lonely. Daily haunted by memories of her past, her failures, and facing a dull and lifeless future. Since she'd gotten dragged into this adventure with Sav, she hadn't felt the same haunted feeling. She hadn't taken out her alchemistry set once to experiment on a cure, and she realized that somewhere along the way, she'd accepted Sav's belief that the cure for the plague lay in defeating the Plague King, something he seemed to believe she could do.

She was just an apothecary, and perhaps not a very good one. And yet, the voice that whispered that negative belief to her sounded so weak compared to a few short weeks ago.

Sav believed in her. Nels did, too. Even Fiametta had sensed something different about her. And the Three had visited her.

Apothecary was her title, the role society had placed her in. But what if there was more to her? What if she was meant for a greater path?

Her body trembled so hard she had to sit down, holding on to the table for dear life.

At that moment, the door clicked open, and Jayce looked up to see who had entered.

Not the Guild protectors. Not even Head Dame Tsega.

It was Fiametta.

CHAPTER TWENTY

FIAMETTA HESITATED NEAR THE door, which she'd shut tight. A small shadow scampered down her arm, leapt down onto the floor and climbed onto the table, coming close to Jayce. This time, Jayce didn't flinch.

"What are you doing here?" Jayce asked, spreading her hands out on the table to stabilize herself. Mortimer's tiny wet nose touched the tip of her finger, and then he scampered off the table and back to Fiametta, who brought him to her chest and stroked his tiny back.

"Saving you from one man's poor choices," Fiametta said.

"Do you mean Sav?" Jayce asked.

"Yes. The man suffers from chronic recklessness and doesn't care who he takes down with him. Dame Tsega knows he was behind the break-in last night, and she knows you and your friend were involved. I can convince her to drop her charges against you both, but I need something from you first."

Fiametta pulled something from a satchel hanging off her shoulder and set it down on the table. The blue glass bottle gleamed innocently in the lantern light, a dark liquid sloshing around inside.

Jayce's breathing hitched. "Is that..." She licked her lips. "The truth tonic?"

"It is," Fiametta admitted, clasping her fingers together in front of her.

"You were making that for Sav. For me to tell Sav my story."

"I do need your story. And anything you know about Sav. Tell me, taking the truth tonic if you have to, and I will negotiate your release with the Head Dame."

"Does she know you're here?" Jayce locked eyes with Fiametta, searching for the truth in her brown-eyed gaze, but the woman wore her usual cold mask of indifference. "You work for her, don't you?"

"I'm not a traitor, if that's what you think. Sav knows I've been close to the Head Dame for many ages. He never demanded loyalty, only information. It worked out well, so long as what Sav wanted didn't conflict with what the Head Dame wanted. Now he's crossed a line he never should have crossed, and I will do what is in my best interests."

"I thought you believed in the rebellion? Isn't that why you joined?" Jayce insisted.

Fiametta laughed and took the chair across from Jayce, tossing her beaded hair over her shoulder. "Of course not. Savage Alighieri is an irresponsible attention-seeker who only looks out for himself and doesn't have a healthy aversion to danger."

Jayce's stomach clenched. She had thought that once, too. But her opinion of him *had* changed after finding out who he truly was. Heir to the throne, intending to help Neldor recover from the plague. Not hide the truth, but put everything out in the open for the people to see.

So they could heal.

"You're wrong," Jayce blurted. "Sav cares. He cares most about the truth, but that doesn't mean he doesn't care about others."

About this realm, she almost said, but she clamped her mouth shut. She didn't know what Fiametta knew, and she wouldn't be the one to reveal Sav's most closely guarded secret.

Fiametta raised her eyebrows. "I wondered how close you had gotten to him. He is convincing, isn't he? One has to wonder how you always end up getting into situations and agreeing to do things that you never would have before."

"Sav doesn't have any abilities," Jayce said carefully.

"No, of course not. But these things are bred into people of a certain status. He can't help but use you. He bought you."

Jayce turned away from Fiametta's smirking expression. Her ears and cheeks burned, and her breath came faster. Fiametta knew Sav had paid her life debt, of course. Sav had told everyone in the rebellion the details of how he'd met Jayce and why she was there.

Jayce turned back, glaring at Fiametta. "He didn't buy me. I chose to come with him to Enterea. To help with the rebellion."

"You choose it because you feel beholden to him. I know, Jayce. I didn't have a life debt as you did, but my family was desperate. They spent everything they had to send me here, and then the plague struck, cutting us off completely. Half of my family died of the plague. The others had to flee our homeland, where they burned homes with families still inside in an attempt to stop the spread of the plague. Sav helped me send money to my family to bring them here. He's never said a word about it, but I cannot forget it, and he uses that."

Fiametta's clenched fists relaxed, and Mortimer seemed to sense her distress, snuggling onto her chest in a curled-up position.

"I thought he might have a chance with his scholarly little rebellion—uncover the truth, take it to the queen, and ask her to step down. Peaceful. No war. The problem is, he has no authority to make the queen listen."

"What does Head Dame Tsega want from me?" Jayce asked.

"I want the truth." Head Dame Tsega's voice floated through the room, and Jayce realized with a start that the woman had entered without her realizing. She'd been so focused on Fiametta she hadn't noticed the door open to let the woman in.

Fiametta immediately stood. "Head Dame, I told you I could handle her myself. You didn't need to—"

"No, but I wanted to. I want to hear what she has to say. Based on what I heard as I came in, I haven't missed the juicy bits yet. Besides, don't you think it would be wise for me to use my abilities before we risk using yours?" Head Dame Tsega gestured at the truth tonic on the table.

"The plan was for you to speak to Sav. You wanted to focus your full strength on him," Fiametta stammered.

"Yes, well, he's proving a harder nut to crack than we thought, and I needed a diversion before I do something I would regret. But Jayce, here, I imagine, won't give me so much trouble, will you dear?"

The room filled with a terrible pulsing energy that Jayce recognized. With dread mounting in her chest, she moved away from the Head Dame, backing up until she hit the wall.

It was her. The Head Dame was the one with the powers of manipulation.

Jayce had felt it when she met the Head of the Guilds for the first time. Then again, last night at the Ivory Concord.

Jayce glanced from the Head Dame to Fiametta, who looked smaller than she had before, cowering before the powerful woman now occupying the chair she'd been in.

"Oh, don't look at me like that," Head Dame Tsega pouted, her arms resting on the table before her with her fingers clasped. She tossed her long red hair and smiled widely. "We can be great friends if you'll just answer a few teensy questions for me."

The initial wave of power had faded, leaving smaller waves in its wake that pressed against Jayce, corroding her will. She wanted to say that of course she would answer any question the Head Dame had, but she resisted with everything she had.

Once she let the woman's magic in, she would never regain control.

How could the Three give a gift like this to someone?

Head Dame Tsega's lips pursed. "Now, then, let's begin."

Jayce braced herself, still leaning against the cool, smooth wall behind her. She had to do something. Escape, yes, but until she found a way to do that, she had to throw off the Head Dame and Fiametta. Make the first move.

"I've only known Sav a little over a turn. Why do you need me to answer anything?"

Fiametta found her own spot against the wall, cupping her hands around Mortimer and looking disappointed that the Head Dame had interrupted her interrogation.

Jayce continued, "Because he hasn't told me the real reason he went to Neldor in the first place. He claims it was to find you and get information about the Plague King, but I think there was a different reason. He keeps hinting at it, but he won't trust me enough to say what it is."

"Yes, yes, you can explore Alighieri's trust issues on your own time. What I'm interested in is what you know of the baron, Jayce Keenstone."

Another wave pulsed through the room. Jayce would have staggered back had she not been relying on the wall. "Must you use so much of your power against me? It's nauseating. I can hardly think." Which was, to some degree, true, but she wanted to gauge the Head Dame's reaction.

Head Dame Tsega put a hand to her chest. "Me? Using my power? What are you talking about?"

Then it was a secret. Or intended to be. How could anyone who had been around her for any length of time not sense the overwhelming amount of magic the Head Dame gave off? Either she was oblivious or she could force others to forget about how she manipulated them into giving her what she wanted.

"Now then, tell me everything about the baron. Start with how you met."

"We met for the first time in Loshar, though I didn't know it was him at the time. He rescued me in Eastmill from Sir Dray. He's—" Jayce cut herself off before she could speak the secret he had told her in confidence last night. That he was the lost heir to the throne of Neldor, that he thought the Plague King might be his father, King Reginald. She put a hand to her mouth, eyes stretching wide and taking in the Head Dame's sly smile.

The Head Dame waved at Fiametta. "Take notes."

"Yes, mistress," Fiametta said, scrambling to remove quill and parchment from her satchel. She looked helplessly around the room for a surface to write on, then brought the chair Jayce had occupied around the side and sat next to the Head Dame.

"I'm certain in the time you've spent with him he's told you more than that. I'm looking for secrets. Things he told you in confidence, perhaps asking you not to tell anyone else?"

Despite her determination not to tell the Head Dame anything, Jayce's mind raced to find the answer to her question. She wanted to give her an answer. Wanted it more than anything. Her throat burned.

"I don't know him well. We only just met," Jayce blurted.

The Head Dame frowned and looked at Fiametta. "I thought you said she would have more information for us."

"About the baron's research. He went to Neldor to find her because she had seen the Plague King," Fiametta said. "He wanted a first-hand account."

Head Dame Tsega shifted in her seat, clasping her hands before her and resting them on the table. “Well, then, that will have to do. We will get from her what he was unable to and see what we can do with it. Perhaps afterward, she will be more amenable to telling us more. Go on, then. Tell us your experience with the Plague King. And start from the beginning. I want to hear the entire tale.”

Jayce’s vision tunneled. Part of her answered the Head Dame’s manipulative powers, and the other fought against the tide of anxiety that made her palms sweat and her head pulse with a pounding sort of pain.

Her mouth opened and all that came out was a sort of squeak and a series of grunts as she tried to form words but was stopped by herself at every turn.

“She has a psychological block from the trauma, and is unable to speak of it,” Fiametta said, sounding irritated. “That is why I made the truth tonic.”

Head Dame Tsega didn’t take her eyes off Jayce. “She will tell me. Won’t you, Jayce? You trust me. You feel safe around me.”

A more soothing energy filled the room, drifting around Jayce, stroking her mind. For a moment, her mind went blank and dark. When she came to, the room was spinning and she was on the floor, Fiametta leaning over her, her rat peering at Jayce from her shoulder with his tiny beady eyes.

“—no use, I told you.” Fiametta was saying, reaching out a hand to help Jayce up.

Jayce sat, but released Fiametta’s hand and didn’t come to standing. Her head still spun. “What happened?”

“You are of a delicate constitution, my dear,” the Head Dame said, sounding regretful. “My question upset you. As much as I dislike it, we must resort to more… medieval efforts."

Fiametta snorted and snatched the truth tonic from the table. "Now you see the value in my abilities."

The Head Dame looked affronted. "Do not forget to whom you are loyal, Miss Tofana. Those connections you wish to foster with the elite will not come on their own."

Fiametta crouched down with the bottle, her eyes searching Jayce's. She seemed… regretful?

Jayce's gaze flicked to the blue glass bottle and back to Fiametta's face. The list of symptoms ran through her mind.

Hallucinations. Heart palpitations. Death…

"I don't want to take it," she said. "As a healer, don't you have oaths of protection to uphold?"

Fiametta looked away.

"You don't have to do this," Jayce pressed.

In answer, Fiametta unstopped the bottle. "Please do not make me force you."

"We have your friend in the other room. What's his name… Nels Martin. I haven't seen him yet, but from what I hear he is refusing to cooperate as well. If you don't take the tonic, we will have him brought here, and I'm sure there are things we could do to convince you to comply." Head Dame Tsega stood, moving toward the door.

Jayce wanted to stop her—she didn't want Nels anywhere near this woman again if she could prevent it. But if they were in the same room, perhaps they could escape together.

She pressed her lips tight and turned her face from the bottle.

"Very well," the Head Dame said, and she spoke to one of the Guild protectors outside the door.

The three of them sat in silence as they waited, and a few moments passed before there were voices at the door, and then a Guild protector entered, pushing Nels, hands bound, into the room.

"I told you, I hardly know the man. I—" He stopped when he saw Jayce, his expression filled with concern. "What are they doing to you? Jayce?"

"Silence him," Head Dame Tsega said coldly. She looked back at Jayce, her face a hard mask. "Now, then, will you make this easy? Or difficult?"

Jayce locked eyes with Nels, who seemed to have assessed the situation. He shook his head ever-so-slightly and mouthed the word *don't*.

The consequences of refusal were too terrible to picture. Whatever the Head Dame had in mind for him, Jayce didn't want to find out. The thought of Nels in pain twisted something deep inside her. She wouldn't let that happen—not because of her.

Besides, she had been willing to take the truth tonic before. The only difference was, she would be taking it for Nels's sake, rather than Sav's.

"I'll do it. Just don't hurt him."

The Head Dame's mouth widened into a predatory smile. "Reason has won the day. Fiametta, if you would."

Jayce tilted her head back and opened her mouth.

Fiametta poured a portion of the tonic in. "Swallow," she instructed.

She considered spitting it out, but realized that would be useless, since the bottle wasn't empty. They would carry out their threats against Nels and force her to drink the rest.

Closing her eyes and praying to the Three that she hadn't made the biggest mistake of her life, Jayce swallowed.

CHAPTER TWENTY-ONE

AS THE SMOOTH POTION moved across Jayce's tongue, a tingling numbness overcame her mouth, and then the whispers of a plant she had never encountered began.

Glassroot. The truth is sharp. Are you prepared to bleed?

Bitterness coated the back of her throat, and she swallowed.

I have met liars before. But none lie to themselves as convincingly as you.

Jayce closed her eyes briefly, moving her tongue in her mouth to try to bring back some sensation, but it still felt thick and numb. How would she speak?

"The effects shouldn't last long," Fiametta said, stepping away. Was she speaking comfort to her, or addressing Head Dame Tsega?

The red-haired woman came forward with an almost jittery eagerness. "Tell me about your experience with the Plague King. Don't leave anything out."

The memory flooded in, and Jayce braced herself for the dizziness and headache that usually followed and prevented her from sharing her story, but something loosened inside, and then her mouth opened, and words flowed off her tongue. As if someone else spoke for her.

"We were recruited by Queen Lyra to come to the palace and train."

"There was someone with you?" Head Dame Tsega interrupted.

"Myself, and my brother, Javin Keenstone," Jayce said without hesitation, though she had guarded his name close to her heart the past two ages and had rarely spoken of him.

Nels knew him, though, and he startled at the name. They had been friends, too.

Before Jayce could process further, her thoughts were interrupted.

"Continue," Head Dame Tsega snapped. "What were you training for?"

Jayce swallowed past the thickness in her throat and shoved her hand into her pocket, touching the wishing stone for comfort as more of the truth was taken from her.

"To be heroes of the realm. To save everyone from the Plague King."

"Who is the Plague King?" Head Dame Tsega asked, tapping her foot impatiently.

"He is the harbinger of the plague."

"How was he made?"

"I... don't know," Jayce replied. Her tongue still tingled, a distinctly uncomfortable feeling, and her head spun with dizziness, although not the same as what she usually experienced when she tried to talk about her brother.

Images flickered at the edge of her vision. Dark tendrils, reaching for her. Jayce flinched away, clinging to the wall.

Head Dame Tsega frowned. "Tell me the part where you saw the Plague King. What was he like?"

Her eyes turned to black, endless pools, and Jayce screamed as the walls turned from wood to rough stone covered in yellow, bioluminescent lichen, and the floor moved, lapping like water against Jayce's feet.

"What's wrong with her?" Head Dame Tsega asked.

"She is hallucinating. It's a side effect some individuals experience. The texts say it's worse when trauma is involved. I suspect she is seeing the memories she lived through come alive in this room," Fiametta explained.

There was no escape. Jayce's fingertips scratched the walls, and she ran until she found the farthest corner of the room and crouched down, shivering and trembling.

"Jayce!" Nels's voice pierced the darkness of her memories like an arrow of light.

She let the world blur around her and found her breath again. In and out.

"Stop asking her questions," he demanded. "It's hurting her."

"There is possibly no one else the world over who knows what she knows," Head Dame Tsega hissed. "This is our only chance. Tell us now, girl. Who is the Plague King? How can he be defeated?" She loomed over Jayce, tall and terrifying, waves of her manipulative power pulsing through the room and clashing with the terror in Jayce's heart.

"He killed him. He killed him and he's dead," Jayce muttered, rocking back and forth. Her hand found her pocket again, the smooth stone warm to the touch. *Anything you want.*

I want my brother back.

I want the plague gone.

I want to be happy again.

Her eyes snapped open, and the tendrils of darkness reached for her. A hand clasped her arm, fingernails digging into her skin. Beyond them both, Nels struggled against the guards, shouting for her.

The palm-sized wishing stone didn't have the power to grant wishes on such a scale. She knew that. But Nels had given it to her as a gift, and he believed it could do something to help her, perhaps grant her a small wish.

I wish something would happen to distract the Head Dame and Fiametta. The stone heated until it felt too hot to touch, but Jayce held on to it.

A third guard rushed forward to help his comrades hold Nels back. His hip struck the table, knocking over the lantern.

Oil spread across the table, and flames licked across the wooden surface like liquid fire.

The guards holding Nels stared at the table, gaping, and their hold relaxed.

Nels yanked his arms free and pulled several rocks from his pocket, throwing one at the Head Dame. It struck her shoulder, and she shouted.

Her grip released from Jayce's arms.

Jayce ducked around the Head Dame and crawled toward Nels. One guard fell, struck in the head by one of Nels's stones. The small stone shouldn't have been enough to do more than annoy him, but Nels must have managed to enchant it somehow.

She reached him, and he offered her a hand, which she took, letting him pull her up beside him.

They ran for the door.

Fiametta stepped in front of them, spreading her arms to block their passing.

"Let us through," Nels pleaded. "She's no use to you like this."

"We can try again. I'll adjust the dosage," Fiametta insisted, one side of her face lit with firelight. The table was ablaze, and the heat and smoke were growing more intense.

Jayce's mind and vision spun. She clung to Nels. The light and smoke had at least chased the hallucinations away—for now. Would they return? Or was the potion wearing off so quickly?

"Haven't you done enough damage?" Nels snapped. He raised his other arm, preparing to throw his last stone.

"She isn't truly harmed. When it wears off, she'll be fine. Ending the plague is worth the discomfort of one woman. I imagine she would agree with me."

Jayce would have at one point. But something had changed in her. Sav, showing her the kindness of a stranger, treating her like a lady, like someone important. And Nels, holding her, fighting for her, looking at her now like she was his whole world.

The Three, telling her they gave her power for a purpose.

She locked eyes with Fiametta, and inside, the part of her that felt like an unyielding wall cutting her off from her true power, cracked open a little farther.

"If you wanted to control me, you never should have told me I could be more than I am," Jayce said.

She sensed the grass and trees outside, the vines curling up the walls outside this room, and she pulled them to her with as much force as she could muster.

The wall beside them exploded as a branch shot through, knocking Fiametta over. She shrieked, falling to the floor.

Nels and Jayce ducked under the branch and stepped over the fallen woman, throwing open the door and escaping into the corridor beyond.

CHAPTER TWENTY-TWO

NELS'S BREATH CAME HEAVY beside Jayce. He could have run far faster than her, but she knew he wouldn't leave her behind.

Jayce had the thought to look for Sav and try to rescue him, too, but before they'd gone halfway down the corridor, Guild protectors spilled out of the room they had left, shouting for them to halt.

They passed the Head Dame's assistant and two more Guild protectors standing in the hall, but they were too shocked to stop them before they'd passed, making straight for the outer doors of the Guild Hall.

Bursting out into the cold night air, they paused for the briefest moment to catch their breath.

"Where can we go? Our rooms?" Nels asked.

Jayce shook her head. "They'll look there first. We need to hide before we go back for our things."

She scanned the moonlit grounds, her eyes catching on a glinting spire. She pointed. "The Temple of the Three beside the Mana Guild. We'll be safe there."

The wooden doors swung open behind them, and she grabbed Nels's hand, relying on him for stability as they raced down the stairs and sprinted across the grounds.

The biggest flaw in their plan was that the Guild protectors would see where they were headed and would no doubt send a much larger group after them. Their only hope was that Keeper Solmere would offer them sanctuary protection. It wouldn't go entirely above the law if Head Dame Tsega pressed charges against them, but it might bide them time enough to find a way out of the Guilds and back to Neldor.

Jayce's lungs burned, and she tried not to think of how often she'd run from the authorities recently. She was becoming quite the criminal. No, not a criminal. A rebel. Like Sav.

Would she suffer the same fate as Dagric Wortcunning? Banished and outcast from society? Living on her own in a forgotten corner of the realm?

They hadn't even secured the translation of his journal yet. Perhaps that was something she should leave to others, now, but her heart stubbornly held on to it.

She had to find a way to get the journal back, translated or not. If Sav was correct, it held the only access they had to the prophecy that Queen Lyra had tried to keep secret.

They passed the outer stone wall that surrounded the temple, the prismvine gleaming with dark purple and blue hues even under the moonlight.

They slowed to a rushed walk, weaving around flower beds and statues until they came upon the temple.

The doors were locked.

No doubt Keeper Solmere was asleep. Should they wake him?

"Let's hide around back," Jayce said, shivering in the cool night air made worse by the several instances her arms had brushed against leaves and branches in their hasty dash through the garden.

The Guild protectors weren't far behind. Moving to the back of the temple wouldn't delay their discovery for long.

Nels pulled her around the corner of the temple, then guided her gently until her back was pressed against the stone wall. He glanced the way they had come, checking for their pursuers, then he turned to face her.

His hands cupped her face, drawing it up to look at him. The moonlight cast its silver light on his concerned expression.

"Are you all right?" he asked, eyes searching hers.

Jayce's throat had closed. She couldn't find the words to speak, much less say them. She'd been drugged against her will and threatened. Everything had gone so wrong.

"I'm sorry," Nels whispered, his voice breaking.

"It's not your fault," Jayce whispered back. Her body felt alert and warm. Was it his proximity or the impending risk of discovery?

Nels's hands slackened, ready to retreat. Jayce caught his arms and held him there. She drew a slow breath, anchoring herself in his presence. His patience and care felt undeserved after everything she had put him through.

“We should hide better. Maybe climb over the back wall and head into the forest?” Nels said. He kept his hands on her face, even stroking her cheek with his thumb.

Jayce licked her lips, finally finding her voice again. “No, I can hide us here. Just... give me a moment.”

She breathed deep and relaxed her grip on him, tugging her gloves off. She deliberately touched the prismvine climbing up the stone.

Prismvine. I bend the light. I break it apart. You only see what I allow.

I need you to hide us, Jayce thought back. The vines felt pleasantly cool to her touch.

Nels moved closer, hands dropping from her face. He pressed himself against her, as if to share his body heat.

He *doesn't know about the Three's gift*, she realized. He was trying to help counter the effects of using her magic.

She warmed at the thought, her cheeks flushing.

The prismvine rustled, the vines growing at a rapid and impossible pace, crawling to surround her and Nels. Moonlight filtered through, and Jayce worried it wouldn't be enough. She hastily thanked the prismvine, then pulled her gloves back on and leaned into Nels.

It would be enough. It had to be enough. She had to protect him.

“Are they close?” she whispered.

“I can't see anything,” he replied, lifting his head away from hers and looking down.

She couldn't see his expression anymore, but in their curtained, ivy-formed alcove, the fear of discovery paled in the face of how safe and secure she felt in his arms.

"I never should have asked you to leave," she said, so quietly she wasn't sure he could hear her.

His arms tightened around her. Voices carried across the distance. The Guild protectors were nearing the temple.

"You were right about the jealousy. I just—" His voice broke, and he paused, swallowing hard as he gazed down at her. "I couldn't stand to see you putting yourself in danger. But I realized that I have to let you make your own choices. If I hold you too tightly… I'll lose you."

The voices drew nearer.

"I should have appreciated what I had in you sooner," she whispered, searching his eyes, trying to read his expression.

His hand rose to her face, tenderly stroking her cheek, as if to convey what words couldn't say.

He forgave her. Somehow, despite her ingratitude, her rudeness, her inadequate apology, he forgave her.

And there were no secrets between them, except what she hadn't been able to say of her past. He'd never pushed her for it or tried to manipulate her into telling it. He just loved her, as he always had. Quietly, without expectation.

She felt no expectation from him now, except…

The tilt of his face as he lifted it from the top of her head, looking down at her. The question that hovered between them as he hesitated. He wouldn't close that gap the rest of the way, she knew. He was waiting for her to choose it.

To choose him.

Breathless, Jayce lifted her chin. Still not close enough. She pressed her hand to his chest, traced upward to his neck, and pulled him in.

For all his usual bluster, there was no showmanship when he kissed her—just a raw confidence in the way his lips moved on hers, and the way his body responded, pressing into hers until they couldn't get any closer.

He kissed her like he had all the time in the world, like he wasn't afraid of what came next.

When she kissed him, it felt like coming home.

She could have stayed like that forever, all her problems pushed so far to the back of her mind she barely remembered why they were hiding.

Jayce sensed the prismvine wrapping tighter around them, creating a sort of cocoon. It did nothing to drown out the sound of the tromping footsteps of Guild protectors fanning out in the gardens, searching every corner.

Several passed right by their hiding spot, but the prismvine hid them well, somehow disguising the bulk of their bodies against the wall without creating any suspicion from those on the outside.

Nels trembled as he held her, his forehead pressed against hers.

She wanted to talk to him, to explore what they had done and felt together, but they couldn't risk even a whisper without drawing the attention of the Guild protectors.

The gardens grew quiet again, the only sound the breeze rustling leaves and the distant, eerie hoot of an owl.

Nels moved first, creating space between them.

Jayce immediately wanted him back as the night air brushed her skin. She kept her hands on his chest, resisting the urge to rub her arms, wanting to stay connected as long as possible.

"I have loved you for ages, you know."

The words hung in the air. It felt like a curtain between them had been drawn back.

Nels sighed. His fingers moved across her back, stroking. She felt comfortable in his arms, like she could stay there forever.

"It happened so gradually, I didn't notice at first. I liked hanging out with you when my family's caravan drove in for the summer markets. When I got older and started my own route, I made sure Loshar was on it. It wasn't just a business decision, Jayce. If you ever left your apothecary, I would have gone out of my way to see you wherever you were. One time, I came back and found you in your shop, falling asleep over your books, that alchemy set of yours bubbling away. You always had one foot in the past, trying to save the future for the people of Neldor, and I..." He shook his head. "I wanted to be the one to pull you back to the present."

"Why didn't you ever say anything?" Jayce asked, her throat clenching at the thought of all the missed opportunities, all the time they wouldn't get back.

"I didn't want to lose your friendship. I knew once we crossed the line, there would be no going back to the way things were. When Dray threatened you, and then you left so abruptly, it shocked me. I knew I had to try, even when you told me it wouldn't work out between us and you only thought of me as a friend. Even with my rival being some high-born fancy-britches like Sav. I guess I have a competitive streak."

"You don't say," Jayce replied, smiling up at him.

"Speaking of," Nels said, drawing out the words and tilting his head so a streak of moonlight fell across it, highlighting his raised eyebrows. "Do you want to tell me what I saw last night? Will I have to challenge him to a duel for your honor?"

"It's not like that, I—" Jayce fought to find the words that would clear up what had happened between her and Sav, and what she felt for him.

"I've spent so long feeling guilty for failing to destroy the Plague King when I had the chance, that I didn't allow myself to feel anything else. Feelings became the enemy of my focus on paying off my debts, on researching the plague. I didn't prioritize anything else because I didn't think I was worthy of it. Not until I found the cure and could fix my mistakes."

She glanced away from him, staring out at the moonlit garden.

"You know, I don't think Sav remembers who he is without the masks he wears. It's hard to fully trust a person like that. I thought I could, but there are too many secrets still between us. I can't believe I was so blind to it. You saw the signs before I did, I just didn't want to admit it."

"I'm not the only one with a stubborn streak," Nels said, smiling. Then he cleared his throat. "I want to hear you say what you feel, so there's no mistake." He sounded nervous.

Of course he did. He'd followed her across an ocean to find out if she could share his feelings, not knowing whether she had already committed her heart to another.

Jayce put her hand against his cheek. "I'm still healing. I can't promise myself to you when I don't... feel whole."

He leaned into her touch, his throat moving as he swallowed.

The question still lingered between them. She hadn't answered it, and she knew that if she didn't, she could lose him for good. She would have to be brave. To be willing to move forward into the unknown, not knowing what might happen or how long they would have.

"I do love you, Nels." Her breath whooshed out of her at the admission. The truth of it rang deep in her soul, all the way to the depths of her being.

He slid his arms around her once more. His breath tickled her ear as he spoke. "Good enough for me."

It was time to face reality once more. Nels seemed to sense it, too. They separated, and the vines fell back to hanging naturally against the wall of the temple.

He jammed his hands into his pockets and glanced around the garden. "What now? We could find Bentley and leave this place. Head to the docks and catch the first boat back to Neldor," he said.

She shook her head. "Even if we find Bentley, and he agrees, I don't have money for passage. I might be out of debt, but I'm completely broke."

Nels grinned. "I'll cover you. I might not be as wealthy as that Sav bloke, but I've been saving for ages, and I brought some of my more precious stones with me just in case."

She hesitated. "What about the journal?"

"What about it?" he asked.

Jayce bit her lip. "We came all this way to have it translated, to hopefully unlock the clues that would lead us to some answers about being rid of the plague forever. I-I can't leave until I know what it says."

“Staying means imprisonment. You can’t spend your life chasing something that isn’t even your responsibility to resolve. Let Sav and his rebellion deal with escaping prison and saving the realm. You could come home with me. Let someone else save the world.” His fingers interlocked with hers, and she could imagine his gray-blue eyes, like pools as deep as a lake, wide and pleading.

“We couldn’t go back to Loshar. Head Dame Tsega has connections there, and I doubt Queen Lyra would be so quick to pardon me the second time, especially as I’m guilty of the charges this time. We would be on the run.”

“On the run with you is better than prison,” Nels jibed.

Jayce squeezed his hand. “Yes, but I’d rather make things right instead. I can’t just leave Sav imprisoned here. I owe him too much.” The truth of who he was burned on the tip of her tongue. She had to tell Nels. She could trust him, and she wouldn’t have any more secrets between them.

So she explained the events of the Ivory Concord and the information she had learned. About the man with the cane, Leth Alend, and her connection with him as well as her theory about him being the infamous L.A. they had been searching for. When she finished, the night’s chill had set into her bones, and she was shivering uncontrollably, her teeth chattering.

“It sounds like Sav has gotten himself into a load of trouble. With all his friends and resources, I’m certain he can get himself out. Even if we did try to free him out of some misplaced loyalty for a bastard son of a dead king, why would the Head Dame listen to us?”

Jayce frowned. She didn’t care for the way he talked about Sav, but she couldn’t blame him. She was asking a lot of him, of their relationship, new as a fledgling in a nest. But she couldn't leave things the way they were. Her conscience wouldn't let her.

"If we get the journal, we have something to bargain with. She wants information about the Plague King, same as us."

"How can you be sure she won't take the journal and keep Sav imprisoned?" Nels asked.

"I can't," Jayce said, looking beyond the walls around the temple, noting the Warrior and Arcane Guild towers in the distance and thinking of the other friends Sav had. Friends they could recruit to help them.

"But we don't have to do it alone."

CHAPTER TWENTY-THREE

JAYCE FINGERED THE OUTLINE of the small honeybee key as the forest, hushed and gray in the dawn's half-light, pressed close on all sides. Every branch, leaf, and root seemed to be alive and reaching for her, like the fern from the ambry.

Nels cursed as he stumbled over a gnarled root.

Vines unwound from the undergrowth, stretching across the ground toward her. Thin branches dipped low, brushing her shoulders. Ferns, heavy with dew, leaned in. Their fronds touched her ankles, her waist, her fingers, curling around them, futilely trying to get her attention. She could imagine the cacophony of whispers she would hear if most of her skin wasn't covered.

She swatted them away, then stopped in frustration, wrestling with a stubborn branch that held a lock of her hair.

The plants took advantage of her standing still and drew nearer, a thorny vine coiling around her boot.

Nels reached past her and yanked a branch away from her face with more force than necessary, nearly breaking it. “They’re all over you. This isn’t normal, is it?”

Jayce shook her arms and yanked her boot out of the vine’s grasp. “No, it isn’t.” She stumbled back a step, running into Nels, breathing hard.

He gripped her arms, holding her close and eyeing the plant life that reached for her again.

“I’m not sure we can make it to the hideout like this. Can’t you tell them to stop?”

Jayce shook her head. In reality, she was frightened. Something had happened in the Temple of the Three to make the plants react more around her.

“Are you all right?” he asked, brushing stray leaves from her hair. “I’ve never seen this happen to you.”

Jayce grimaced. She needed to tell him, and now was as good a time as any. “I went to see the head of the Mana Guild yesterday. She agreed something was wrong, but she couldn’t fix it. She sent me to the Temple of the Three on the grounds.”

She paused and yanked a vine off her wrist.

Another branch creaked as it reached for her.

Nels stepped in front of it and snapped the limb back. “Back off,” he growled at the trees. “Come on, let’s keep moving.”

He walked beside her this time, and they kept a quick pace, moving faster than the plants that yearned to be close to her.

"I was guided through some kind of prayer, or ritual, to commune with the Three. I... I felt them, Nels. Heard their voices. They told me I had to visit the Well in Thengroth. Their presence filled the temple, and I think they cracked the block on my magic. I can feel the plants now—louder. Needier. It's like they want something from me." She shuddered.

"Want what?" he asked, glancing warily at the nearest sapling that had begun leaning in again.

"I don't know," she whispered, her throat tightening. She had a sense that the Three had a purpose for her, but could she rise to meet their expectations?

Nels's hand brushed hers, and she jerked away, thinking it was another over-eager piece of foliage.

He ran a hand through his hair. "If you're more in-tune, then they ought to listen to you. No harm in trying, right?"

The idea of more magic waiting just beneath her skin made her want to run, not reach for it. What if letting it out meant losing control?

Jayce stood still, trying to ignore the slight tug on the hem of her skirt as another branch or vine no doubt tried to climb her. She breathed, imagining she was a tree herself, part of the forest, soaking in sunlight and turning it into food, breathing out air that humans could breathe.

Her first instinct was to ask as she had in the past, using thought to communicate with the forest. But something about that didn't seem right anymore. Could she use images, too?

She pictured herself walking between the trees, with branches gently and naturally swaying, leaves fluttering, and nothing reaching for her.

Heat blossomed across her skin, reaching her core and warming her through.

A sense of stillness washed over her, and relief followed. She heard a quiet gasp from Nels, but he didn't intervene with whatever he saw happening, and Jayce was glad. She could have existed in that peaceful, relaxing state for hours, simply existing in the awareness of the life all around her and being part of it.

She opened her eyes and was shocked to find the branch of a maple tree touching her cheek.

Touching her without the freezing and numbness that usually followed. And instead of intruding whispers, a quiet murmur, like an undercurrent flowing through her consciousness. She felt as if she could give the tree permission to speak, and it would, but there seemed to be more of an understanding between them now.

She tugged her gloves off her hand and stroked the leaves of the maple, deliberately not asking it for anything. Experimenting with the new sensations that came from contact with its veiny green leaves.

"It's like, my whole life, the plants have been screaming to get through this block on my magic, and now it can whisper," she said, releasing the branch and moving forward.

Nels slipped his hand into hers as they rounded the bend. This time, she didn't jerk away but grasped his hand in hers, relishing the other kind of warmth that bloomed inside her.

The hidden entrance to the rebellion's safe house lay just ahead, the wooden door carved with a bee peeking through the trees.

"That's far enough."

Cold steel kissed Jayce's throat. An arm clamped around her ribs, rough and unyielding. She froze, breath catching as the blade pressed harder—enough to warn, not yet to break skin.

"Yamalda," she forced her voice to remain level. Recognition struck as sharply as the knife. "There's no need for this."

She didn't dare move, but her eyes flicked toward Nels. *Don't do anything foolish.*

"The Guild protectors came for me this morning." Yamalda's breath was hot on her ear. "I barely escaped. And here you are—walking free. Why?"

"They questioned us, too," Jayce said. "We got out."

"She set the room on fire," Nels added.

Yamalda hesitated. Then the blade lifted. Her arm unwrapped from Jayce's chest. She stepped around to face them and crossed her arms, knife still in hand.

"What did you tell the Head Dame?"

"Nothing," Jayce said, too quickly. "But I know what she wants."

Yamalda's eyes narrowed. "Where's Sav?"

Jayce hesitated. Her heart lurched, and the forest seemed to tilt around her.

"We had to leave him behind."

A sharp breath from Yamalda. "How convenient." Her mouth twisted. "Let me guess—the Head Dame sent you to earn back our trust. Draw us out. Make it easy for her to gut us all in one strike."

"That's not it," Jayce said, the words tumbling over each other. "We came here to get your help. To get him back."

She almost said more. The truth about who Sav really was burned on her tongue, but she didn't know if it was hers to give. Had he told them?

"I know who he is," she said finally. "Who he really is."

Yamalda went still. Her hands dropped to her sides. "So. He told you."

Before Jayce could answer, a crack of thunder rolled low and close.

A shadow moved behind the trees—and then Corbin stepped forward, eyes storm-lit, hair windblown, and rising as if caught in an invisible current. "Just say the word," he said. Lightning flared in his irises.

Nels stepped in front of her without hesitation. "No one has to get hurt. Jayce is telling the truth."

Corbin didn't lower his hand, but his eyes flicked to Yamalda. "You believe them?"

The woman stared at Jayce. Her gaze was unreadable, but something shifted there.

Then Yamalda gave a single, sharp nod. "Bring them in. I want to hear what they have to say."

Corbin moved behind Nels, silent and watchful. Yamalda turned and led them through the underbrush until they reached a wooden door half-swallowed by ivy and shadow. She unlocked it with a key identical to Jayce's.

The hinges creaked. Cool air breathed out.

They stepped into the musty dark.

Bentley sprang to his feet the moment they stepped inside, running into an armchair in his rush.

"Yamalda, you were gone so long, and then Corbin just—" His eyes landed on Jayce and Nels. His mouth snapped shut. "What are they doing here?"

"Claiming they need our help," Yamalda said, settling on the arm of a chair with the casual air of someone who could still kill them in three moves or fewer. "We'll see."

Jayce's heart thudded against her ribs. She took a step forward, hands open. "Yamalda, I swear on the Three—"

"Spare me," Yamalda cut in, eyes cold. "Sav might've trusted you. Doesn't mean we should. Start talking. Tell us everything that happened last night, and what the Head Dame wants."

Jayce sank into the nearest chair. Her legs didn't want to hold her anymore. But she couldn't rest—not yet. Not with Sav imprisoned, not with the journal lost.

She told them everything—how the Head Dame cornered her, the interrogation, the escape. Nels chimed in, his account rougher, filled with graphic detail.

As Nels spoke, Jayce's eyes caught on the dark smudge along his jaw. She'd thought it was stubble earlier, but now she saw the swelling, the bruise coming in. Without thinking, she reached up and touched it lightly.

He flinched, but still gave her a half-smile.

Her fingers curled back into her lap.

The Head Dame hadn't just threatened him. She'd hurt him.

Her stomach twisted. Nels had always stepped in to shield her. And she hadn't been able to stop any of this.

"Jayce?"

Nels's voice dragged her back. He crouched beside her chair, hand brushing hers. His touch lit something in her chest that had nothing to do with the conversation.

"I'm fine," she said too quickly. Her body knew better. It leaned toward him as if pulled.

"She's been up all night," Nels said to Yamalda, voice edged with concern. "She needs sleep."

"We'll wake you when we've made our decision," Yamalda said. She flicked a dagger from her belt and twirled it. "Don't try to leave. Corbin has the wind watching."

"Then you believe us?" Jayce asked. "What about Fiametta?"

Yamalda's mouth twisted. "We've always known where her loyalties lay. We warned Sav, but he didn't want to hear it." She turned and stalked toward the door.

Bentley hesitated, lagging behind. He leaned down, voice low. "If you need to run, I can get you to Starfall by nightfall. One ride. One way. No fare."

"Why?" Nels asked, blinking.

"You saved my life," Bentley said. "And Berma's. Consider it a debt paid."

"Thank you," Jayce whispered.

"Bentley!"

He flinched at Yamalda's bark. Gave them one last nod.

Then he was gone, and the door clicked shut behind him.

Nels stood, running his hands through his hair and scanning the room. After shuffling a few seats around, including sliding one up to Jayce's and having her prop her legs up on it, he'd rigged up two bed-like places for them to nap.

Jayce rested her head on her hands, looking across the thick chair arms that separated them as Nels climbed in on the other side.

"You feel so far away," she said wistfully.

Nels snorted. "That'll be the sleep deprivation talking. You'll change your mind after you hear me snoring."

"How would you know if you snored?" Jayce asked incredulously.

Nels laughed. "I suppose you'll tell me." His face turned serious, and he reached hesitantly across the distance to take her hand in his. "I didn't dream it, did I? What we did in the ivy?"

His fingers felt cool, but Jayce welcomed his touch. Feeling bold, she pulled herself up over the arm of the chair and leaned in to kiss him again. This time, his lips were sweeter, slower, tugging and pulling at her with a more subtle hunger than she'd noticed before.

She loved every moment, and when they finally pulled away, she sank happily into the cushioned chair, still gripping his hand as she closed her eyes and relished the warm feelings coursing through her.

Nels cleared his throat. "We should get some rest, I guess."

With some regret, she agreed, and a few moments later, she had drifted off, dreaming of moonlight kisses and a world where the Plague King, and all the trouble it had brought to her life, didn't exist.

The sound of shuffling feet and voices in the corridor outside startled Jayce awake some time later. It must have been hours, as the oil lamps had burned down.

Nels woke beside her. He touched her shoulder, putting a finger to his lips, then left the armchair bed he'd made and crossed to the doors, reaching into his pocket.

He stopped before the door, a sizable rock in his hand. He turned the handle.

The door burst open, sending Nels stumbling back to avoid getting hit in the face.

Corbin, Yamalda, and Bentley stood in the doorway.

"Sorry to startle you. I thought the handle was stuck when I turned it," Bentley said. "Corbin rammed into it with his shoulder."

Jayce's shoulders relaxed slightly.

Bentley helped Nels off the floor, dusting him off.

Yamalda crossed the room and stood in front of Jayce. "We need your help to rescue Sav. He's being held in the Dame's offices, still, and from what I've gathered, he's going on trial in the morning. We can't let that happen."

It was unspoken, but Yamalda wouldn't be asking for their help if she didn't think they could be trusted.

"Trial? For what?" Jayce asked.

"Breaking and entering. Loitering on school grounds. Disturbing the peace. I don't know. I just know he's crossed the Head Dame and has held out giving her the information she wants. No doubt your escape has soured her mood as well." She shot a glowering look at Jayce, as if the entire situation were her fault.

Arguing that last night had been Sav's idea wouldn't help matters.

"So we rescue Sav, and then what?" Nels asked, joining Yamalda near Jayce's chair. Bentley and Corbin followed.

"I take us to Starfall, and we book passage on the first ship that will take us," Bentley interjected.

"But the journal," Jayce said. "We don't have it."

"Sav met with the translator last night. He has the information," Yamalda said.

"He's the only one who does. If something happens to him, or the translator, no one else will know. That isn't wise," Jayce insisted.

"If something happens to him, the rebellion is doomed," Yamalda said, locking eyes with Jayce.

Because Sav, as the hidden heir of Neldor, was the figurehead. Without him, would the rebellion fall apart? And if it did, could anyone else hope to discover the truth behind the Plague King?

A truth, Jayce realized, that Queen Lyra had been trying to hide behind the restrictions and fees placed on researching the plague.

I suspect my father's disappearance has something to do with the Plague King.

The implication sent Jayce's thoughts reeling. If what Sav had said was true, then she needed the translation of Dagric's journal more than ever.

"We could use the information in the journal as collateral to free Sav."

"I wasn't planning to ask nicely, much less *trade*," Yamalda spat.

"Besides that, we don't know what information the Head Dame might have gotten from Sav while we've been chatting," Corbin added. "She might know everything, making the journal useless."

A lump formed in Jayce's throat at the thought of Sav going through what she had with the truth tonic, and the Head Dame's persuasion powers, and possibly worse. She swallowed.

"Then it's even more critical that more than one person knows what Wortcunning's journal says. If we fail to rescue Sav…"

"We won't fail. We can't," Yamalda said, her eyes gleaming with conviction. She gripped the sword at her hip. "Sav is the only one who can challenge the ones covering everything up. We have to rescue him, or all is lost."

"I agree with Jayce," Bentley piped up. "Sav valued knowledge above everything, even his own life. When I thought he was crazy for returning to Loshar to find a certain apothecary, every time he said '*the right information is worth the sacrifice.*'"

Sav had said the same to her, when he'd first introduced her to his literary rebellion. His value of knowledge and the way he built everyone around him up might just be enough to convince the queen to listen, but would it be enough to end the plague?

"Fine," Yamalda yielded. "A quick stop to get the translation, then we go get Sav."

Murmurs of agreement rippled through the group.

Nels moved behind Jayce, his presence grounding her. She glanced up at him, then faced the others. "Does… anyone know who the translator is?"

Yamalda raised a brow. "Didn't Sav tell you?"

"Only that he trusted them," Jayce said. "He didn't share a name."

Corbin threw up his hands. "Of course he didn't."

"I think I know," Bentley offered, lifting a hand. "My uncle. Dire Isen Pell. He teaches here—ancient languages, obscure stuff. Sav would go to him for translation, no question."

"Then I guess we're paying him a visit," Jayce said, already rising to her feet.

They had a name. Now they just had to hope he had the answers.

CHAPTER TWENTY-FOUR

JAYCE HAD NEVER SEEN the campus so still. Rain clung to the stone paths and pooled beneath benches, and the usual chatter had gone quiet—replaced by the hush of people pretending not to notice something was wrong.

Jayce kept her head down, but every whisper seemed to be about her, and every glance lingered a bit too long. She and Bentley walked a few paces behind the others, doing their best to look like strangers on a shared path. Smaller groups drew less attention—at least, that was the idea.

Would someone report them to the Head Dame? Paranoia was getting the better of her. The borrowed cloak itched at her neck, but she tightened it anyway, hunching as a gust of wind drove cold rain beneath the hem. The hood helped hide her face, but it did nothing for her fear.

The Lore Guild stood a bit shorter than the others, a massive owl with spread wings carved out of limestone or granite—Nels would know which—staring down at them with disapproving eyes.

She had to focus.

Dire Isen Pell wouldn't hand over information easily. Even with Bentley there, the man might refuse. If he hadn't known what the journal held before, he did now. And if his loyalty lay with the Guilds, or the Crown, he might have already gone to Head Dame Tsega with the information. They could all be arrested the moment they walked through those doors.

Outside sounds vanished behind the thick stone walls. Only the faint shuffle of feet, quiet turning of pages, and barely perceptible whispering of students could be heard.

"Bentley?" she murmured, drawing closer.

He pulled his hood down and gave her a look. Right—hers needed to come off, too. She hesitated, then lowered it.

"Is your uncle… loyal to the school?"

Bentley frowned. "He's unmarried. Lives here full time. From what I've seen, the staff is basically his family."

Jayce swallowed, the hope that had risen inside her falling. "But he helped Sav. He'll help us, too, won't he?"

He shrugged. "For the right cause, I think so. My uncle is a good man, and Sav trusted him."

Sav had trusted Fiametta, too. And he thought Jayce held some secret to defeating the Plague King. Perhaps they shouldn't be relying on his judgement.

She didn't reply to Bentley as she, instead, focused on climbing the third flight of stairs

The stairwell quieted as students peeled off, floor by floor, until only their group remained. At the third-floor landing, the others waited as Jayce and Bentley caught up.

Nels took Jayce's hand when she reached the top. "Wasn't sure I'd make it up that last stretch," he said.

Jayce raised an eyebrow. "Don't you climb mountains and mine stone for a living?"

"There's less climbing involved than you think," Nels replied with a crooked grin.

"Cut the banter," Yamalda snapped. Her gaze swept the corridor. "We don't know what we're walking into."

"My uncle isn't a threat," Bentley said, bristling.

Yamalda didn't soften. "You don't know that. For all we know, he's already sent the translation to Head Dame Tsega, and there are Guild protectors waiting in his office. Everyone has their price."

So, Yamalda had been thinking the same thing. Jayce relaxed slightly. Knowing someone as skilled in combat as Yamalda and Corbin were on their side gave her confidence. If something went wrong, they had a good chance of getting out of it.

The plush purple rug softened their footsteps, and the lanterns on the walls glowed softly. It was almost enough to lull Jayce into a false sense of safety, but her blood still rushed in her ears, her senses heightened, ready to alert at the first sign of danger.

They stopped before a door with Dire Isen Pell's name on a brass plaque. Bentley stepped forward and knocked.

"Come in," a male voice called out.

Bentley seemed to hesitate, but he turned the handle and stepped inside.

The curtains were drawn shut, and only one lamp lit the room, the one closest to the door. The dim light didn't reach the desk, where Dire Pell sat staring at the wall behind his desk, his back to the door.

"Close the door," he said.

Nels obeyed, the latch clicking shut behind them.

"Something doesn't feel right," Bentley muttered, leaning in toward Yamalda. "I'm not sure this is—"

"I know why you've come," the man said, slowly turning in his chair. "Unfortunately, you're too late."

Jayce gasped.

Leth Alend.

She knew him in an instant—the man with the cane. The one who had blocked her magic years ago, the one her parents had paid to silence a part of her.

He sat in Dire Pell's chair like he belonged there.

Her pulse seemed to skip, then rush to catch up.

Where was the Dire?

The room narrowed. The air thinned. Her body moved without thought, and she backed into Nels. His hands held her shoulders, steadying her, but her balance had already tipped.

This wasn't right. None of it was right.

"What's wrong?" he whispered in her ear.

Jayce didn't respond, her mind reeling. How was *he* here? And why?

"Who are you?" Bentley asked, sounding confused.

"Ask your companion, Jayce. We've met before."

The three in front turned to Jayce, their stares accusing.

Jayce opened her mouth, but her voice caught. For a breathless moment, nothing came out.

Nels shifted beside her, hand still steady on her arm, as if preparing to speak on her behalf.

She had to say it—to face him, to name what he'd done.

"You've been following me since I arrived," Jayce said. Her voice came out confident and clear—exactly as she'd hoped. "What I don't know is why."

Leth smiled, and it chilled her more than it should have.

Her voice dropped but stayed steady. She stepped forward, slipping from Nels's grasp and passing Corbin, Yamalda, and Bentley without looking back.

"Oh, I've been following you far longer than that. A twin, born under the blood-red moon. I suspected you were the one the prophecy spoke of—and made sure others wouldn't find you before the time was right."

"Who is this, Jayce?" Yamalda asked behind her.

Jayce kept her eyes locked on the man in front of her. "His name is Leth Alend. He works for the queen, but I don't know anything else."

He tsked softly, moving out from behind the desk. The lantern light caught his features as he passed—creased face, neatly trimmed mustache, gold buttons gleaming. Then he moved back into the shadows. The effect made her stomach twist.

"I must take responsibility for that," he said. "You see, my magic lies in memory. I can erase myself—and any memory tied to me—from those I've touched. I didn't want you coming to find me. Safer for both of us."

Jayce's fists clenched at her sides. So that's why she'd reacted to him without understanding why. Her body remembered what her mind couldn't. A cold tremor ran through her.

"I know you blocked my magic when I was little."

He waved a careless hand. "Yes, I did. Or rather, I manipulated your memories of your magic, creating a sort of bypass so you wouldn't be able to access the fullness of your powers. Your parents asked me to. They were afraid of what you could do. Afraid the Three would take you from them."

"The Three?" Jayce murmured. She wouldn't have expected him to be so direct.

Leth Alend nodded. "Yes, they recognized the signs of one goddess-touched at birth. They were convinced your brother was, as well, but his magic was nothing special. You are the one the Three chose. And since you don't remember, I will tell you that I'm the one who recruited you and your brother to the palace to train to defeat the Plague King."

The pieces clicked into place, like gears sliding together in perfect synchronization. Her mother had taken her to him—back then, he didn't have a cane, and his hair had been darker. She remembered how it felt to have his magic inside her, her mother holding her down while she screamed for him to stop.

And she recalled the turn he'd knocked on their door. Javin had answered, had come to get her, dragging her from her work bench to talk to the man who told them the queen requested their presence.

He had made her forget it all.

"Why keep my magic blocked if you thought I could be the one the prophecy spoke of?" Jayce said, disbelief still swirling through her mind. It had always been about Javin, not her.

Leth Alend chuckled. "Prophecies are tricky things, you know—hard to interpret, harder still to control. That fool Wortcunning had to have been goddess-touched. The most incredible remedies, the deadliest of poisons. Ones that gave him visions, told him things. The goddesses gave the wrong man the power. Did you know he refused to tell anyone the full text of the prophecy? Dangled it over all of our heads. He wanted immunity from his past actions, to be reinstated, his banishment revoked. Queen Lyra refused, and he disappeared, taking the prophecy with him."

He adjusted a paper weight on the Dire's desk, picking it up and hefting it before setting it back down with a thud that made Jayce jump.

She hardly dared to breathe, to break whatever spell was in place to make Leth Alend reveal the truth.

"We had a fraction of the prophecy. Based on that, everyone believed it spoke of your brother. A quiet apothecary-in-training didn't fit their expectations, so they ignored you. They wanted a sword. A hero. A legend.

"But I knew there was more to it. So I waited. I watched. You wouldn't believe how powerful someone becomes when they're forced to fight against their own limits."

Jayce inhaled slowly. The air felt thick, like it was pressing in against her skin. "You thought you could control me," she said.

Leth didn't flinch. "I gave you room to survive. I shaped the conditions that allowed you to become what you are now. You should thank me."

Anger, pure and clear, shot through her. Like an arrow to its target.

"Thank you? For sending my brother to his death? For allowing thousands to suffer while you played a game with fate?" Her shoulders rose and fell with each strong breath.

"This is how we fix everything. Purge the rot. Start again. And you get to be part of it all." His eyes held a mad gleam.

He was insane, filled with some sort of over-inflated sense of self-importance, as if he held the power of the Well, rather than the benevolent Three that had governed it for thousands of years.

"What did you do with my uncle?" Bentley asked, breaking the tense silence.

Leth Alend's attention turned to him. "He gave me the information I sought, and therefore, outlived his usefulness," Leth Alend said with a casual flick of his hand, as if shooing a fly from his face rather than talking about the death of a person.

Horror filled Jayce.

Bentley leapt past her, his face a mask of rage. "He was all I had!"

Corbin darted forward and grabbed Bentley by the arms, holding him back.

Bentley struggled for a moment, then stopped, chest heaving, tears streaming down his face. "Uncle Isen never did anything to harm anyone. He gave knowledge freely and loved teaching. How could you just... just... end him?" His voice cracked.

"He held illegal, unreported knowledge. He would have stood trial for distributing restricted information to those who oppose Queen Lyra's rule."

Jayce couldn't speak. Bentley's grief sat heavy in the air, settling on her skin like ash. She couldn't let it drag her under. Couldn't let the revelation that Leth Alend had been manipulating her whole life paralyze her.

"Last I checked, the penalty for that is imprisonment, not death," Yamalda spat, drawing her sword. The metal gleamed in the lantern light, and she paced a few steps away from the group, as if trying to find the best angle to attack from.

"Big mistake, admitting to murder in front of five witnesses," Corbin added, releasing Bentley's arms and swirling one arm upward in front of his face.

The air in the room stirred, responding to the mage's call.

Leth Alend's haughty expression faltered as the thin gray hair on his head fluttered. His eyebrows drew together, and his face fell into a more serious expression. "As one of her most trusted advisors, Queen Lyra granted me authority to remove any threat to her rule. That includes treacherous translators who go directly against her dictates."

Nels shifted behind Jayce. She wondered what he was prepared to do. Could he use the stones in the walls?

There weren't any plants in the room. Unless the dead wood in the furniture and fibers in the carpets would respond to her magic, but that seemed unlikely. Especially with the block on her magic still in place.

Bentley's sobs broke through the stifling silence.

She had to try.

Reaching into that place inside her, she listened for the voice she had heard before—the one that felt like the whole forest spoke to her—but nothing stirred.

"I doubt Queen Lyra meant you could kill without cause," Corbin said.

Leth Alend glanced between all of them. “Come, now, this is getting out of hand. I came for Jayce Keenstone. She is key to ending the Plague King’s rule over Neldor. Surely you all want that?”

“We want Dagric’s journal, the translated pages, and Savage Alighieri returned to us,” Yamalda said boldly. “If we have to trade Jayce for them, we will.”

Jayce’s pulse thudded in her throat, and the truth swept through her like a frigid north wind.

They would sacrifice her to save Sav. And she couldn’t blame them. After all, he was the lost prince; the hidden heir of Neldor. She was only an apothecary of little renown who had failed to destroy the Plague King and save the realm.

CHAPTER TWENTY-FIVE

JAYCE STARED AT THE back of Yamalda's head, half-expecting her to turn around and wink or give some other indication that she was bluffing. But the warrior stood, sword at the ready, her stance fixed and her eyes locked on Leth Alend.

"No!" Nels shouted, pushing Jayce behind him. "That isn't what we agreed."

Yamalda turned on him, her lip curling into a snarl. "As far as I'm concerned, you are both strangers who have done nothing to further our cause. You're expendable, and I would trade both of your lives for Sav's in a heartbeat."

"Yamalda?" Jayce said, peering around Nels to lock gazes with the warrior. Her heart raced as she tried to assess the situation. There were too many players, too many motivations and agendas, and so much fear. She swallowed past her own, trying to stand tall.

Yamalda broke their shared gaze, glancing at the floor. "Sorry, Jayce. You know how important he is to me. To us." She turned back to Leth Alend.

"Ah, yes, he is important to you, isn't he? The secret prince, tucked away out of shame."

Jayce startled. He *knew* about Sav? But how?

Leth Alend continued. "Reginald likely never expected that he and Lyra would fail to bear a legitimate heir when he hid his son away. But alas, the queen remained childless, a fact I know broke her heart."

"How do you know about Sav?" Yamalda growled, adjusted her grip on her sword.

"When Head Dame Tsega first started writing about the rebellion forming on Guild grounds, I took interest. When our sources uncovered that their leader claimed to be a lost heir, I decided to pay the Guilds a visit. How fortunate that Jayce happened to be arriving at the same time—and in the company of that very man. Queen Lyra will be very interested in the information we've extracted from him. I could have you all imprisoned for your participation in the rebellion. You are in a poor position to bargain with me." His mouth spread into a wide, self-satisfied grin that only deepened Jayce's hatred of him further.

"The way I see it, it's five against one. If we kill you, no one will know it was us, and we can retrieve Sav ourselves," Yamalda spat.

Leth Alend looked entirely unshaken by the threat. He spread his arms before him. "You could go to all that trouble, but why, when he's already here?"

The door behind them opened, and Sav stumbled through, his hands bound behind his back and Guild protectors on either side.

Jayce stepped toward him, concerned about the way he was leaning, the pallor of his face, and how ragged his breath seemed.

He glanced at her, flashing a smile despite the pain written on his face.

What had they done to him?

She took another step, and Nels braced a hand on her arm warningly as Head Dame Tsega and Fiametta came through the doorway, looking no worse for the wear despite how they had parted.

"There now, together again. I suggest, young lady, you reconsider your odds."

Yamalda's quiet curse made it to Jayce's ears, and she had to agree with the warrior. Three advanced magic-users, plus the Guild protectors, who would be a formidable threat even if they couldn't use magic.

Head Dame Tsega laughed. "I cannot believe you were right, Leth. I was certain they wouldn't be foolish enough to come after the princely bastard, but here they are, like heroes in a story. Master Thorenvale, I thought you, at least, had more sense than this." She tsked, tilting her chin in a condescending way.

Jayce couldn't see Corbin's expression, but the air around them grew cooler as a supernatural breeze stirred up.

Head Dame Tsega's expression darkened. "We've been gentle with you until this point, don't push us to our worst."

"I don't think we're to that point yet, Velora, it's all part of the negotiation," Leth Alend soothed.

Jayce shouldn't have been surprised that he was on first-name basis with the Head Dame. Two powerful people, both in positions of influence with the queen. If Sav and the others weren't careful, this could end very badly for them all.

Sav straightened up. "What are you proposing?"

The lanterns gleamed off his sweat-soaked brow, and Jayce could tell that staying upright, much less speaking, was taking an immense amount of effort.

"Negotiation?" Head Dame Tsega sneered. "I vote we take him out now. Cut the head off the snake, and it dies." She gestured hard to the right, and one of the Guild protectors rammed their spear butt into Sav's side.

He crumpled.

Jayce glanced helplessly around the room. Not a single plant. Could she summon a plant from outside? She opened her senses, casting about for any whisper or hint that help was nearby.

Yamalda gave a yell of rage, and the warrior sprinted past, her sword aimed for the Head Dame.

Head Dame Tsega smirked. "So much aggression. But you don't *want* to fight me, do you?"

Yamalda's arms slowed mid-swing, the sword halting halfway to its target. Her brow furrowed in confusion, as if she had suddenly decided to reconsider killing the Head Dame.

The Head Dame's manipulative abilities had a strong effect, even on someone as passionate as Yamalda.

Jayce shuddered, remembering what it felt like to have the Head Dame's influence pressing on her own mind.

"We have to do something!" she whispered fiercely to Nels.

"The walls are made of stone," he replied, "but I'll have to be cautious and not tear the building down on top of us."

"Just one or two, enough to take out the Guild protectors and stop the Head Dame," Jayce replied. "Can you do that?"

He nodded, then cocked his head and looked at her with a goofy grin that seemed out of place in the tense situation. "Anything for you."

Jayce stared at him incredulously, but a smile twitched at the corners of her mouth. She would talk to him about the timing of his flirtations later. For now, they had to get out of this mess.

One of the Guild protectors left Sav and rushed Yamalda, who stood locked in a battle of wills against Head Dame Tsega's manipulative power. She was so caught up she didn't notice the man coming until it was nearly too late. She spun and deflected his blow but was thrown off balance and onto the floor.

Corbin charged forward, waving his arms in a wide circle, and the air pressure in the room increased, making Jayce's ears pop. A damp mist rose up around them, thickest at its central point around Corbin.

Nels crept closer to the edge of the room. He gestured at the wall, then toward the Guild protector still guarding Sav. Jayce caught a quiet grating sound. It was working.

Jayce needed to get Sav's attention. If he could use the mist as a distraction, maybe get out of the room... but Head Dame Tsega and Fiametta still blocked the doorway.

With the mist as a cover and so many of the enemy distracted in combat with Corbin and Yamalda, perhaps she could take a moment to sense nearby plants again.

Just as she closed her eyes, and a hand wrapped around her mouth, drawing her head back in a strong grip.

Her eyes flew open, the mist so thick it obscured almost everything. The sound of fighting, then a solid thud and a woman's scream was heard. Jayce didn't know who it was, and for a moment she couldn't think of who might have grabbed her.

She had forgotten about Leth Alend. His hairy arm rubbed roughly against her cheek, and his hand remained clamped over her mouth so she couldn't scream.

"You're going to come with me. Once the fighting is over, I'll take you back to Neldor with me. We're going to pay the Plague King a visit."

Jayce tugged at his arms and twisted, trying to free herself. She wouldn't be going anywhere with him.

"Don't make this harder for yourself. You don't know what I'm capable of," he said, breath heavy in her ear as he held her tighter. "Why do you think you couldn't remember me? I made you forget. And I can make you forget again. Make you forget your friends, where you came from, your purpose, even who you are."

She had wanted to forget, once. Had done her best to numb herself, to keep so busy finding the cure for the plague that she didn't have to think about her parents being gone, or her brother's horrible fate, or the fact that she had survived it all and was alone.

But now she had people who cared about her. And they had given meaning to her purpose again. She couldn't throw it all away now.

More terrifying even than Leth Alend's threats to take her memories was the thought of going with him willingly and leaving the people she cared about to find the cure on their own.

The mist cleared in one part of the room, revealing Nels hurling another stone from the wall into the chest of one of the Guild protectors. She couldn't see Sav; he was gone from the wall where he'd been standing. Had he escaped?

Yamalda's sword glinted. There was a body on the floor. More than one.

How had it all gone so terribly wrong? And what could an apothecary do about it?

"Come along, now," Leth Alend muttered. "Calmly."

He pulled her toward the opposite wall, away from the bulk of the fighting, then made a dash for the door with her in tow.

Sav stepped up in the doorway, leaning back against it with a casual air. "Where do you think you're going, Leth?"

"It's high time someone dealt with you," he sneered, releasing Jayce's arm and drawing a dagger from his belt.

Jayce cried out in warning, but it came too late, or Sav was too exhausted to dodge. He tried, but Leth Alend's blade caught him in the side mid-leap.

He fell to his knees, gasping and holding his stomach. His hand came away bloody.

Anger flooded Jayce. She moved to stand between Sav and his attacker, fully aware of how vulnerable she was. No weapon, not even a plant to call on like she had in the recent past.

But there was more power inside of her—she could feel it waiting beyond the block that had been placed on her as a child. When she'd approached the Three in the temple, they had done something to that block. Cracked it, or thinned it out.

She sank deeper into herself, her magic spreading like roots in search of water.

Water, like that found in the Well.

The sound of fighting faded away as she dug down inside herself, as if she were a tree putting down roots, searching for water in a drought.

The band in her chest tightened. Her brow furrowed and she pushed harder, her hands clenching into fists.

Down, down she went, until the tendrils of her soul brushed something that shimmered in the dark.

The power had always been there.

And it was time she learned to wield it.

Her left arm started to itch. She resisted scratching it. Then her right arm started, in the fingertips at first, then winding up her arms. When the sensation reached her chest, a bright light burst before her eyes and they snapped open, but she didn't see the dimly lit office, nor did she see Sav or Leth Alend or any of the others. She couldn't hear them, either.

She was somewhere else, transported to another place, perhaps through a vision, and as the blinding light faded, a new scene lay before her.

Hidden beneath an unbroken canopy, a forest glade lay in shadow, a motionless pond at its heart, reflecting nothing but the dark.

Jayce approached the water, but she didn't touch it. Some instinct warned against it. Footsteps crashed through the undergrowth, startling her, and she darted away from the water's edge, hiding behind a tree trunk.

Multiple voices spoke, garbled at first, but as they drew nearer, she could make out some of what they were saying.

"I tell you, I don't recall why we're in this forest," claimed a deep male voice. It reminded her somewhat of her own father, but the timbre of it had a different quality and it clearly wasn't him.

"To save your people from war, Sire. What more do you need to know?"

That voice was familiar, but Jayce couldn't put her finger on why until the first man spoke again.

"Everything, Leth. What could we find in these blasted trees that could end a war?"

Her heart rate increased. Surely it was a coincidence? She moved her head, trying to catch a glimpse of the approaching party, but the trees were too thick.

If one of those voices belonged to Leth Alend—the man trying to kill Sav and capture her in the present day—then she had somehow traveled back in time in a vision.

As if that weren't shocking enough, Leth had called the man with him *Sire*. The only person she knew who went by that title was the late King of Neldor—King Reginald Donovanu.

The King, and Sav's birth father.

Rumor had it the king had sought out a hidden magic to turn the tides of the war in his favor, but that he'd died trying to access it. Had the Three granted her a vision of that very moment?

She glanced at the water again. Not so much as a ripple crossed it. Nothing floated on its surface—no leaves, no twigs, no skittering water bugs. The pond seemed dead, except for the fact that it glowed faintly.

The figures came into view, now, the two men alone. She had expected a retinue of guards, at the least.

She crept around the curve of the tree trunk to stay out of sight, peering through the misty gloom at the two men.

Leth Alend walked confidently, somewhat more fit than his current state, but with the same self-confident bearing he carried now. The man at his side, cloaked and tall, bore a regal presence even aside from the thin gold circlet on his brow.

Reginald Donovanu, once ruler of Neldor, now a name whispered in shame and sorrow. He looked weary, holding his arm close to his side like it pained him, and his boots dragged through the damp leaves.

"This is it?" the king asked, staring at the still, glowing surface of the Well. "It doesn't look like our salvation."

"It is," Leth said smoothly, folding his hands. "The Well of Origin—according to legend, this water is a source of magic. The Well answers to those bold enough to ask."

The king hesitated. "I imagine this magic comes at a price."

"Only that you mean what you say. Speak truly, and you will have your wish." There was no malice in his expression, no obvious tone of manipulation in his voice. He sounded sincere, but what he said about the Well didn't sound right.

Jayce remembered the legends differently. Her father had told many stories around the village fire, most notably the Legend of the Three, which told about how Damaris had traveled to the Well to seek a cure for her dying mother and had ended up being gifted the powers of deity along with two of her sisters.

But the Keeper of the Well was recorded as saying that anyone who sought to use the power of the Well for their own gain—even if they presumed the reason to be selfless—would be destroyed. Certainly, King Reginald seeking the Well's power to end the war in favor of his people would count as selfish.

Besides that, where was the Keeper of the Well? The Well should still be protected by Damaris, but no figure—deific or otherwise—appeared to warn the king and his counselor of the dangers of using the Well.

Movement dragged Jayce's attention back to the present—or was it past?—moment.

King Reginald stepped to the water's edge. "I hardly know what to ask for." He fell to his knees, ignoring the mud sullying the rich material of his pants. His voice dropped to a hoarse whisper, almost like a prayer. "My people are dying. My children will grow up in ruins. I would give anything to stop it."

Leth Alend stepped up beside him. "You could wish for immortality, your grace. For power to dispel the evil that assaults your realm."

"I don't want power. I don't want immortality. I just want the war to end," King Reginald turned toward his counselor, brow furrowing.

Jayce blinked back the tears that pricked the corners of her eyes at his passion and sincerity. Surely that would be selfless enough for the Well. It would find him honorable, worthy of holding its power to save his people.

"This is the only way," Leth Alend insisted. "You must ask for great power to drive off your enemies."

The two men went back and forth for some time, King Reginald seeking counsel on how to word the request, and Leth Alend patiently suggesting a variety of options, while always steering the king toward a request for power.

At long last, King Reginald turned back to the Well. He filled his lungs and shifted his shoulders, as if presenting himself to someone with greater authority even than a king.

"Grant me this wish, oh sacred Well: that I might receive unto myself a power great enough to put a stop to the war, to destroy those who murder and torture my people and destroy our cities. I ask not for myself, but for the citizens and families under my care. In the name of the Three I cast this wish forth. Receive it and deliver it unto the one who can grant my wish."

Jayce held her breath.

The surface of the Well rippled.

King Reginald leaned forward as if mesmerized by something in the water, then reached in.

The moment his fingers touched the water, it recoiled—then pulsed outward in concentric rings of dark light. The glow above the water deepened, turning the color of bruised blood. Steam hissed around the king, and Leth Alend stepped back, a look of terror and awe twisting the expression on his face.

King Reginald's shoulders convulsed. He screamed.

Jayce was rooted in place. She couldn't look away from the horror unfolding before her.

The king's body twisted, his skin turned gray, and his veins blackened like ink bleeding through parchment. His cries became unnatural—echoing, fractured. The crown of his head tore open, spilling light and plague and rot.

And the Well—the Well turned black.

Jayce choked on the air. It smelled of decay and something acrid, almost like some poisons she had encountered.

Where was Damaris? Where was the Keeper of the Well? Had the Well been tainted somehow? Why hadn't the Three stopped this?

She finally found her feet again. She turned as if to run from this place, the birthplace of the Plague King, when she slipped on the wet ground and, in catching herself on a nearby tree, happened to glance up and see someone else watching.

A young man who appeared near her age, pale and waif-like, swaying as he stood perhaps thirty feet away, farther into the trees.

Javin.

Her brother, lost to the Plague King two years ago, somehow stood there. His hair was longer, and his face hollow, but it was him. His eyes locked on hers, the dead expression in them brightening as soon as he recognized her.

She didn't question his presence, only ran to him, dodging tree roots, skimming the edge of the Well.

Behind her King Reginald climbed from the water, his new form vast and robed in shadows. He floated across the surface of the Well like oil on water, a spiked bone crown where there once had been gold.

Jayce ran harder, wondering why Javin didn't move toward her. And then she saw that his legs were wrapped in dark roots, grown like vines. He strained against them, teeth gritted.

She leapt the last few feet and caught his hand in hers before a wind ripped through the clearing with the might of a violent storm, threatening to tear them apart.

With her other hand, she grabbed the roots binding his feet and willed them to release him.

Please save him! She screamed, to the Three, to the void, to any power that would listen. *Save him!*

The roots around his legs recoiled, snapping back into the Well as if repelled. A surge of power roared from her chest, down her limbs, through her fingers and into his.

The vision of the clearing dissolved. Jayce cried out as the world folded inward and she fell, and every sensation vanished except the solidity of Javin's hand in hers.

She landed on all fours, breathing heavily and staring at the patterned blue, maroon, and gray rug in Dire Pell's office.

Except it hadn't been maroon, had it? No, that shape looked like a pool of blood, and the body slumped next to it was Sav's.

That thought snapped her back to the present, and she stared at the scene before her. The mist was gone, and everyone present stood frozen, gaping at her.

A man groaned at her side. Her skin prickled, and she turned her head slowly.

Javin lay on his back, so thin, frail, and pale that he didn't seem like he could be alive. But he was moving, rubbing his eyes and blinking, making sounds. His chest rose and fell as he breathed, and then his eyes opened and he, too, stared at her.

"Jayce? Where are we?"

CHAPTER TWENTY-SIX

He was alive.

Relief loosened Jayce's limbs. She bent to hug her brother, careful not to jostle him too much. He was certainly too thin, and who knew what else. She would have to give him a full check up as soon as the opportunity presented itself.

She was so consumed, she hardly noticed Nels arrive at her side.

"Jayce? How is this—Javin! In the name of the Three..."

"I was in a vision, and he was there. I don't know how, but I brought him with me—"

"That isn't all you brought with you," Leth Alend growled from beside Sav, pointing a quivering finger at something behind her.

Jayce turned and gaped up at the rift in the air, splitting Dire Pell's office in half as if hovered like a tear in the fabric of reality. Shadows bled from the unnatural wound, uncoiling in tendrils that poured toward the ground.

A high-pitched whine made Jayce press her hands to her ears and bend over. A sick, twisting wrongness that made her ribs tighten, and she knew beyond all uncertainty that something worse was coming.

A wave of black spores rushed from the rift in the air and rushed about the room as a stream. It moved as if it had intelligence of its own.

Jayce barely managed a gasp before Nels tackled her, arms wrapped tight as if he could protect her from something as intangible as a plague.

"Don't use your magic!" she cried, remembering the theory she had formed in Loshar several weeks ago—that the plague was only passed to those who had magic.

Then the screaming began.

Through a gap in Nels's arms, she saw Head Dame Tsega crumple, clutching her throat as she staggered against the wall, hacking and coughing. Her eyes rolled back, and she collapsed as her skin grayed, blotched and cracked like dry clay.

Fiametta made a choking noise, tried to raise her hands—but her fingers had already stiffened beyond use. She hit the floor with a dull thud, her skin going gray and her eyes going blank.

Corbin backed into the wall, mouth open in shock, arms raised before him. Jayce felt the wind he had summoned.

"Corbin, stop—!" she cried out. He couldn't fight this with magic, no matter how powerful he was.

"What—" He managed before his knees gave out. His hands sparked with wild, uncontrolled wind, then fizzled as his eyes turned milky and his chest began to heave and the pallor of his skin faded.

The one Guild protector left standing shrieked—a sound cut off halfway by a wet, guttural gurgle—and dropped to the floor.

They had all perished, every one of the Guild protectors, the Head Dame and Fiametta, even Corbin...

She shuddered at the crawling sensation on her skin. No, not her skin... inside her. Like the rot brushed up against her soul. Hungry. Searching.

Jayce's heart pounded against Nels's chest. She didn't dare move, didn't dare breathe.

The plague had never acted like this before. It had always been a slow, creeping illness. An invisible killer no one had a defense for. And the Plague King was only a legend made up to frighten children into washing their hands and going to bed early.

Except she had always known the Plague King was real. And now she had unleashed his power on Enterea through a vision that she was somehow responsible for.

The cloud of spores finished circling around the room and gathered into a tight cloud at the location of the rift in the air. They swarmed and pulsed like a living thing, growing as more and more spores joined their number.

Then they drifted outward, revealing a tall, dark being at their center.

The Plague King.

Robes of ragged black flowed around it; the only visible parts of its body were two bony, gray hands. Its face remained hidden in the swarming black spores—or perhaps it was made of the spores. A twisted, bone-white crown rested atop its head.

It pointed a finger at Jayce—no, behind her. She glanced and saw Sav, his breathing labored, his eyes closed as if sleeping.

He was dying.

The Plague King swept toward them.

Nels shouted, dragging her and Javin both out of the way. They collapsed in a heap and watched as the Plague King slowed its approach to Sav, hovering in the air in front of him.

Could the man inside the horror recognize his son?

The Plague King's skeletal hand reached out toward Sav.

A memory flashed through Jayce's mind.

Javin approached the Plague King with that copper sword raised, determined to put an end to the plague once and for all.

The Plague King putting its hand through him. Absorbing him into itself until her brother vanished, his scream echoing through the cave, telling her to run.

So she ran.

She had to save Sav from the same fate. Had to *do* something. But she was frozen, holding Nels and Javin, cut off from her magic for fear of the plague.

And Sav, helplessly alone, his friends dead and injured, near death himself.

Jayce couldn't do anything but watch as that bone hand descended, landing on Sav's shoulder.

The spore particles swarmed him, wreathing him in writhing shadow.

The Plague King Straightened, looking bigger somehow.

"No!" Jayce shouted. She struggled against Nels's arm around her middle, then fell back against him.

Nothing remained of Sav except the dark blood stain on the carpet.

The Plague King made no advance toward them, only turned and walked back into the rift it had come from. That jagged black line sealed back up behind it, and everything returned as it was before.

And yet, nothing was the same.

Dark clusters of plague spores lingered at the corners and edges of the room, trembling as if they didn't know what to do now that their master had gone. They slowly crept along toward each other, gathering into a new cloud.

Once they had combined their strength, would they sweep through the rest of the Ivory Guilds and infect all of Enterea? No one would be expecting such an attack from within...

Jayce didn't want to look, but she forced herself, counting the bodies.

Among them, Yamalda was still alive, though wounded and leaning against one wall.

One of the dead twitched. Memories flooded Jayce's mind, pushing sorrow for Sav and fear for the distant future out of her mind.

She shoved Nels's arms away, struggling to stand and bring Javin with her.

"We have to go, now."

"Hold on, Jayce. We have wounded, and the dead—" Nels started.

"They aren't dead anymore!" Jayce cried. "They're becoming moribund!"

Nels froze, then glanced around the room at the bodies, all of which were now moving. They always took a few moments to rise, but once they did, they would become unstoppable, and she had no way to fight them this time.

Yamalda dragged herself off the ground and grabbed Bentley by the arm, forcing him to his feet. They moved far faster than Jayce had expected.

Leth Alend stood at the doorway between them and freedom, his fine coat soaked in sweat, his face pale as wax. Pale, but not gray. His gaze locked onto Jayce, and he raised a shaking, accusatory finger toward her.

"You," he breathed. His voice rose to a bellow. "You've unleashed the horrors of the Plague King on Enterea. They die at your hands!" Then he turned and fled.

Jayce flinched, cringing at the accusation echoing off the stone walls. Her feet felt fused to the stone, her fingers curled uselessly at her sides.

She had thought—she had assumed—the vision had come from the Three. That it had meaning. Purpose.

But the Three hadn't been there to stop King Reginald. They hadn't prevented the Plague King from rising.

Something was horribly wrong with the Well that sourced all magic. How long had its waters been tainted, and what had tainted them?

Bentley limped toward the doorway, looked more ghost than man, his face covered with blood from a wound on his head. His eyes met Jayce's, and then he pulled the hood of his cloak back up. "If we get separated, meet me at the covered bridge behind the Warrior Guild stables. I'll have

Berma hitched and ready." He disappeared with Yamalda into the hall.

Nels helped Javin get steady on his feet.

Jayce fought off the fear and numbness that threatened to keep her standing and staring at the rising moribund. Scenarios ran through her mind from her past, and projections of possible futures.

A hand landed on her shoulder, and she startled. "Come on, Jayce," Nels said, his voice low and calming.

"We can't just leave them unleashed on the Guilds. We need to tell someone, warn the students," Jayce stammered.

"If we stay to warn them, they'll accuse us of being responsible for the deaths that occurred and imprison us. We might never get free with the evidence against us," Nels said.

Jayce followed Nels and Javin, the last one out of the room, and the last one to see as the first moribund staggered to its feet wearing Head Dame Tsega's body and face.

Helplessness and guilt weighed her down like she'd eaten a stone. It was the same feeling she'd gotten after her parents had died of the plague, after so many had been killed by moribund, and after Javin had perished at the hand of the Plague King. She had survived, and the others hadn't.

The students, Dires, and Dames of the Ivory Guilds might have incredible knowledge and wisdom, and they might be some of the greatest magic users alive, but they couldn't fight what they didn't know was coming.

Jayce halted in the middle of the corridor, heart thudding at the thought that had just occurred to her.

She might not be able to stay and make sure the moribund stayed trapped. But she could keep others from walking into danger.

Jayce gently unlooped Javin's arm from her shoulders, ignoring his muffled protest. Her gaze locked with Nels's.

"Take him. Get to the others."

Fear flickered in Nels's eyes.

She didn't give him time to argue. Turning away, she ran—boots thudding on the carpet, each step pounding with purpose.

"What are you doing?" he shouted. "Jayce!"

"I'm going to close the building," she shouted over her shoulder. "I'll meet you at the stables!"

She prayed to the Three that he would listen and not try to play protector. She made it to the stairs and took them two at a time, holding on to the railing so she didn't trip.

No footsteps followed her, and she breathed a sigh of relief that the others trusted her with this, knowing that Nels would take care of her brother in his weakened state.

Evening had fallen over the Lore Guild. Classes were over, but there was no telling how many students were still inside the massive building.

Jayce breathed deep and started shouting. "Get out of the building! It's not safe! Moribund awakened on the third floor in Dire Pell's office! Leave now!"

Several confused people poked their heads out of various rooms, some even shushing her for disturbing their studying. She continued yelling, not caring what they thought of her.

A man she assumed must be a Dire stepped out of a room, blocking her path. She tried to dodge him, but he gripped her arm, preventing her escape.

"What is the meaning of this disturbance, young lady?"

Jayce stopped pulling away and tried to catch her breath. "I don't have time to explain, but several moribund have awakened on the third floor in Dire Pell's office. They'll break through the door any moment and spread the plague to everyone they can reach. Please, help me get everyone out."

His hard gaze analyzed her for a moment, perhaps ascertaining her sincerity, then he released her, raised both hands and the air wavered around them.

"Please exit the building. Take only what you can carry. Stay at the risk of your life." His voice boomed far louder than humanly possible, and everyone scrambled to obey. He waved his hands again, bringing them up in a lifting gesture, and a sound like a high-pitched inhuman wail filled the building.

The Dire turned back to her. "If this is a false alarm, you'll be heavily reprimanded, young lady."

"Thank you, thank you," Jayce stammered, thanking the Three in her mind that she had found this man who had magic that could do something so incredible that would warn the entire building.

A stream of people poured out of the building, Jayce in the midst of them. Once outside, she made her way through it and stood off to the side, watching as the stream thinned, then stopped. She caught no sign of the others. Hopefully they were far from here.

She closed her eyes, feeling for the presence of the trees that surrounded the Lore Guild. Sweat soaked her clothes and dripped down from her forehead.

Had Nels, Sav, and the others made it out? Had she given them enough time? She couldn't wait much longer.

A few last stragglers left the building. People milled about, everyone asking what had happened. Some claimed a fire had broken out and looked for smoke to rise.

Whispers of *moribund* and *plague outbreak* moved through the crowd in waves.

Jayce already knew what she was going to do, but it would take all her courage and strength to do it.

Please, surround this building. Trap the sickness and rot inside. She pictured the trees and vines growing to wrap their branches around every window, door, and potential exit, encasing the Lore Guild in a case of wood and leaves.

Her arms itched. She glanced down and watched with awe as the swirling marks—now on both arms—lit up with a soft effervescent glow. The itching spread to her shoulders and chest and the glow increased, shining through her clothes.

With a deep breath, Jayce plunged into the power coursing across her skin and through her veins.

The trees didn't speak to her, but an enormous creaking and cracking filled the air, and then the screams and shouts of surprise started.

The trees were growing, stretching, doubling, tripling, increasing far beyond their natural height, becoming sheer giants. The canopies stretched, covering the top of the building, and then branches crept into place, crisscrossing to block every window and door. It was like watching time fast forward as the trees nearly consumed the Lore Guild's white stone walls. Red and gold leaves cascaded to the ground, falling among the onlookers.

The itching-burning sensation of the power faded from Jayce's limbs, and she slumped back against the nearest tree, staggering with exhaustion. The front steps of were covered with roots, the grand front doors sealed shut and barely visible through the tree branches.

She had done it. And the Dire knew about the moribund—he could tell whoever else needed to know so they could eliminate the danger and save the rest of the Ivory Guilds.

For now, all the students and staff would be safe. Perhaps the cloud of black spores she had seen would dissipate on its own before it caused an epidemic to break out on Enterea.

Putting her cloak hood up, she wove through the crowd, avoiding eye contact to hopefully get away unnoticed. The Dire she'd spoken to didn't know her name, but if he saw her, he would demand more of an explanation. And that was something she couldn't risk if she was going to use her knowledge to find a cure for this plague and save the lost heir of Neldor.

She raced for the stables behind the Warrior Guild, passing the Mana Guild and the Temple of the Three resting beside it. She longed to enter, to try to reach the Three again and gain more understanding about her powers and what she was meant to do, but that would have to wait until a less pressing time.

A bell tolled as she rounded the corner of the Warrior Guild building. Loud gongs that ruptured the otherwise peaceful air.

A second toll followed, then a third.

Yamalda spotted her first, propped up as she was against a haystack. Her eyes were murderous as she ripped fabric from the end of her cloak with her teeth to wrap the wound in her thigh.

No doubt she blamed Jayce for Sav's loss.

"That means lockdown," Bentley announced, walking out with Berma. "We practiced when the plague first spread through the mainland."

Nels rushed up to Jayce and pulled her in tight, squeezing her a touch too hard.

"I wish you wouldn't have gone off on your own," he whispered. "You scared me."

"I know. I'm sorry. But all those people… I had to do something," she said, stepping back from his embrace, allowing his arms to stay around her. "I warned them, I think they all got out. Then I sealed the entrances."

Nels's eyes lit up. "I wish I could have stayed to see that."

Jayce held up her arms. "Here's the evidence." Brown swirls, not unlike vine tendrils, worked their way up her skin. Based on where she'd felt the itching, she assumed they covered her entire body. She still didn't know why the magic affected her this way, or what it meant, but she was going to return to the mainland and find the Sacred Well and find out.

Jayce's gaze landed on Javin next. He sat on the other side of the stable entrance, looking paler than ever.

"How is he?" she asked Nels.

"Weak. We got him a little water, but he needs food."

Bentley cleared his throat. "Sorry to break this up folks, but we need to get moving. Lockdown will prevent anyone leaving through the main roads, and my cart can't take us through the forest. If we hurry, we'll pass the final guard before the road shuts down."

Nels climbed into the wagon and helped Javin up, then Jayce.

They all looked to Yamalda, who was flexing her leg, still sitting on the ground.

"Are you coming?" Bentley asked.

Yamalda's gaze went straight to Jayce, then glanced at Javin, sitting next to her. "Where did he come from?"

"This is my brother, Javin," Jayce replied, her throat thick with emotion. "He tried to defeat the Plague King two years ago and was absorbed. I don't know exactly how, but I pulled him from my vision."

"Then you can do the same for Savage," she replied. Not a question.

"I—" Jayce started, her voice faltering. She didn't know how to get back to that place. And even if she managed it, she didn't know what she'd done or if it would work for Sav.

Yamalda's eyes narrowed. "You *will* save him. It's your fault he's gone, and the rest of us can't afford to accept your brother in trade for our future king."

Jayce only nodded. She would try. If she got the chance... If she could find the Three, perhaps they would tell her how it could be done.

Apparently, it was good enough for the warrior. She struggled to her feet and limped to the wagon, pushing away Bentley's offered hand as she dragged herself into the seat beside him.

"I'm coming to make sure you follow through," she replied. "Getting Sav back is our sole purpose now."

Bentley called to Berma, and the wagon lurched into motion, creaking as it passed over uneven ground.

Jayce hadn't noticed the nip in the air until then. She shivered, and Nels looped his arm over her shoulders, bringing her close to him.

A brief flash of guilt consumed her. She and Nels and Javin had made it out alive. Corbin had lost his life, and Sav... He was as good as dead. It was hard to feel like she deserved any happiness in the face of those tragedies.

Even though Sav wasn't there with them, Jayce could imagine what he would say in a moment like this.

Something about how they would find a way, and that knowledge was always worth the sacrifice.

The translation was lost. She tipped her head back and exhaled, fighting the sting behind her eyes.

They had gone to Dire Pell to retrieve the translation to avoid this exact situation. Sav was the only one left alive who knew what Dire Pell had uncovered.

"What's wrong?" Nels asked, adjusting his grip so he could look down at her.

"We didn't get the journal," she said, swallowing past the thick emotion in her throat. "After all that... we failed."

Something thudded into the bed of the wagon at Jayce's feet. She sat up and grabbed it, the black leather warm as if it had been hidden close to someone's body. A thick folded stack of parchment made the journal flare open. No doubt notes from the Dire's translation work.

Bentley twisted in his seat. "I grabbed that from my... from the desk." He stumbled, as if saying his late uncle's name was too much to handle. "I had time to look during the fighting when everyone was distracted. I hope you find something useful in it. I'm not convinced the sacrifice was worth the knowledge in this case."

He returned his attention to driving, not waiting for Jayce to respond.

She couldn't see anything in the light of the Blood Moon rising over the trees. Reading would have to wait for daylight, and a safer location.

Purple Bell season was over, and autumn had come to Enterea. The Ice Moon wouldn't be far behind. Could they confront the queen and end the plague before then?

Carefully tucking both loose pages and the journal into the waistband of her skirt, Jayce leaned back against Nels again, prepared to close her eyes and try to sleep.

Beside her, Javin stirred, shivering. He was skin and bones, and probably far colder than her because of it.

A blanket lay folded in the corner. Jayce crawled over and grabbed it, then tucked it around her brother. His eyes flickered open, and she sensed his gratitude. She laid a kiss on his brow and returned to Nels's side.

She fell asleep at some point, the rocking of the wagon and the cool night air soothing her exhausted mind and body. She rested in the darkness of a dreamless sleep until Nels shook her awake.

It was the middle of the night, but they had reached Starfall. Waves lapped against the docks, and men shouted as they passed crates and ropes and other items up to those on the nearest ship, a bustle of activity that didn't match the stillness of the houses and shops behind them.

Jayce stood, stretching out her tight and sore muscles, then accepted Bentley's help from the wagon and supported Javin as he climbed off. He felt far too light, her warrior brother. Where was his strength and stamina? He didn't seem to be able to access his abilities. Perhaps once he had regained some of his health, those abilities would return.

For now, Jayce supported him on one side, Nels on the other, and they followed Bentley and Yamalda as they approached a dock worker and asked to speak to the owner of the ship that seemed to be preparing to launch.

Jayce couldn't focus on the animated conversation happening between Yamalda and the captain of the ship, once he appeared. His face held a permanent frown, and he shook his head several times, keeping his arms crossed.

Nels went over, producing a few select rocks from his pockets. Even with everything that had happened, he still had rocks in his pockets. Apparently valuable ones, too, because once the captain saw them his face lit up.

The exchange went on a little longer, and by the end of it, the captain clapped Nels on his shoulders, then walked away shouting for his men to prepare for passengers.

Nels came back to Jayce and Javin, shaking his head. "That man sure knows how to bargain. I doubt he's ever gotten more in payment for passage. He didn't like the look of us, all roughed up and bleeding. Plus, he's not set up for passengers; they were meant to do a cargo run only. But I brought out my nerithite—"

Jayce gasped. He had told her about the nerithite before. Its other name was skyglass, only found at the tops of incredibly high mountains, and therefore, an extremely difficult mineral to obtain.

Nels nodded at her understanding. “He not only knew what it was, but he’s a trader of valuable minerals. He has a customer in mind for it already. Can you believe it? I have a feeling we’re being watched over, Jayce. Only the Three could have coordinated such a fortunate circumstance.”

If she hadn’t been visited by them herself in their temple, she might not believe they had anything to do with their fortune. But perhaps they were watching, doing what they could to ease their journey to the Well.

CHAPTER TWENTY-SEVEN

THE LIGHTS OF STARFALL faded behind the *Seafox*, the last traces of civilization swallowed by a light fog that had descended around the ship.

Jayce stood at the railing, wind tugging at her hair as she watched the shore of Enterea grow smaller.

She ran her fingers along the worn edge of Dagric Wortcunning's journal. The translated pages waited inside—but part of her wasn't ready to face whatever truths they held.

Chasing the truth had already cost her so much. She couldn't return to the cozy, quiet life she had left behind when she'd sought the truth about the noxbrosia remedy. Might never be able to, now that she had blatantly defied Queen Lyra's orders and had illegal information in her possession.

And Sav was gone. She kept expecting him to come up beside her at the bow, to talk about their next steps and tell her that he believed in her.

She wished she had his confident words now.

She felt guilty all over again—if she hadn't discovered the journal, she wouldn't have come to Enterea and had that vision, unwittingly unleashing the Plague King. But if it somehow led to finding a cure, perhaps she could be forgiven.

She gripped the journal tighter. She would make sure Sav's sacrifice wasn't in vain.

At last, the only lights she could see were the crimson moon and a few stars peeking through an overcast sky. Dawn would be coming soon, but she would be asleep before the sun appeared. She hoped.

That little gleam of hope was short-lived.

Soon, they would be back on the mainland of Neldor again. Word would arrive from the Ivory Guilds, and those who knew them would note their absence and how it coincided with the deaths of the Head Dame, Fiametta, Dire Pell, and the Guild protectors.

And if Leth Alend stayed in the Guilds, he would likely plant seeds about their role in what happened and write a letter to Queen Lyra. If he did, Loshar wouldn't be safe for them either.

Footsteps sounded on the deck, swift and sure and headed toward her.

Jayce turned and found Nels approaching. "Is Javin all right?"

She had left him watching her brother, who she had assessed and found severely malnourished, but had no sign of being infected by the plague or any other injuries. He just needed rest, food, and water. It would take time for him to heal physically, not to mention emotionally.

"He's sleeping," Nels replied. He rubbed his jawline, which was covered in stubble. He looked rugged, like how she imagined him in the mountains and hills listening for the stones and precious gems he loved so much. How would it feel to kiss him with that facial hair?

Her throat bobbed, and sudden shyness stopped her from reaching out to feel it.

"Yamalda is insisting on a meeting with everyone," he said, holding out a hand toward her.

Jayce wrapped her cloak tighter around herself. She knew they had to come up with a plan for when they reached the mainland, but couldn't it wait until they'd all had some rest?

She took Nels's hand and went with him below deck, where the sleeping quarters lay. The sailors had been particularly cranky about the captain commanding that they make room for the passengers, but they had given up two rooms—one for the men, one for the women.

Sharing a room with Yamalda would be interesting. Jayce would be surprised if the woman didn't try to kill her in her sleep. Perhaps she should trade Bentley places... but it would hardly be an appropriate request.

Nels knocked on the door, a subtle rhythm to the gesture.

The door swung open, and Yamalda stepped aside, allowing them to enter. She looked as exhausted as Jayce felt and was apparently too tired to even glare at her as she passed.

Javin lay on one of the wooden bunks, bundled in blankets and fast asleep, as Nels had said.

Nels stood against the frame of the bunk, and Jayce pressed herself against him. He wrapped his arm behind her and kissed her forehead.

Bentley sat on the bottom bunk on the other side of the tight room, staring at Yamalda, who paced along the narrow space between the beds.

"We are in a predicament. The literary rebellion could fall apart if word gets out about Sav. The only ones who know are the four of us and Leth Alend." She paused, making eye contact with each of them. "As long as he keeps the information to himself, we can control if, and when, the news gets out."

"Don't they deserve to know?" Jayce asked.

"As long as you can save him, there is nothing for them to worry about. I see no point in telling any of them unless you fail," Yamalda said, her green eyes glittering.

Fail. Like she had every other time she had encountered the Plague King.

"So the rebellion carries on," Bentley said. "What are we doing?"

Yamalda sat down, and everyone looked at Jayce, who blinked in surprise.

"Why is everyone looking at me?"

Yamalda snorted, crossing her arms. "As much as I'd like to take charge, I don't know the first thing about the Plague King or how to retrieve someone he's taken. You've already done it once. Tell us what to do."

"That was an accident. I-I don't know if I can do it again," Jayce admitted. She hadn't meant to enter that vision, hadn't meant to find Javin. How could she do it on purpose?

"It was *your* magic that summoned him before. You can do it again. And you will. Right now," Yamalda snapped, her lip curling into a snarl.

"And bring the plague to this ship, this crew, in the middle of the ocean? Very wise. I like that plan," Nels said, a defensive edge to his voice.

Yamalda shrugged. "So we wait until we get to the mainland."

"I imagine that before doing anything else, Jayce needs to get that block on her magic removed." Nels interjected.

She glanced gratefully at him. "I don't know if I can do it again. But if we go to the Well, the Three can tell me how to save Sav. I know they can."

"The Three?" Bentley asked, looking between the three of them, confusion wrinkling his brow. "Where do they come into this?"

Nels raised his eyebrows at Jayce.

She licked her lips. It was time to tell the full story about her encounter in the Temple of the Three. Nels already knew, but Bentley and Yamalda... If they were going to help, they deserved to know everything.

So she told them. About Keeper Solmere and the ritual he had guided her through. About the images of the Three that had appeared in the candle flames.

"Do you think they would show up again if we got some candles and the items you mentioned?" Bentley asked, a thoughtful hand on his chin.

Jayce wished for a cup of water, her mouth thoroughly dried out. She licked her lips before she spoke. "It's probably worth a try. I'm not certain we could procure all the items we need on this ship, and we might have to visit a temple for the ritual to work."

"There's one in Loshar," Nels said.

"Surely there's one closer to the port in Crotos," Yamalda insisted.

"There might be, but we can't risk getting caught there. The port is the first place the queen will send guards if Leth Alend gets a message to her before we arrive. We could have our work cut out for us as it is," Nels replied.

"We'll go to Loshar and attempt to contact the Three there. Nels and I both have homes there," Jayce cut in.

"Yours will be compromised. It's the second place they'll look," Nels argued. "Look, I'm nobody. Just some random gem merchant. I doubt Leth Alend even knows my name. My place is the safest."

"Regardless," Yamalda cut in, her foot tapping the wooden floorboards impatiently. "Loshar is the last place we can go. Your faces are known, and Leth Alend could return there and come after us."

"There's nowhere else," Jayce argued, her voice rising despite her attempts to keep it down. "If the temple doesn't work, the only place left is the Well. For a journey like that, we need supplies."

"Not to mention a wagon," Bentley muttered, looking thoughtful. He had been able to convince the captain to allow his mule on board, and fortunately they were able to procure supplies for her before shoving off. But his cart had been left behind. They would have to find another on the mainland.

"We can get everything we need in Loshar," Nels said. "I have a second house. I've been fixing it up over the years.

No one knows it's mine, and the neighbors haven't been too nosy. If we are smart about it, we could stay there as long as we need to without anyone finding out."

Silence fell between them all, the only sound the muffled lap of waves against the hull of the ship outside.

"I don't like it, but I see no other option," Yamalda admitted, slapping her thighs as she stood. "Good night, everyone."

They all murmured their replies as she left the room, and Bentley followed after, muttering some excuse about checking on Berma.

Jayce was alone with Nels, unless she counted Javin, who still appeared to be sleeping.

Her body ached with fatigue, and she knew she needed to go to bed, but her mind wouldn't settle. They had a plan now—a fragile, dangerous plan—one that everyone else was expecting her to lead.

Sav had been the leader, not her. Could she do this? Could she be responsible for everyone's lives as they traveled with her to the sacred Well?

Nels tugged her down to sit on the floor. She curled up beside him, laying her head in his lap and closing her eyes. She could almost have fallen asleep that way, cradled in his warmth and rocked by the movement of the ship.

"None of you have to come with me," she started. "To the Well, I mean. We might not survive another encounter with the Plague King."

He wrapped both arms around her, pulling her in tighter. "You've already survived twice. I consider those fantastic odds."

“If I fail again, I could lose all of you.” She imagined the Plague King consuming them all, one by one, as she watched. Losing Javin again.

Losing Nels.

Nels turned her face toward him and met her gaze. The amount of love in his eyes threatened to overwhelm her.

“I’m not leaving you to do this alone. And you aren’t going to fail. With the translation and your full powers, there’s no telling what you’ll be able to do if you try.”

Jayce blinked, her throat tight. “But what if trying isn’t enough?” *What if* I’m *not enough*? The familiar fear echoed inside her.

He brushed his thumb over the back of her hand, his voice soft. “Then at least we’ll be together at the end.”

Jayce turned her body and leaned into him. “I don’t think I deserve you, Nels Martin. Not by half.”

Nels leaned in, touching his forehead to hers, still gazing earnestly into her eyes with his deep blue ones. “Then I’ll make it my mission to ensure you know, beyond any doubt, that you deserve more than me, so much so that I’ll have my work cut out trying to keep hold of you.”

He grinned, and Jayce giggled. The giggle turned into laughter, and tears mixed in as the suffocating bubble of stress that had been hovering over her burst.

Nels pulled her up into his arms, hugging her tightly.

She nuzzled her face into his neck, breathing in the linen of his shirt, and it occurred to her that she couldn’t hear the usual simpering chatter of the fabric beneath the bare skin of her hands and arms. She ran her hands along his back then moved to his shoulders, rubbing as if to provoke the flaxen fibers of the fabric into speech.

Nels started laughing and leaned away. "Not that I mind, but what are you doing?"

"Shh," Jayce replied, breathless with excitement. She concentrated, and still hearing nothing, used her thoughts to ask the flax to speak to her from the linen fibers.

Flax. I remember the sun... I drink only salt now.

The voice was quiet and fragmented, as if the flax itself were a distant memory due to the process it had gone through to make the shirt. She had often found manufactured items to be this way, but never so quiet. Never waiting until she requested to hear from them. Always a quiet hum in her mind.

Ever since the Three had cracked the barrier Leth Alend had placed on her magic, she had felt relief from the cold and their voices. She had a glimpse of what it would be like to have her full ability returned to her.

"Jayce?"

"I think," she said slowly. "The Well is the source of the power of the Three, the same power that They gave to humanity so many centuries ago. The Well in my vision seemed tainted somehow, and if it is, that might be how the plague is infecting people. Through our magic."

He stared at her with amazed wonder in his expression. "If that's true, how do we fix it?"

"By healing the Well," Jayce replied. Could it really be so simple? "Before you ask, I have no idea how to do that."

Nels laughed and laid a kiss on her brow. "I have no doubt you'll figure it out."

Equal parts of fear and excitement bled together inside of her. She might not have the answers, but she had enough pieces that perhaps she *could* figure it out.

She might not fail this time.

The lantern light made wide, shifting shadows on the wall as it swung from its spot on the ceiling. She closed her eyes and took a deep breath in, filling her nostrils with the faint scent of salt and damp wool clinging to the air. The rush of waves against the hull mixed with the sound of Javin's quiet breathing behind them.

When she opened her eyes again, the cabin was still dim. The future was still uncertain.

But she wasn't alone.

Nels's hand remained wrapped in hers, steady and warm. Javin stirred behind her, alive. The ship creaked onward through the dark, and Jayce let herself believe—just for a moment—that moving forward was enough.

She didn't have all the answers. Maybe she never would.

But she had Dagric Wortcunning's journal. Dire Pell's translation. The weight of power stirring inside her, waiting to be unlocked by the Three.

And she had the will to keep going.

Perhaps that was enough.

The ship slipped through the Atean Sea as she set her heart toward Loshar, the Sacred Well, and the truths waiting to be unearthed in the deep, wild heart of the world.

The End

ACKNOWLEDGEMENTS

THANK YOU, DEAR READER, for continuing the Plague King Chronicles series! You make it all worthwhile, and I'm so grateful for your support. Please consider leaving a review on your favorite platform so other readers can find this story.

A special thank you to my Kickstarter backers! You continue to make my dreams come true, covering editing costs and enabling the production of the special edition of The Arrow and the Ivy. I couldn't do it without you.

A thousand thanks to Heather Q. for being my sounding board, alpha reader, and best friend. This book is better because of you.

To Sam, Amy, Beth, Jenny, and Kaylee, for feedback on the manuscript in various stages of development.

Many thanks to Claire Ashgrove, my copy editor, for cleaning things up.

To the Lost Canvas, Blue Umbrella Bakery, and Swed & Co. for providing me with all the brain food, tea, boba lemonade, and Lotus I needed to finish this book. If you are ever in this little corner of southeastern Iowa, they are all well-worth the visit!

Unending love and gratitude, as always, goes to my husband, who never fails to support this writing habit of mine, and refuses to let me quit when things get hard.

These acknowledgements wouldn't be complete without a shout out to a teenage crush of mine, the namesake of one of the love interests in this series.

(Nels, if you're reading this, you'll be relieved to know that all of the magical items in this book actually do something.)

Shadows of Camelot

The Lady's Last Song

The Queen's Quiet End

Shadowed Minds Series

Prequel: Thief of Lies

Thief of Magic

Thief of Aether

Thief of Bones

Wings of Rebellion Series

Prequel: Raven Blood

Raven Born

Serpent Cursed

Coven Bound

Serpent Turned

Siren Called

Rebel Sworn

The Plague King Chronicles

The Keeper of the Well

The Quill and the Vial

The Arrow and the Ivy

Of Dusk and Dawn Collection

Sacrifice for the Standing Stones

Vows Beneath the Frozen Stars

Bree Moore lives in Iowa with her husband, seven children, and two cats. When she's not busy homeschooling or folding laundry, she sneaks off to write more fantasy.

Bree writes urban and epic fantasy to explore different worlds with amazing creatures and magic systems. She enjoys giving her readers a story that is both entertaining and emotional, with a healthy dose of romance. When she's not writing, Bree can be found foraging for edible plants, watching fantasy shows and movies, or hanging out with her husband and kids.

Visit www.authorbreemoore.com for a FREE fantasy book!

tiktok.com/@breenovels

instagram.com/breenovels

www.ingramcontent.com/pod-product-compliance
Lightning Source LLC
Chambersburg PA
CBHW020338310726
48979CB00015B/2423/J

* 9 7 8 1 9 5 6 6 6 8 7 6 6 *